SPIRITS UNWRAPPED

SPIRITS UNWRAPPED

edited by
DANIEL BRAUM

LETHE PRESS
AMHERST, MA

Published by LETHE PRESS
lethepressbooks.com

Copyright © 2019 by Lethe Press

ISBN: 978-1-59021-695-8

Cover art
by PATRICIO BETTEO

Cover and Interior design
by INKSPIRAL DESIGN

TABLE OF CONTENTS

INTRODUCTION

DANIEL BRAUM

WELCOME TO *SPIRITS UNWRAPPED*, an anthology of stories about mummies. Within these pages, fourteen authors—bestselling and award-winners, exciting new-comers—have thrown off many of the old and cinematic trappings of these monsters to create tales that encompass more than the dust of ancient Egypt.

The mummy as contemporary horror aficionados know it from popular culture is a curious thing. A slow-moving figure, wrapped in frayed bandages, motivated by ancient curses and vengeance. Growing up, most Hollywood depictions induced a groan from me. While I did appreciate the performance of Boris Karloff in the principal film from 1932, I've always felt that the rest of the mummy's cinematic canon mostly abandoned the strange, opting instead for a shambling but simple threat.

This is a monster created by ancient rituals. Undead. Who were these men? (20th century films always portrayed the mummy as a male doomed to embalming because of a forbidden love affair.) The wonders and marvels and mysteries of pharaohs and high priests of the Nile loomed large in my young imagination, as did the stories of cursed tombs and the fate of Howard Carter's expedition. What I could not find in the movie theater or on television, I sought at my local library. And still my yearning for wonder was never sated.

Until 2004, when I read Karen Joy Fowler's short story "Private Grave Nine." Here was the mummy story I had been missing all my life! A clever, heartfelt, and dangerous depiction of human emotions and the supernatural condition of being a wrapped spirit. Inspired by Fowler, I gathered all the books containing mummy stories I could get my hands on, from the classics (Stoker's "Lot No. 249" and Bradbury's "The Mummies of Guanajuato" among others) to volumes of contemporary work. I wrote a mummy story of my own that appeared in *Cemetery Dance Magazine*. And I recommended "Private Grave Nine" to every reader who would listen.

And yet, my imagination yearned for more. There remained an untapped potential for the mummy beyond Egypt, beyond sentimentality. Where was the monster straddling the distant past, woken in the present, entities that have glimpsed the span between life and death. Where are the mummies of other cultures, the folklore new to me?

It is said that some archeological finds are happy accidents. So is this book: while working on another project together I learned that publisher Steve Berman shared my excitement and enthusiasm in seeing more diverse mummy stories. And thus *Spirits Unwrapped* crossed the underworld to its fitting home at Lethe Press.

The authors you are about to read deliver a rich mix of stories spanning cultures, time periods, and settings around the globe…and even beyond our planet. These are treasures of speculative fiction, the horrific and the weird. Prepare yourself for dark mysteries. Our present is in your hands, and you are cordially invited to its unwrapping.

Daniel Braum
May 2019
New York

THE UNWRAPPING PARTY

JOANNA PARYPINSKI

To our dearest Mr. and Mrs. James and Vera Babcock—
It is with exceeding pleasure that we announce the return of Ms. Claudia Evers and Ms. Hattie Evers from their Egyptian holiday. In their travels, the Misses Evers have encountered mysteries of an ancient and exotic nature and wish to share with their friends the wonder they have experienced abroad. You are therefore most cordially invited to attend an unwrapping party hosted by the Misses Evers, featuring the preserved remains of one anonymous Egyptian whose body has not seen the light of day in several thousand years. The party shall take place at the Evers Estate on Friday the fifth of September, 18—. We hope for your attendance and request that you post your response at your convenience.
Gratefully yours,
Claudia Evers and Hattie Evers

Vera finished reading the invitation and sniffed disdainfully. "Well, what do you make of that?" she asked James, who lay swathed in the bedclothes. "An unwrapping party, of all things! It sounds like a gruesome affair, don't you think?"

James' lack of response elicited a scowl in the mirror, which deepened considerably as she went about her embellishments. Despite the pastes and powders, the years had left their mark on her once youthful visage: crow's feet wrinkled the corners of her eyes, beneath which her pale skin sagged hopelessly.

"Well, I'm going." She snatched some paper from the drawer beneath the vanity and set to writing her response.

"Dear Misses Evers," she muttered as she wrote. "It pleases me to confirm that I will be attending your unwrapping party, however without my husband James. Unfortunately, while you were away, he took ill and remains bedridden. The physician assures a full recovery. I am very much looking forward to the party. Yours sincerely, Mrs. Vera Babcock."

"I'm off to post my response," she announced as she stood up, donning a hat. "You just lie there in your own filth, then." The air was lighter in the hall, and Vera hummed to herself as she walked through the house, feeling quite grand already about the whole affair.

WHEN VERA KNOCKED, Hattie Evers swung open the door wearing an arrangement of golden beads over her red curls. She might have called the Evers old spinsters, but they were actually several years younger than herself—still perky and vivacious into their thirties, which Vera despised.

"Vera, my dear!" Hattie greeted. The gold beads clinked together. "So sorry to hear about James. Is he getting on all right?"

"He'll be fine," said Vera as she stepped inside, removing her coat. "Lovely to see you, Hattie. I don't suppose you brought back a husband from the desert?"

"Not unless you count old dry-bones from Thebes. Come, have a look." She led Vera to the parlor, where a small gathering of guests already mingled, glasses in hand. Vera recognized the young Judith and Walter Devereux, a dark-haired pale-skinned couple, and wealthier than life itself; Fanny and Harold Spooner, a middle-aged plumpish woman and her lump of a husband; and Agnes and Nathaniel Hardgrave, one a tall red-haired beauty, the other a bespectacled and often tongue-tied scholar. How utterly drab, she thought, to invite only couples when the hosts themselves were nothing but a pair of old maids.

Hattie sidled up next to Vera, a glass in hand with one olive skewered in the center. She handed it to Vera, who took a sip of the strong cocktail, and called for a toast. "To the spoils of life—and those of death." A chuckle went around the room. "And to that poor Egyptian fellow who is now to be this evening's entertainment!"

"Aye," Harold shared quietly with Walter. "Never thought he'd end up here in heart of civilization, eh?"

"How very Christian of you," said Agnes with what Vera thought was a note of sarcasm.

Vera took a small sip from her drink. Where *was* that blasted mummy, anyway? Old dry-bones from Thebes—the closest the Evers sisters would ever get to a man, Vera suspected—did not appear to be in the parlor at all. She gazed about at the hearth with its lustrous urns perched on the mantle, at the oriental tapestry on the wall that depicted a violent scene of war, at the Gothic candelabras lining the walls. The room held in it a sort of dark, enchanted mystery. It was, she had to admit, the perfect parlor in which to denude an ancient mummified corpse.

Suddenly the lanterns dimmed, and in the unsettling gloom the pale form of Claudia Evers strode into the room.

"Thousands of years ago, there lived a civilization of mysticism and pagan worship. Though they lived on the fertile banks of the Nile, they housed their dead in the desert sands, to be preserved for all time."

The group had gone quiet; Claudia's presence was nothing like her sister's but seemed to cast an eerie pall wherever she walked.

"In their superstition, they placed curses upon their dead to keep prying hands away from their sacred relics. Of course, none of us here believes in curses...do we?"

Vera saw Nathaniel nervously adjust his spectacles as he glanced around the room. Not all here shared Claudia's macabre sense of humor.

The heavy rap of the doorknocker echoed three times from down the hall. Vera looked around. The Devereuxs, the Spooners, the Hardgraves... who else might be arriving? And so tardy?

"Hattie—the door, if you please," said Claudia, and her sister hurried down the hall.

"You know," said Fanny as she wandered up to Vera, her nose in bad need of a powder, "we really shouldn't be using this body as entertainment. It seems a bit ... cruel. But how are you getting on? Shame James couldn't be here. Have you ever been to the Mediterranean? The sun, the sea—oh, it does wonders for the constitution. Perhaps you'd best follow the Evers' lead and take a holiday. It might help his recovery."

Vera smiled thinly and sipped her gin. No, of course she had never been to the Mediterranean—only the cold, gray drab of England, with its mist-draped moors and its rocky shorelines and its endless rainy days.

She was still thinking of a witty retort when Hattie returned to the room with a figure behind her, an older gent with a looming stature. When he spoke, it was in a rusty croak. Vera detected a faint accent—German? Austrian? "My apologies," he said.

"Mr. Wagner is an historian," Claudia supplied to the group. She drawled over the man's name, *Vaauuug*-ner. "Ancient history, if I'm correct."

Meanwhile, Hattie had approached a table in the center of the room, clutched the edge of the velvet cloth that covered it, and pulled it away to reveal what Vera saw now was not a table at all, but a sarcophagus—hieroglyphics carved into stark, crude shadows upon the stone. A thrill went through her; within that stone coffin lay the body of an ancient man, his body outlasting even the memory of him.

"Before we begin," said Claudia as the others gathered. Instead of finishing her thought, she lifted a chest and opened it, revealing four compartments within, each containing what appeared to be a carved figurine.

"These are Canopic jars," she said as she lifted the first one. It bore the head of a bird, perhaps a falcon. She passed this to Walter Devereux, who inspected it with care. "They contain the dried organs of the deceased." As Claudia held out one with the head of a baboon to Harold Spooner, he shook his head and stepped back. Fanny also declined. Claudia handed it to Judith Hardgrave, who held it slightly away from her while Nathaniel looked on. The next one, with a man's head, was passed to Mr. Wagner. "This was the only way the ancient Egyptians could preserve the mummy without allowing the liquefied innards to decompose the body from the inside out." She removed the final jar from the box—this one with the head of a jackal—and handed it to Vera.

Vera liked the idea of the jars; they kept everything so tidy and organized, like a well-kept wardrobe. Not like the barbaric Christian burials of today, where they dumped the body underground to fester amongst the worms. She couldn't think of a more gruesome thing. Was it blasphemous to think so? Was it sacrilege to want your body, your most prized possession, preserved for hundreds—even thousands—of years beyond death? To outlive death itself? She wondered.

"Now, let us gaze upon the face of death," said Claudia. At her request, Walter and Mr. Wagner positioned themselves on either side of the sarcophagus and endeavored to lift the lid. Stone ground against stone, an awful sound that set Vera's teeth on edge, and she fairly buzzed with anticipation.

A cloud of dust rose into the air, then dispersed. Shrouded in the musty darkness within the coffin lay a human shape wound head to toe in strips of brownish, rotting linen. Vera had a prickling sensation that anyone could be under that cloth.

Fanny pressed a hand over her mouth and nose. "That stench," she murmured behind her cupped palm.

"Smells like the nest of dead rats I found in the cellar last year," said Nathaniel. He glanced at Anges. "You remember?"

"Yes, it was the highlight of my winter," she replied drolly.

Vera willed the lights in the parlor to brighten, to banish the dread that filled her with fantastic notions. Somehow she imagined if she could see the mummy in better light, it would not seem as weighted with the terrible mystery of death, but now it lay within a shroud of shadow, separated from the living, somehow, beyond a veil.

The room quieted as Claudia produced a small knife and sliced the cloth. She unwound it with difficulty, the linen sticking to the corpse, but after some effort the mummy's feet appeared. They were black and shriveled, like abused leather, and they twisted unnaturally together. The skin had shrunk over the bones. Vera imagined Claudia proceeding to peel away the dead skin now, tearing it off until the bones beneath came to light. Stripping the mummy bare and barer still, down to the very skeleton of its frame, the last thing holding the expired body together as it had been in life.

A gagging sound pulled Vera's attention from the feet to Fanny, whose face had gone sickly. The hand over her mouth quivered.

"Well, did you expect it to smell like roses? It's been dead a few thousand years," Harold reasoned, eliciting a glare from his wife. Despite his light tone, however, Howard also looked a trifle uneasy.

Dead a few thousand years—Vera could hardly believe she was gazing upon the remains of a being so ancient, so far removed from her own reality. It was hard to believe the thing had ever been a human being, and she had the distinctly unsettling feeling that perhaps it *hadn't*, that it had been something *else*.

After snipping away portions of linen still clinging to the feet, Claudia continued unraveling the ankles. Fanny retched dryly and swooned, stirring everyone's concern. As they attended to their friend, Vera turned her back and tried to pry open the Canopic jar, wondering at the possibility of holding an organ—a formerly functioning, pumping organ—in her hand.

"May I try?" Wagner's voice startled her. She reluctantly handed over the jar, distrusting the stranger even more than she distrusted her so-called friends. His meaty fingers pulled and strained until the lid came free.

Darkness within. Vera took the jar, momentarily afraid to reach in and touch what lay in the shadows; however, with Mr. Wagner watching, she reached gingerly into the opening, held her breath, and closed her fingers over a dry, shriveled, and shapeless thing. Irrationally, she dared not let her hand linger in the darkness, and she pulled the organ free.

Wagner said, "The stomach. One of the four organs known to be stored this way."

"How foul. I was hoping for the heart."

"No, the Egyptians never removed the heart. They believed it was the seat of the soul," Wagner replied. "Without the heart, you would cease to be yourself—cease to be anything but an empty vessel."

Vera noticed Fanny and Harold waving goodbye across the room.

The others returned to the sarcophagus, murmuring about Fanny, the *poor thing*, who was simply overwhelmed by the foul reek of death. And Harold, what a gentleman, escorting her home in the middle of the party.

While Claudia resumed unwrapping, Judith asked if they might raise the light a bit. "No," said Claudia. "The vendor who sold us this mummy said to keep it out of direct light. It might speed the deterioration." Thus, in semi-darkness they remained, where colors faded, leaving the edges of the parlor in a web of shadow.

A flutter of unease went through Vera. Perhaps it was the darkness, or the liquor, which continued to alternately dull and sharpen her senses. Perhaps it was that creeping sensation that they were going to unwrap the linen, and someone…some familiar face, which she could almost perceive in her mind's eye, would appear. For even the living someday would wear the face of death.

The mummy emerged from the feet to the knees now, and Claudia pulled away layers of cloth over those knobby bones, proceeding up the thigh.

"Fanny was right. Ghastly smell," Walter whispered to Judith, though the whisper carried through the silence and cut somehow more easily through the darkness than the light. When Vera looked up, she found Judith looking positively spectral.

"Aren't you having fun?" Judith asked. Her smile wavered a touch. Too much for her pretty little head, thought Vera. Her pretty little *young* head, unable yet to comprehend mortality. The couple stepped away, conversing in low tones. Walter announced they would be leaving, and off they went.

Claudia resumed unwrapping the pelvis. Vera was mildly disappointed when the elephantine skin bore little sign of a penis.

"What a shame," she said. "Hattie's new husband won't be able to provide her any children."

She looked up through the semi-darkness and saw Hattie's eyes glistening. Had her barbs finally nicked a nerve in the poor lamb? Just as well. Hattie could have any husband she wanted, but she chose to remain a spinster—her own fault. "Excuse me," Hattie said before leaving the parlor.

"Hattie loves the idea of children," Claudia murmured. "I should think you'd be sympathetic to the matter."

Vera supposed Claudia was referring to the rumor of her infertility. Had she wanted children, once upon a time? Perhaps. Children, after all, were meant to continue the lineage, so that some form of the parents might live on forever. Yet it was not to be, and she wouldn't for a moment feel sorry for herself. Children, after all, were nasty brats, and good riddance. She had carried a child, once, but it had been dead in the womb. James had always been disappointed.

Claudia's careful fingers continued unraveling the cloth, winding it around and around the corpse's chest. The stench grew more intense the more skin emerged, and Nathaniel had to step back, gagging. Agnes snorted a very unladylike laugh.

Vera felt as if she were entering a dream, down the long tunnel of the parlor's darkness into the hazy liquored light where lay the shriveled body. She clutched her Canopic jar, feeling that it was a token stolen from Death itself, and wasn't that the ultimate triumph? To take for her own what belonged rightfully to Death, when Death was always taking, taking from humanity?

The stiff linen cracked and crumbled in Claudia's hands, and a halo of dust arose.

"There's nothing like the pyramids," said Claudia as she unwrapped the arms. She picked at the linen stuck between the fingers—twisted into claws, little more than bone. "Filled with the dead. Sacred spells carved into the stone. They leave food and libations. All this to preserve the husk of former human beings whose souls have fled. Empty vessels." She looked up, her eyes catching Vera's. "Waiting to be filled."

"With what?" asked Agnes.

Vera had to squint through the miasma of dust made foggy by the liquor; she had continued refilling her drink and now could not remember just how many she'd had. Suddenly she felt quite drunk, and she gazed into her cup, trying to recall whether it was she or Hattie who had last refreshed her drink. It was a good deal stronger than she had expected. The room spun around her, and she felt too warm. Were they in the interior of a pyramid? Was the Egyptian sun baking on the stones that encased them in the dark, hot tomb?

Claudia began to unravel the cloth from the skull. Vera trembled with exhilarating terror—now, yes, now she would see the face of death!

The bandages came loose, crumbled away, and left behind the mummified visage of—Vera! It was her very self—but ancient, shriveled, ghastly. She stumbled back, gasping and believing then that the sarcophagus was indeed cursed, that she was now cursed with the black shadow of death. She let out a strangled cry and dove at Claudia, hands scrabbling on the woman's neck and closing around it. She wasn't able to strangle her for long, though, as two hands grabbed her from behind and two more pried hers free. Wagner and Nathaniel dragged her back, still struggling, from Claudia, gasping as she bent over the sarcophagus. Over the mummy with its blank face.

Vera looked again.

It wasn't her face. She did not recognize the face the mummy wore, its blank features brown and leathery and eerily inhuman.

"We ought to leave," murmured Agnes, pulling Nathaniel away. The last remaining couple made their hasty retreat.

"What is it?" murmured Vera, for the corpse indeed was not human, this she could see now—its skull was too elongated, its eye sockets gaping vast holes, its jaw wrong, all wrong.

"A very special mummy," said Claudia soothingly. "No need to fear, my dear. Come closer. You see? It is not a man at all, but a god."

"What?" Vera shook her head, uncomprehending.

"Hattie is dying." She placed a hand on Vera's shoulder and led her to the sarcophagus. "It's why we went on holiday. If all goes well tonight, however, we shall learn secrets from the God of Death himself, and we shall save her." Her eyes glittered knowingly. "And you shall save James."

Vera shook her head again, trying to control herself, but she could not help the words that spilled from her: "No. James is going to die!" She tried to stem rogue tears. "He will die, and I will be alone—and then I will die alone."

The alien mummy stared up at her with its endless black hole eyes that contained an abyss, and she wondered what this unnatural thing had been in life. Whatever it was, she felt sure it was no god.

"What if you could live forever?" said Claudia.

Vera had no chance to reply, for at that moment, Hattie reappeared.

At least, she thought it was Hattie. The person who entered the room wore a jackal mask that encompassed her entire head. The effect was altogether unsettling, but even more so when Wagner donned an identical mask.

The Hattie-jackal stepped up to the sarcophagus and started speaking a language Vera could not place—chanting, humming some pagan mass. She produced a knife and began cutting into the mummy's chest, peeling back old leathery skin while she spoke. At last she extracted the final dried-up organ within—the heart.

"The body of a dead god, now an empty vessel. Waiting to be filled again with its immortal spirit," said Claudia. "Anubis."

The Wagner-jackal took the heart and presented it to Vera, speaking in a distant voice. "Come. Look upon the majesty of time. See what we have seen, and live forever."

She could not stop herself; she reached out and took the heart from him.

The moment her fingers touched it, she lost the thread of time.

She flew disembodied on the air, backwards, watching buildings deconstruct themselves into farmland; she soared across the ocean while the world turned over and over like an hourglass, and she found herself in desert sands beneath a golden sun, which gleamed upon massive stone pyramids. She saw a creature from the stars, come to teach the mysteries of death, worshipped by the people. When it died, priests brought it into a dark chamber, emptied it, rinsed the body in wine, salted the corpse, and let it dry; time passed, a week, a fortnight, forty days; they stuffed the deflated body with sand, they wrapped the body with linen, they placed the body in a sarcophagus and left it in the pyramid. Time sped up. Sun and moon alternated on the blowing sand. She watched the erosion of the years, what felt an eternity. People forgot the dead god, died themselves, turned to skeletons, turned to dust, and still she stood and watched, an endless consciousness beyond time. Endless... endless... and bringing with it madness—to be a god herself, a mad god! What had she become? She was hardly herself anymore; she was an unnamed being out of time;—it was unbearable! She wished for death. She wished to turn to dust, but she was immortal now; she had gotten what she wanted. Please, she wanted to cry out, please help me—but there was no one to hear, for billions perished continually before her rolling eyes. She burned forever like the stars, whirling in an endless dance, and she understood, now, the necessity of consciousness dissolving after death, for eternal life was utter madness.

She flew from Egypt now and traveled across the world, watched modernity take hold: impossible steel towers, boxes that spoke, sentient devices: a terrifying future where people lived in a world that was not quite real, a world that existed somewhere in the crackling ether around them. And finally they conquered Death, and the people were the gods now, and they lived forever: skeletons ruled the earth, hungry and insatiable, worshipping Anubis, who was called by a different name in this future. We have done it, they said, and Vera wanted to tell them that they have made the ultimate mistake, that the crawling hungry corpse of the earth would travel through the cold dark recesses of space forever now, forever, with them trapped upon it. The sun turned red and bloated and burnt them to a crisp, but they could not die, and so the writhing tortured corpses lived, and the world had become Hell, and the endlessness of time made all men mad and mindless creatures; the earth was a gross infected blight on the universe, and the universe regretted giving life at all when life itself had turned out to be a clawing parasite, a grotesquerie, a horror—a horror!

Vera let go of the heart.

She could hardly remember where she was. She shook her head and trembled; had she been a chattering demon driven mad by the wastes of time? Had it been an eternity, or had she been standing here only a moment?

Claudia placed her jackal mask over her head and transformed into a beast. The three demons gathered around the sarcophagus.

"Put it back," Vera murmured, gesturing to the heart now forgotten on the floor. "Put it back! Oh God, put it back!"

Ignoring her, they spoke in unison, in some ancient foreign tongue.

"Stop!" said Vera. "Stop, you can't—"

But they did not stop.

Chanting rose from the three jackal-headed pagans, and beneath their voices Vera heard a terrible creaking sound—old bones shifting, stretching from millennia of slumber to bring some ancient beast back from the great beyond. Vera took a glass and dashed it against the wall; it broke in her hand. She charged forward and drove the jagged shards into the nearest jackal. It sank into Wagner's side. The broken glass came loose as he whirled around, and she slashed it across his throat. A line of red opened beneath the mask. As he fell, the other two grasped at him, trying to help him. Vera made to slash at these two jackals as well, but she detected movement from within the sarcophagus, the lifting of a desiccated hand—and, dropping the bloody glass, she fled into the cold black night.

VERA ARRIVED HOME still drunk and half-wondering if she hadn't hallucinated the entire ordeal. Her nerves clanged as she opened a bottle of whiskey and took a small, burning sip. The house was dark; she stared about her, flinching at every small noise—the groan of a floorboard, the whistle of wind. Was it Anubis, coming for her now? Come into the world in the dark, empty spaces?

She stumbled to her bedroom in the dark, holding panic just beneath the surface of her crawling skin.

"James?" she whispered. She sat beside him on the bed. "Oh, James. You would hardly believe..." She bent over him, peering through the darkness at his face. "James?" She placed a hand on his cheek; it was cold. "James?" She felt for a pulse; all was still.

Gasping, she fell to her knees. No, she did not disdain her husband— she did love him, after all.

And wasn't love a kind of immortality, the sort of love that endures for eternity? Such a notion might have brought comfort only yesterday, but today the mere thought of anything being allowed to exist forever was a cold nightmare.

In the darkness, she drank with the hope for oblivion and mercy from the secret knowledge of those alien gods that once walked this earth—and those that will walk it again, in the guise of humanity, or whatever humanity will become.

ANTIQUITIES

JOHN CROWLEY

"THERE WAS, OF course," Sir Geoffrey said, "the Inconstancy Plague in Cheshire. Short-lived, but a phenomenon I don't think we can quite discount."

It was quite late at the Travellers' Club, and Sir Geoffrey and I had been discussing (as we seemed often to do in those years of the Empire's greatest, yet somehow most tenuous, extent) some anomalous irruptions of the foreign and the odd into the home island's quiet life-small, unlooked-for effects which those centuries of adventure and acquisition had had on an essentially stay-at-home race. At least that was my thought. I was quite young.

"It's no good your saying 'of course' in that offhand tone," I said, attempting to catch the eye of Barnett, whom I felt as much as saw passing through the crepuscular haze of the smoking room. "I've no idea what the Inconstancy Plague was."

From within his evening dress Sir Geoffrey drew out a cigar case, which faintly resembled a row of cigars, as a mummy case resembles the human form within. He offered me one, and we lit them without haste; Sir Geoffrey started a small vortex in his brandy glass. I understood that these rituals were introductory-that, in other words, I would have my tale.

"It was in the later eighties," Sir Geoffrey said. "I can't remember now how I first came to hear of it, though I shouldn't be surprised if it was some flippant note in Punch. I paid no attention at first; the 'popular delusions and madness of crowds' sort of thing. I'd returned not long before from Ceylon, and was utterly, blankly oppressed by the weather. It was just starting autumn when I came ashore, and I spent the next four months more or less behind closed doors. The rain! The fog! How could I have forgotten? And the oddest thing was that no one else seemed to pay the slightest attention. My man used to draw the drapes every morning and say in the most cheerful voice, 'Another dismal wet one, eh, sir?' and I would positively turn my face to the wall."

He seemed to sense that he had been diverted by personal memories, and drew on his cigar as though it were the font of recall. "What brought it to notice was a seemingly ordinary murder case. A farmer's wife in Winsford, married some decades, came one night into the Sheaf of Wheat, a public house, where her husband was lingering over a pint. From under her skirts she drew an old fowling piece. She made a remark which was later reported quite variously by the onlookers, and gave him both barrels. One misfired, but the other was quite sufficient. We learn that the husband, on seeing this about to happen, seemed to show neither surprise nor anguish, merely looking up and-well, awaiting his fate.

"At the inquest, the witnesses reported the murderess to have said, before she fired, 'I'm doing this in the name of all the others.' Or perhaps it was 'I'm doing this, Sam [his name], to save the others.' Or possibly, 'I've got to do this, Sam, to save you from that other.' The woman seemed to have gone quite mad. She gave the investigators an elaborate and horrifying story which they, unfortunately, didn't take down, being able to make no sense of it. The rational gist of it was that she had shot her husband for flagrant infidelities which she could bear no longer. When the magistrate asked witnesses if they knew of such infidelities-these things, in a small community, being notoriously difficult to hide-the men, as a body, claimed that they did not. After the trial, however, the women had dark and unspecific hints to make, how they could say much if they would, and so on. The murderess was adjudged unfit to stand trial, and hanged herself in Bedlam not long after.

"I don't know how familiar you are with that oppressive part of the world. In those years farming was a difficult enterprise at best, isolating, stultifyingly boring, unremunerative. unremunerative. Hired men were heavy drinkers. Prices were depressed. The women aged quickly, what with continual childbirth added to a load of work at least equal to their menfolk's.

JOHN CROWLEY

What I'm getting at is that it is, or was, a society the least of any conducive to adultery, amours, romance. And yet for some reason it appeared, after this murder pointed it up, so to speak, dramatically, that there was a veritable plague of inconstant husbands in northern Cheshire."

"It's difficult to imagine," I said, "what evidence there could be of such a thing."

"I had occasion to go to the county that autumn, just at the height of it all," Sir Geoffrey went on, caressing an ashtray with the tip of his cigar. "I'd at last got a grip on myself and begun to accept invitations again. A fellow I'd known in Alexandria, a commercial agent who'd done spectacularly well for himself, asked me up for the shooting."

"Odd place to go shooting."

"Odd fellow. *Arriviste*, to speak frankly. The hospitality was lavish; the house was a red-brick Cheshire faux-Gothic affair, if you know what I mean, and the impression it gave of desolation and melancholy was remarkable. And there was no shooting; poured rain all weekend. One sat about leafing through novels or playing Cairo whist—which is what we called bridge in those days—and staring out the windows. One evening, at a loss for entertainment, our host—Watt was his name, and..."

"What was his name?" I asked.

"Exactly. He'd become a student of mesmerism, or hypnotism as he preferred to call it, and suggested we might have a bit of fun probing our dark underminds. We all declined, but Watt was insistent, and at last suborned a hearty local type, old squirearchical family, and—this is important—an inveterate, dirt-under-the-nails farmer. His conversation revolved, chiefly, around turnips."

"Even his dark undermind's?"

"Ah. Here we come to it. This gentleman's wife was present at the gathering as well, and one couldn't help noticing the hangdog air he maintained around her, the shifty eyes, the nervous start he gave when she spoke to him from behind, and also a certain dreaminess, an abstraction, that would fall on him at odd moments."

"Worrying about his turnips, perhaps."

Sir Geoffrey quashed his cigar, rather reproachfully, as though it were my own flippancy. "The point is that this ruddy-faced, absolutely ordinary fellow *was cheating on his wife*. One read it as though it were written on his shirt front. His wife seemed quite as aware of it as any; her face was drawn tight as her reticule. She blanched when he agreed to go under, and tried to lead him away, but Watt insisted he be a sport, and at last she retired with a headache. I don't know what the man was thinking of when he agreed; had a bit too much brandy, I expect. At any rate, the lamps were lowered and the usual apparatus got out, the spinning disc and so on. The squire, to Watt's surprise, went under as though slain. We thought at first he had merely succumbed to the grape, but then Watt began to question him, and he to answer, languidly but clearly, name, age, and so on. I've no doubt Watt intended to have the man stand on his head, or turn his waistcoat back-to-front, or that sort of thing, but before any of that could begin, the man began to speak. To address someone. Someone female. Most extraordinary, the way he was transformed."

Sir Geoffrey, in the proper mood, shows a talent for mimicry, and now he seemed to transform himself into the hypnotized squire. His eyes glazed and half-closed, his mouth went slack (though his mustache remained upright), and one hand was raised as though to ward off an importunate spirit. "'No,' says he. 'Leave me alone. Close those eyes-those eyes. Why? Why? Dress yourself, oh God...' And here he seemed quite in torment. Watt should of course have awakened the poor fellow immediately, but he was fascinated, as I confess we all were.

"'Who is it you speak to?' Watt asked.

"'She,' says the squire. 'The foreign woman. The clawed woman. The cat.'

"'What is her name?'

"'Bastet.'

"'How did she come here?'

"At this question the squire seemed to pause. Then he gave three answers: 'Through the earth. By default. On the *John Deering*.' This last answer astonished Watt, since, as he told me later, the *John Deering* was a cargo ship he had often dealt with, which made a regular Alexandria-Liverpool run.

"'Where do you see her?' Watt asked.

"'In the sheaves of wheat.'"

"He meant the pub, I suppose," I put in.

"I think not," Sir Geoffrey said darkly. "He went on about the sheaves of wheat. He grew more animated, though it was more difficult to understand his words. He began to make sounds-well, how shall I put it? His breathing became stertorous, his movements..."

"I think I see."

"Well, you can't, quite. Because it was one of the more remarkable things I have ever witnessed. The man was making physical love to someone he described as a cat, or a sheaf of wheat."

"The name he spoke," I said, "is an Egyptian one. A goddess associated with the cat."

"Precisely. It was midway through this ritual that Watt at last found himself, and gave an awakening command. The fellow seemed dazed, and was quite drenched with sweat; his hand shook when he took out his pocket-handkerchief to mop his face. He looked at once guilty and pleased, like—like—"

"The cat who ate the canary."

"You have a talent for simile. He looked around at the company, and asked shyly if he had embarrassed himself. I tell you, dear boy, we were hard-pressed to reassure him."

Unsummoned, Barnett materialized beside us with the air of one about to speak tragic and ineluctable prophecies. It is his usual face. He said only that it had begun to rain. I asked for a whiskey and soda. Sir Geoffrey seemed lost in thought during these transactions, and when he spoke again it was to muse: "Odd, isn't it," he said, "how naturally one thinks of cats as female, though we know quite well that they are distributed between two sexes. As far as I know, it is the same the world over. Whenever, for instance, a cat in a tale is transformed into a human, it is invariably a woman."

"The eyes," I said. "The movements—that certain sinuosity."

"The air of independence," Sir Geoffrey said. "False, of course. One's cat is quite dependent on one, though she seems not to think so."

"The capacity for ease."

"And spite."

"To return to our plague," I said, "I don't see how a single madwoman and a hypnotized squire amount to one."

"Oh, that was by no means the end of it. Throughout that autumn there was, relatively speaking, a flurry of divorce actions and breach-of-promise suits. A suicide left a note: 'I can't have her, and I can't live without her.' More than one farmer's wife, after years of dedication and many offspring, packed herself off to aged parents in Chester. And so on.

"Monday morning after the squire's humiliation I returned to town. As it happened, Monday was market day in the village and I was able to observe at first hand some effects of the plague. I saw husbands and wives sitting at far ends of wagon seats, unable to meet each other's eyes. Sudden arguments flaring without reason over the vegetables. I saw tears. I saw over and over the same hangdog, evasive, guilty look I described in our squire."

"Hardly conclusive."

"There is one further piece of evidence. The Roman Church has never quite eased its grip in that part of the world. It seems that about this time a number of R.C. wives clubbed together and sent a petition to their bishop, saying that the region was in need of an exorcism. Specifically, that their husbands were being tormented by a succubus. Or succubi—whether it was one or many was impossible to tell."

"I shouldn't wonder."

"What specially intrigued me," Sir Geoffrey went on, removing his eyeglass from between cheek and brow and polishing it absently, "is that in all this inconstancy only the men seemed to be accused; the women seemed solely aggrieved, rather than guilty, parties. Now if we take the squire's words as evidence, and not merely 'the stuff that dreams are made on,' we have the picture of a foreign, apparently Egyptian, woman—or possibly women—embarking at Liverpool and moving unnoticed amid Cheshire, seeking whom she may devour and seducing yeomen in their barns amid the fruits of the harvest. The notion was so striking that I got in touch with a chap I know at Lloyd's, and asked him about passenger lists for the *John Deering* over the last few years."

"And?"

"There were none. The ship had been in dry dock for two or three years previous. It had made one run, that spring, and then been moth-balled. On that one run there were no passengers. The cargo from Alex consisted of the usual oil, dates, sago, rice, tobacco—and something called 'antiquities.' Since the nature of these was unspecified, the matter ended there. The Inconstancy Plague was short-lived; a letter from Watt the next spring made no mention of it, though he'd been avid for details—most of what I know comes from him and his gleanings of the Winsford *Trumpet*, or whatever it calls itself. I might never have come to any conclusion at all about the matter had it not been for a chance encounter in Cairo a year or so later.

"I was en route to the Sudan in the wake of the Khartoum disaster, and was bracing myself, so to speak, in the bar of Shepheard's. I struck up a conversation with an archaeologist fellow just off a dig around Memphis, and the talk turned naturally to Egyptian mysteries. The thing that continually astonished him, he said, was the absolute thoroughness of the ancient Egyptian mind. Once having decided a thing was ritualistically necessary, they admitted of no deviation in carrying it out.

"He instanced cats. We know in what high esteem the Egyptians held cats. If held in high esteem, they must be mummified after death; and so they were. All of them, or nearly all. Carried to their tombs with the bereaved family weeping behind, put away with favorite toys and food for the afterlife journey. Not long ago, he said, some *three hundred thousand* mummified cats were uncovered at Beni Hasan. An entire cat necropolis, unviolated for centuries.

"And then he told me something which gave me pause. More than pause. He said that, once uncovered, all those cats were disinterred and shipped to England. Every last one."

"Good Lord. Why?"

"I have no idea. They were not, after all, the Elgin Marbles. This seemed to have been the response when they arrived at Liverpool, because not a single museum or collector of antiquities displayed the slightest interest. The whole lot had to be sold off to pay a rather large shipping bill."

"Sold off? To whom, in God's name?"

"To a Cheshire agricultural firm. Who proceeded to chop up the lot and resell it. To the local farmers, my dear boy. To use as fertilizer."

Sir Geoffrey swirled his nearly untouched brandy and stared deeply into it, watching the legs it made on the side of the glass, as though he read secrets there. "Now the scientific mind may be able to believe," he said at last, "that three hundred thousand cats, aeons old, wrapped lovingly in winding cloths and put to rest with spices and with spells, may be exhumed from a distant land—and from a distant past as well—and minced into the loam of Cheshire, and it will all have no result but grain. I am not certain. Not certain at all."

The smoking-room of the Travellers' Club was deserted now, except for the weary, unlaid ghost of Barnett. Above us on the wall the mounted heads of exotic animals were shadowed and nearly unnameable; one felt that they had just then thrust their coal-smoked and glass-eyed heads through the wall, seeking something, and that just the other side of the wall stood their vast and unimaginable bodies. Seeking what? The members, long dead as well, who had slain them and brought them to this?

"You've been in Egypt," Sir Geoffrey said.

"Briefly."

"I have always thought that Egyptian women were among the world's most beautiful."

"Certainly their eyes are stunning. With the veil, of course, one sees little else."

"I spoke specifically of those circumstances when they are without the veil. In all senses."

"Yes."

"Depilated, many of them." He spoke in a small, dreamy voice, as though he observed long-past scenes. "A thing I have always found-intriguing. To say the least." He sighed deeply; he tugged down his waistcoat, preparatory to rising; he replaced his eyeglass. He was himself again. "Do you suppose," he said, "that such a thing as a cab could be found at this hour? Well, let us see."

"By the way," I asked when we parted, "whatever came of the wives' petition for an exorcism?"

"I believe the bishop sent it on to Rome for consideration. The Vatican, you know, does not move hastily on these things. For all I know, it may still be pending."

PRIVATE GRAVE NINE

KAREN JOY FOWLER

EVERY WEEK FERHID takes our trash out and buries it. Yesterday's was chicken bones, orange peels, a tin that cherries had come in and another for peas, a comb I sat on and broke, two prints I overexposed and several discarded drafts of Mallick's letter to Lord Wallis about our progress. Meanwhile, at G4 and G5, two bone hairpins and seven clay shards were unearthed, one of which was painted with some sort of dog, or so Davis says, though I'd have guessed lion. There's more to be found in other sectors, but all of it too recent - anything Roman or later is still trash as far as we are concerned. G4 and G5 are along the deep cut and we pull our oldest stuff there.

I'd spent the morning in the darkroom, feeling lucky that my work demands this privacy. I'm an only child; the constant companionship of the expedition house is sometimes hard on me. The photographs I was printing were of infant skeletons. There's an entire level of these, all laid out identically on their sides with their little legs pulled into their stomachs. My pictures were of all different children, but all my pictures looked the same.

Davis had cleared each tiny skull and ribcage with his breath because they were so delicate, and I wondered if he'd felt any attachment to one more than another, but it seemed a rude thing to ask. I had some philosophical thoughts that I shared at lunch, on how much sadder a single child would have been and how odd that it should be like that, you feeling less with each addition. Mallick, our director, said when I'd put in a few more seasons I'd find I didn't think of them as dead people at all, but as the bead necklace or the copper bowl or whatever else might be found with the body. Mallick's eyes are all rimmed in red like a basset hound's, which gives him a tragic demeanor, though he's really quite cheerful. The whole time he was speaking, Miss Jackson, his secretary, was seated just past him with her head down, attending to her plate. Miss Jackson lost her husband in the trenches and her son to the flu after. Remembering that, and remembering how each of her losses was merely one among so many they might as well have been stars in the sky or sand on the beach, made me wish I'd kept my thoughts to myself.

FERHID HAD CARVED us a cold lamb for lunch and had the mail lying under our forks. Ferhid has the profile of a film star, but a mouth full of rotted teeth. I often wish he smiled less; his mouth is a painful thing to see while eating. We each had a letter or two, which was fair and companionable, though most of them mentioned Howard Carter's dig, which was not. Mine was from my mother who pretends not to miss me as unpersuasively as she can. Being her sole support kept me out of the army, but it's a role I've found burdensome since the war ended. Last month I wrote to her that a man must have a vocation and if nothing comes to him, then he must go looking. Today she responded by wondering if it was necessary to travel half a globe and 4500 years away. She said that Mesopotamia must be about as far from Michigan as it's possible to get. How wonderful it must be, she said, to be so unattached that you can pick up and go anywhere and never mind the people you've left behind. And then she assured me she wasn't complaining.

Patwin read bits of the *Times* aloud while we had our coffee. Apparently reporters are still camped at the Tut-ankh-Amen tomb, cataloguing gold masks and lapis lazuli scarabs and ebony effigies as fast as Carter can haul them out. These *Times* accounts have Lord Wallis and everyone else in a spin, as if we're playing some sort of sporting match against Carter and losing badly. Our potsherds, never mind how old they are, have become an embarrassing return on Wallis' investment, though they were good enough before. Our skeletons are too numerous to be tasteful. I'm betting Wallis won't be whimsical about paintings of dogs, nor will anyone else at his club.

As he read, Patwin's tone conveyed his disapproval. He has an anarchist's face, but is actually a French Marxist and, though he'll tell you slavery was a necessary historical phase, shards of good clay working class pots suit him better than golden bowls put by for the afterlife.

"We had a lovely morning in PG 9," Mallick said stoutly. PG stands for private grave and PG 9 is the largest tomb we've found so far, four chambers in all, and never plundered, which is the really exciting part. A woman is laid out in the second of these chambers—a priestess or a queen in a coffin of clay. There's a necklace of gold leaves, a gold ring, and several of the colored beads she once wore in her hair have fallen into her skull. The bodies of seven other women kneel about her, along with two groomsmen, two oxen, and a musician with what I imagine, when Davis reconstructs it, will be a lyre. Once upon a time Wallis would have been entirely content with this. A royal tomb. A sleeping priestess. But that was before Carter began to swim in golden sarcophagi.

ANOTHER AMERICAN, A girl from Rapid City, has come to visit us in the expedition house. Her name is Emily Whitfield and she's a cousin of Mallick's wife or a second cousin or some such thing, some relative Mallick found impossible to send away. She's twenty-nine years old, which is two years younger than I am, unremarkable black hair, cut very short, unremarkable eyes of a watery blue, but a good figure. Because of our similar ages there'd been some teasing before she arrived. "High time you met the right girl," Mallick had said, but the minute I'd seen Miss Whitfield I'd known she wasn't that. I've never believed in love at first sight, but I've had a fair amount of experience with the opposite.

Patwin had claimed to dread Miss Whitfield's visit, in spite of the obvious appeal of a new face. "She'll need to be taken everywhere and someone will always be hurting her feelings," Patwin had predicted. Patwin prided himself on knowing women although when that would have happened I really couldn't say. "She'll find it all very dirty and our facilities insupportable. She'll never have stood before." And then Patwin had a coughing fit; it was such a rude thing to have said in Miss Jackson's presence.

But Miss Whitfield was proving entirely game. Davis took her to see the baby skeletons and he said she made no comment, lit an unmoved cigarette. She was actually an authoress and quite successful, according to Mallick who'd learned it from his wife. Five books so far, books in which people are killed in clever and unusual ways, murderers unmasked by people even cleverer. She was about to set a book at a dig such as ours; it's why she'd come. Mallick told me to take her along and show her the tomb, so she was there when I took my picture. I pointed out an arresting detail or two—the way the workmen chant as they haul the rubble out of the chamber, the rags they tie around their heads, their seeping eyes. She didn't seem interested.

We brought the smell of sweat and flesh with us into the tomb. Most people would have instinctively known to whisper. Not Miss Whitfield. "I thought it would be grander," she said when we were inside the second chamber. "I didn't picture mud." She lifted a hand to her hair and when she lowered it again there was a streak of dust running from the hairline down her temple. It gave her a friendlier, franker look, but like Mallick's eyes, this proved deceiving. What she really wanted to know was whether there were tensions in the expedition house. "You all live so cheek-by-jowl. It must drive you crazy sometimes. There must be little, annoying habits that send you right around the bend."

"Actually things go very smoothly," I told her. "Sorry to disappoint." I set up for the picture. I dragged a stool over and stood on it. Miss Whitfield was beneath my elbow. Davis was in a corner of the chamber on his knees, pouring wax and covering it with cloth. Bits of shell and stone had been found there in a pattern. When the wax dried he would lift them out without disturbing their placement.

Miss Whitfield finally softened her voice. She was so close I could smell the cigarette smoke lingering in her hair. "But if you did murder someone," she whispered, "would it more likely be Mr. Patwin or Mr. Davis?" She might have been asking this at the exact moment I got my shot. Afterwards she looked closely at the priestess's skull. "I hear Tut-ankh-Amen's skull was bashed in at the back," she said. She was clearly disappointed.

Later that night Patwin complained that I was blocking his light while he tried to read. I told him it was interesting that he thought the light belonged to him. I said, that's an interesting point of view for a Marxist to take, and I saw Miss Whitfield pull out her notebook to write the whole thing down.

A CYLINDRICAL SEAL was found on the bier and Davis deciphered a name from it. Tu-api, along with a designation for a high-born woman. A princess, not a priestess, then. We also found a golden amulet, carved in the shape of a goat standing on its hind legs. There'd been a second goat, a matching partner, but that one was crushed beyond mending. Pictures of all the ornaments had to be finished in a rush and sent off to Lord Wallis. The goat is really lovely and my photograph showed it well; no one will have to apologize for that find.

But even better were the stones and shells that Davis had been excavating. Mallick believed there'd once been a wooden box with pictures pressed into its sides. The box had disintegrated and the two sides fallen together, but Davis was slowly putting them right. One side showed scenes from ordinary life. There was a banquet with guests and musicians, farmers with wood on their backs, oxen and sheep. The second side was all armies, prisoners of war, chariots, men with weapons. Before and After, Miss Jackson called it, but Mallick called it Peace and War to clarify that it represented two parts of a cycle, and not a sequence, that peace would follow war as well as precede it. The forgotten artist must have been remarkable as the people were so detailed, right down to the sorry look on the prisoners' faces.

Patwin criticized me for taking more pictures of Tu-api than of the kneeling girls or the poor musician. Tu-api, he guessed, had the good fortune to die of natural causes. He said that I must fight the bourgeois impulse to care more about the princess than about the slave. It would be even harder, he conceded, now that the princess had a name.

Does he always lecture at you like that?" Miss Whitfield asked. "How irritating that must be!"

BECAUSE I WAS busy developing pictures of golden goats and verdigris bowls, because we'd already sent Lord Wallis plenty of photographs of skeletons, I left my shot of Tu-api untouched for a couple of days. It was late at night when I put it through the wash and hung it up. I didn't look at it closely until the following morning. In my photograph, Tu-api had a face. This wasn't part of the picture exactly, but a cloudy, ghostly spot with imploring eyes superimposed over the skull. It made my skin crawl up the back of my neck and I took it out to the dig to show the others. It was a hot day and the air so dry it stung to breathe. I found Mallick, Davis, and Miss Jackson all together in the third chamber.

They were not as unnerved as I was. A human face is an easy thing to find, Davis pointed out, in the paint on a ceiling, the grain in a wooden board. "I once saw the face of God in the clouds," Miss Jackson agreed. "I know how that sounds, but it was sharp and perfect as a Michelangelo. Sober and very beautiful. Racially indistinct, but a thin Chinese sort of beard. I got down on my knees and watched until it melted and blew away."

This sudden display of fancy from solid, cylindrical Miss Jackson obviously embarrassed Mallick. He got scholarly in response, with his dry voice and those sad eyes. "I've heard of places where bodies are naturally preserved right down to the facial expression," he said. "In the Arctic ice, for example. At very high altitudes. I've always thought those discoveries must be rather grim."

"Buried in the bogs," Patwin said. He'd arrived with Miss Whitfield while Mallick was speaking. He held out his hand for my photograph and looked it over silently. He handed it to Miss Whitfield. "I knew a man who'd met a man who'd found a thousand-year-old woman while digging for peat. He said you can't look into a thousand-year-old face and not find yourself just a little bit in love. You can't look into a thousand-year-old face and think, I bet you were an annoying old nag."

"You've just put your thumb here on the print," Miss Whitfield suggested to me. As if I were eight years old and playing with my father's camera.

I imagined myself with my hands about her throat. It came on me all of sudden and shocked me even more than the photograph had. I took my imaginary hands off her and gave her an imaginary and forgiving handshake instead.

In fact, I was angry with them all for refusing to believe the evidence of their own eyes. The woman's face was indistinct, I grant you that. But so beautiful. So filled with longing. I looked into her eyes and I could see that she'd been frightened. I could see that she hadn't wanted to die alone, had surrounded herself with other people, but it hadn't helped her. I thought we all maybe knew something about that. I knew I did.

ON PAYDAY THERE were forgeries to be exposed. A number of intriguing little carvings had begun to show up, all found by the same pair of brothers. The recent ones were simply too intriguing. Mallick made a show of dismissing the culprits as a lesson to the rest. It was all very good-natured. Even the brothers laughed at their exposure, left with a cheerful round of goodbyes. It was, no doubt, a great disappointment to Miss Whitfield who had been looking forward to the confrontation ever since Mallick showed us the tiny forged bear.

None of the workmen would be back until their money ran out, which meant that we would start again in two days time with a whole new crew. Yusef, who'd found the golden goat, had been paid its weight in gold and wouldn't be back for weeks. This was a shame as he was one of our most skilled workers and a natural diplomat as well. Diplomats were always needed on our mixed crew of Armenians, Arabs, and Kurds.

The site was sadly quiet with everyone gone. I missed the rhythmic chanting, the scraping of stone on stone, the frequent pleasure of dim and distant laughter.

Davis and I used the day off to drive Miss Whitfield to the holy shrine of the Yezedis. The Yezedis worship Lucifer and represent him with the symbol of the peacock. We bounced along the road, the dust so thick I had to stop every fifteen minutes and wipe down the car windows. The last few miles can only be done on foot, but by this time you've risen into the pure air and walking is a pleasure. The shrine is breathtakingly, white and intricate as a wedding cake. Streams pour through descending basins in the cool courtyard and acolytes tiptoe in to bring you tea. Clearly their Lucifer is not the same as our Lucifer.

Still we'd done our best to work Miss Whitfield up with stories of Satan worshippers so that the peaceful, bucolic scene would be a nasty surprise. I figured I was getting to know what Miss Whitfield wanted. I whispered to her that the priest, whom we did not see, was said to be kept drugged so that his aunt could rule in his name; I didn't want the trip to be a complete disappointment.

"Tell me," Davis said to Miss Whitfield. He sat holding his small, black cup of tea in two hands and smiling sweetly. I was across from him, sleepy from the sun and the sound of water. Miss Whitfield had knelt by the lowest of the fountain pools. She broke the surface with her hand, so her submerged fingers seemed larger than the dry hand to which they were attached. "When you come to a place like this," Davis asked, "even at a place like this, do you find yourself imagining a murder?"

And I thought how easy it would be to push Miss Whitfield's head under and hold it. It wasn't even a complete thought, just a flicker, really, with no emotional content, no actual desire. I put it instantly out of my mind, which was easy enough since it had hardly been there to begin with.

"Would you think I was a ghoul if I said yes?" Miss Whitfield's black hair shivered in the slight breeze. She smoothed it back with her wet fingers, dipped her hand and wet her hair again.

"I'd think you the complete professional," Davis said politely. "But it's a ghoulish profession."

"So's yours," she answered.

And then to me, "So's yours," even though I hadn't said a thing.

On our way back we stopped in town to buy bread and chocolate to add to our supper of mutton and goat cheese and tankards of wine. Davis had gotten too much sun during our outing; he was as pink as if he'd been boiled. When he came to the table he sat on a chair that wasn't solidly beneath him and fell to the floor with a loud cry of alarm. I'd never seen Patwin enjoy anything so much. He could hardly chew he was laughing so hard.

Miss Whitfield was too tired to eat. Ferhid took her untouched plate back to the kitchen where he dropped knives and slammed pots onto tables to communicate his disapproval until Mallick went out to mollify him.

Before the light went, and when there was no one else about, I slipped away and took six more pictures of Tu-api. I developed them that night, quietly so that no one would hear me up and about. None of the new ones showed her face. I took another print off my original exposure and her face didn't show up there either. Perhaps this should have persuaded me that the image wasn't to be trusted, was a fault of the paper and therefore unreal. Instead it had the opposite effect. I was even more persuaded in the event, which was proving so singular and so intimate. Tu-api had shown her face only once and only to me.

"I HAVE A bone to pick with you." Patwin caught me as I came out of the bathroom. "You're always riding me about my politics."

Patwin didn't often use the sort of American idioms these two sentences contained so I imagined he was merely repeating what some more native speaker had said to him and I imagined I knew who that would be. I was outraged by the collusion, but also by the sentiment.

"You must be joking," I said. "The way you lecture me…"

"Live and let live is all I'm saying." And he brushed by without another word.

I passed Davis on the way to my bedroom. "That really hurt when I fell," he said. "I may have cracked a bone."

"I didn't laugh as hard as Patwin did," I told him.

MISS WHITFIELD ASKED us all what it was about a dig that we liked. We were sitting in the courtyard in the middle of the expedition house and only Mallick was missing, trapped in town by a heavy rain that had turned the roads to mud. The air outside was washed and wonderful and the sky an ocean of cool, gray clouds. Davis and Miss Jackson were playing a game on a stone board more than four thousand years old. Four thousand years ago they would have played with colored stones, but they were making do with buttons. Seven such boards had been found in Tu-api's tomb and the rules were inscribed in cuneiform though not in our dig, but back in Egypt at Carter's. This same game had been played as far away as India. Ferhid was a demon at it.

"Not the fleas," Patwin said. He was scratching at his ankles.

"Not the dust." That was Miss Jackson.

"Not the way the workmen smell," I said.

"Not the way you smell," Patwin added. And then placatingly, "Not the way I smell."

"I like a routine," Davis told her. "I actually enjoy picky, painstaking work. And, of course, I like a puzzle. I like to put things together, guess what they mean."

"I like that it's backwards." Miss Jackson won a free turn and then a second. All six of her buttons were on the board now. "You dig down from the surface and you move backwards in time as you go. Have you never wanted, desperately wanted, to go backwards in time?"

"Yes, of course," Miss Whitfield said. "Erase your mistakes, the stupid things you say without thinking."

"I like the monotony of it." Patwin had his eyes closed and his face turned up to the cool sky. "Day after day after day with nothing at all but your own thoughts. You begin to think things that surprise you."

Davis bumped one of Miss Jackson's buttons back to the beginning. "There you go backwards in time," he said, but Miss Jackson was speaking too, only quieter so it took a moment longer to hear. "You have to be in love with the dead to like a dig," she said. She took two of her stones off the board in a single turn and bumped one of Davis's. A third stone occupied a safe square, leaving Davis no move.

He shook his fist at her, smiling. "You're a lucky woman," he said.

"Do you know how many bodies we've found on this site?" Miss Jackson asked Miss Whitfield. "Almost two thousand. And every single one of those left someone behind, begging their gods to undo it. Bargaining. Screaming. Weeping. You can only manage a dig if you already feel so much you can't take in another thing."

A long silence followed. "Excuse me," Miss Jackson said and left the courtyard.

Miss Jackson seldom made speeches. She never, ever referred to her losses and I only knew about them because Patwin, who'd worked with her three seasons now, had heard it from gossipy Mallick. Patwin had hinted that she was sleeping with Mallick, but I'd seen no signs and hoped it wasn't true. Miss Jackson was not a young woman, nor a pretty one, but she was too young and too pretty for Mallick. Few women wouldn't be.

I thought back on how she'd also told us she'd seen the face of God in the sky and how that speech too had been uncharacteristic. Perhaps we'd come up on the anniversary of something or other. Or perhaps Miss Whitfield was responsible. Miss Whitfield might make me edgy and snappish, but perhaps Miss Jackson had melted in the sympathetic presence of another female.

"Well," said Miss Whitfield. "I hope it wasn't something I said." She wrote a few words in her notebook and then addressed me. "You're very quiet. Are you in love with the dead?"

Since I'd been thinking about Miss Jackson and not about myself, I had nothing prepared to say. "I'm not sure I do like a dig," I answered. "I'm still deciding." My heart was thudding oddly; the question had unnerved me more than I could account for. So I kept talking, just to demonstrate a steadier voice. "I wanted to see some things I wouldn't see in Michigan. Mallick gave a lecture at the university and I asked some questions that he liked and he said if I could make my own way here, he could use me."

Miss Whitfield was staring at me through little eyes. I could see that she didn't believe me and, from her vantage point, I could also see how defensive I'd sounded, how unresponsive to the actual question, and how unlikely my sequence of events was. Mallick in Michigan. Me, asking such good questions from the audience that I was hired on the spot. In fact, it was all true, but pointing that out would be the most suspicious move of all. I felt unjustly accused, but also terribly, visibly guilty. There was a letter opener on a table by the doorway. I pictured myself picking it up and opening Miss Whitfield's throat in one clean swipe.

All of a sudden Patwin laughed. "What?" Davis asked him. "What's so funny?"

"I was just remembering when you fell off your chair," Patwin said. He was still laughing. "How your arms flew up!"

I'D BEGUN VISITING Tu-api's tomb at night when no one would know. I'd like to say that there was nothing at all odd in this, but how defensive would that sound? I won't persuade you, so let's just skip that part.

In fact, I was disturbed by the murderous images coming over me and the tomb seemed a quiet place to figure things out. I wasn't the sort to hurt anyone.

People rarely upset or angered me. I'd never been a bully at school, didn't fight, didn't really engage much with people at all. Didn't care about anyone but myself, my mother had said once after my father died. She'd never said it again, but she hinted it. Buried it in the subtext of every letter. Her own grief had been an awful thing for an eight-year-old boy who'd just lost his father to see.

But mostly I thought of myself as a typical photographer. I was a watcher, a recorder. I was empty inside, always had been. And I thought how these violent images had started up shortly after Miss Whitfield's arrival, and might have come with her. But they'd also begun shortly after Tu-api had shown me her face. In fact, if I remembered correctly, at the moment I had taken my picture the word murder had been hanging in the air. The smell of smoke. "If you were to murder someone," Miss Whitfield had been asking, "who would it be?" Was it possible that the word itself had brought Tu-api back? Perhaps what I saw in her face wasn't longing after all, but remorse. Patwin was always pointing out how she was a murderess. Perhaps she wanted company in some unending world of guilt.

But I found it easier to think Miss Whitfield was to blame than that Tu-api wished me ill. I'd begun to carry the print of her face in my pocket so I could pull it out and look at it whenever I was alone. At night I would sit on the bricks by her coffin and stare until I'd conjured her face out of the darkness.

One night, walking as silently as possible back to my bedroom I nearly collided with Mallick. He was wearing a nightshirt that left his saggy old

---

knees bare. "Going to the lavatory," he explained unnecessarily, so that I knew it was true what Patwin had told me, that he'd been visiting Miss Jackson. I tried to see the good in that, but really, what comfort could sleeping with Mallick have been?

"Me, too," I said with an equal lack of conviction.

We stood a moment, carefully not meeting each other's eyes. "So Miss Whitfield leaves tomorrow," Mallick offered finally. "She's been a lively addition." I realized then that he thought I'd been visiting Miss Whitfield. As if that wouldn't be worth your life!

A woman's face appeared in a doorway, white and sudden.

When my heart began beating again, I recognized Miss Whitfield. She didn't speak to me; merely noted my suspicious, nighttime ramblings, my covert meetings with Mallick and disappeared as quickly as she'd come, no doubt to write it all down before she forgot. "Taking my own sort of pictures," she called it once, as if what she did and what I did were the same, as if her imposed judgments could be compared to my dispassionate records. If I'd wanted to murder her this would have been my last opportunity. Not that I wanted to murder her. Plus Mallick had seen me. I'd never have gotten away with it.

I went to my room and into a night of troubled dreams. Miss Whitfield left the next morning. At Patwin's insistence, I took a picture of everyone before she went. Patwin was always reminding me to document the work as well as the artifacts. "Take some pictures of live people today," he would say. "Take some pictures of me."

Everyone lined up in the expedition house courtyard, staring into the morning sun. In the resulting photo, Davis has his hand on Patwin's shoulder, but no one else is touching. Miss Whitfield couldn't stand still and ruined three exposures before I got one that showed her clearly.

"Was there a curse on Tu-api's tomb?" she'd asked us shortly after her arrival. According to the newspapers Carter had a curse; it was one more way in which we disappointed. (According to Mallick, who had his own sources, no one could find the actual site or text of this alleged curse. Other tombs had them so, of course, Carter couldn't be expected to do without.)

The very day Carter found the entrance to Tut-ankh-Amen's tomb a cobra ate his pet canary. "Some curse," Patwin scoffed when we read this, but Davis had reminded us how canaries in mines were there to die and warn you death had entered a room. And then, just last week, we had a telegram from Lord Wallis that Lord Carnarvon, who sponsored Carter's dig, had suddenly died in Cairo. The cause was indeterminate, but might have been a fever carried by an insect bite on his cheek. Back in England his dog had also died—this curse was most unkind to pets.

It was the dog that put Miss Whitfield over the top. She cared little for mountains of copper, gold, and ebony. She was, as Patwin had noted, being nothing but fair, no materialist. But she did love a suspicious death. She left us for Egypt just as quick as an invitation could be wrangled and transport arranged.

I believe we were all a bit disappointed to realize that none of us was to be the murderer or victim in her next book. All those murderous thoughts I'd obligingly had, all the probing we'd withstood, all the petty disputes we'd engaged in and all for nothing. The one to reap the benefit would, of course, be Carter.

We stood at the entry to the expedition house and waved. She was turned around to us, her face in the window, smaller and smaller until it and then the car that carried her vanished entirely. "A dangerous woman," Patwin said.

"A terrible eater," said Ferhid. His tone was venomous. "A picky eater."

"I can't put my finger on exactly what it was about her," said Miss Jackson. "But there were times when she was watching us, taking notes on everything we said and did, as if she knew what we really meant and we didn't—there were times when I could have happily strangled her."

So we were all glad to see the last of her. It didn't mean she wasn't missed. It was hard to go back to how we'd been before; there was a space left where she'd been and nothing else would fit inside it. Ferhid kept forgetting and setting her plate at the table for four days after she'd gone.

THE NIGHT OF her departure I went again to Tu-api's tomb. The silhouette of the ruined ziggurat shone in the moonlight. There was the hum of bugs; a dog barked sleepily in the distance; my footsteps thudded in the dust. The wind was cool and carried the smell of cooked chicken. My relief was enormous. The only reason I'd thought of murdering Miss Whitfield was that she was an annoying woman who often talked about murder. There was nothing supernatural at work here; it was all perfectly normal and everyone had felt the same.

The moon had risen, round as an opened rose. I walked away from it into the perfect darkness of the tomb. I owed Tu-api an apology. How could I ever have thought, even for a minute, that she'd curse me? I begged for her forgiveness. It was the first time I'd spoken to her aloud.

She was not the only one listening. Mallick had apparently told Patwin his suspicions regarding me and Miss Whitfield, and Patwin, being more discerning and trained to read puzzles far older and more mysterious than I, came upon the truth of it. He'd followed me and when I spoke, he was the one who responded. "What's this about?" he asked and what could I possibly say?

"You can't be coming here anymore at night by yourself." Patwin stepped towards me. "You can't be thinking this way." He took me by the arm. "Come back to bed."

I let him lead me over the moonlit dust to the expedition house. As we went, he analyzed my errors. I was guilty of romanticism, of individualism. I was guilty of ancestor worship. I had entertained the superstition of an ancient, powerful curse. I wasn't even bourgeois; I had barely made it to primitive.

There was no need to lecture me. I knew all those things. He put me to bed as if he were my mother, sitting beside me for awhile, pretending nothing was wrong, just the way my mother would have pretended. "You need a girlfriend," he suggested. "It's too bad Miss Whitfield has gone. It's too bad Miss Jackson is already spoken for."

I stopped listening. I'd just realized something about myself, something so unlikely, so unexpected that no one would ever have guessed it. I myself would never have guessed it. Mother would never have guessed it and she would be so surprised when she found out. The thing I realized was this: I was the sort of person who would do anything for love.

Call it a curse if you like. I've never felt so joyful, so serene. Mr. Davis or Mr. Patwin? Mallich or Miss Jackson or Ferhid? All or none of the above? The choice was hers, not mine. I just had to wait until she made it.

Serenity is, of course, a transitory state. Whatever Miss Jackson may wish to believe, humans being humans, eternal peace is only found in the grave and not always even there. I'm not telling you anything you don't already know.

But why spoil the moment with the long view?

Let's leave me here, filled with love. I had only to turn to see Patwin's concerned, doomed face. I agreed with everything he said. I agreed that my infatuation with Tu-api was at an end. I agreed that, circumstances being different, I would have considered Miss Jackson or even, God forbid, Miss Whitfield. I agreed that when the weather grew too hot and we all went to our separate homes for the summer, I would put serious effort into finding a girlfriend who was alive. I agreed that love could be usefully examined with the tool of Marxist analysis. I handed over my photograph and watched Patwin tear it up, both of us pretending there was someplace he could put those pieces where they wouldn't last forever.

MUMMY FEVER

DAVID WELLINGTON

IT WAS 1923, which was the year the autogyro was invented. It was also the year the first commercial refrigerator was sold, in Sweden of all places—where you would think keeping things cold would be less of a priority. Ice cubes to Inuits, and all that (though, to be technical about it, the ice cube tray wouldn't be invented until 1928). The first one-piece bathing suits were seen on American beaches that year, which raised quite a scandal. Most importantly to our story, it was also the year that Howard Carter breached the inner burial chamber of Tut-anhk-amen, and became the first man in millennia to behold, by flickering lamplight, the golden sarcophagus contained therewithin.

The effect on the popular imagination was as immediate as it was electrifying. The combination of hidden treasure and lost millennia of history filled column inch after column inch in the newspapers, and soon a kind of fever for mummies and golden death masks spread faster than the Spanish Influenza.

Everyone in New York had to have an Ancient Egypt party, with ladies dressing in tight white wrap dresses and the men wearing handkerchiefs on their heads. The Metropolitan Museum of Art, on the Upper East Side—the only place in New York to see authentic mummies—stayed open late on Friday nights and offered light refreshments and activities of dubious educational value. Much amusement was to be had by having one's photograph taken while standing sideways, for instance, one foot in front of the other, and by fanning each other with giant palm leaves.

This was the fourth year of Prohibition, which meant people had to find fun where they could get it.

Ancient Egyptian fashions were all the rage, as long as they met the standards of public decency. Men weren't exactly running around in linen skirts, certainly, but gold jewelry was everywhere and women wore far too much eyeliner. It was considered especially droll, then, if not altogether "too much", when a fellow came into the museum wrapped head to toe in neatly laundered linen bandages. Taking away—just a bit—from the effect was the fact that he also wore a natty grey suit and a celluloid collar, and twirled a felt Trilby on one bandaged finger. Still, his commitment to the mummy look drew cheers and acclaim as he made his appearance. He sketched a quick bow for the crowd in the lobby, then took a glass from a passing waiter and made his way toward the exhibits.

The Met possesses a truly top-notch, world class collection of Egyptian artifacts. Painted wooden coffins lay in state amongst glass cabinets absolutely stuffed full of lapis lazuli scarabs and alabaster ankhs and jade cosmetic pots. It was not, however, the finery of some ancient queen or the massive granite statues of Cheops that commanded this strange visitor's attention. Nor was it the free sandwiches or the souvenir maps of the Valley of the Kings. Instead, he headed directly for a rather dusty and uninspiring collection of tall stone jars, each with a stopper in the shape of an animal's head. Items so uninteresting that they were protected solely by being placed behind a velvet rope, perhaps to keep anyone from accidentally knocking them over with their coat tails.

The odd fellow studied the jars for a while, then proceeded to lift one index finger and point it at each of the jars in turn, exactly like a grocery shopper trying to pick out the ideal pineapple. The bandages over his lips could be seen to move, as if he were muttering to himself.

Elspeth Rose Lieberman-Tubbs found herself drawn, quite ineluctably if unconsciously, toward this man. Perhaps she was simply bored that day, or perhaps some undercurrent of unresolved Oedipal stress motivated her (Elspeth Rose Lieberman-Tubbs, being a devotee of the new fad of psychoanalysis, found Oedipal undercurrents dogging her heels on a regular basis). She sidled up beside him—apparently unnoticed—and sipped at her glass, watching him over its rim.

He nodded politely to her, and knocked back his own drink. Then he reared his head in surprise. "These martinis appear to be malfunctioning," he said. "From the taste I'd say there isn't any gin in them at all."

"On the bright side, there's no vermouth, either." She gestured at the display of jars. "Looking for anything in particular?" she asked.

"I'll know it when I see it," the man said. He had an accent that might not have been born in England but which had definitely taken vacations there. "Ah. This one." He pointed at a jar that looked exactly like all the rest. Its stopper was worked in the shape of the head of a falcon, and it was inscribed with several lines of hieroglyphic text. Elspeth Rose Lieberman-Tubbs saw nothing whatsoever to recommend it.

The bandage-wrapped man reached over the velvet rope and picked up the jar and tucked it under his arm. Then he put his hat back on, pausing only momentarily to tip it in Elspeth Rose Lieberman-Tubbs' direction.

"Good evening," he said, and then he proceeded to walk right out of the museum.

Or at least, he gave it the old college try. Before he could reach the door, a veritable mountain of a man stepped into his path. A good six feet tall and of a width that would make it difficult for him to get through doors, the museum's guard had a pistol on his hip and a complete lack of a smile on his face.

"Where do you think you're goin' with that?" the guard asked, using his chin to indicate the jar.

"To my hotel, actually," the wrapped gentleman replied. "Though I might stop off and get a proper drink first. Now, if you'll excuse me—"

"Alright, pal, hand it over," the guard said.

"This canopic jar? But it's my property."

"I don't see your name on it," the guard pointed out.

"Yes, you do. Right here." The odd fellow pointed at a line of hieroglyphs. "Neferkare-ka-Imsety. Couldn't be plainer."

This exchange had garnered the attention of the crowd and now several red-cheeked men came pressing in, some of them pretending to read the pictograms on the jar, some slapping Neferkare-ka-Imsety on the back. "He's got you there," one of them said.

None of them seemed to take with any seriousness the fact that they were witnesses to an attempted crime. The guard, whose job was to take such things very seriously indeed, squinted and pursed his lips and dropped one massive hand on Neferkare-ka-Imsety's shoulder. Then he did something rather odd. He grunted in frustration. His face turned a liverish sort of color and his eyes widened.

"Anything at all the matter?" Neferkare-ka-Imsety asked.

In fact, there was. The guard had been attempting to grab the smaller man by the shoulder, with the intent of spinning him around and twisting his arm behind his back. It was a tactic that had worked invariably for him in the past. It should have this time, as well. Neferkare-ka-Imsety, or whatever the joker's actual name might be, was rail thin and not particularly tall. The weedy sort of fellow who ought to have to worry about strong breezes sending him cartwheeling down the street.

After straining and huffing and puffing for nearly a minute, the guard had to admit he would have had more luck attempting to restrain one of the granite statues of Cheops.

He therefore proceeded to his second and final gambit of the night, which was to take a step back and draw his pistol. He pointed it directly at the sunken chest of the would be jar thief. "Drop it!" he said.

"I rather think that would be a mistake. It's quite fragile," Neferkare-ka-Imsety pointed out.

The guard cocked his pistol. Then, because he was out of options and had never possessed much imagination, he pulled the trigger.

Someone screamed. Elspeth Rose Lieberamn-Tubbs looked around to see who it was, then realized, to her profound embarrassment, that it had been her. She ran forward, the tails of her stole flapping, her arms out to catch the foolish, funny man. She had time, as she ran, to concoct an entire scenario in her head, of how she would hold the dying man in her arms as he bled out his last. It would give her a great deal to talk about at her next session with her analyst.

Unfortunately for the progress of psychology, by the time she reached Neferkare-ka-Imsety, he had yet to fall down. Nor, in fact, did he seem likely to any time in the near future. He did let out a cry of distress, as he prodded the new and very neat little hole in his vest.

"I quite liked this shirt," he said.

The guard's eyes had been wide before. Now they grew to the size of saucers and his jaw fell open and slack. He raised his pistol once more, clearly intending to empty the barrel into the impossible man, but before he could do so, Elspeth Rose Lieberman-Tubbs grabbed the jar out of Neferkare-ka-Imsety's grasp—clearly, he wasn't expecting that—and tossed it in the guard's general direction.

"Catch!" she said.

The guard had played football for his high school team. Reflexes honed over countless Sundays upon a green and grassy field kicked in and he dove, fingers outstretched, to catch the falling jar. For a moment it looked like he would fumble the reception, the priceless artifact dancing out of his grasp, but at the last moment, his hat swinging forward over his eyes, his knees colliding noisily with the marble floor, he snatched victory from the jaws of defeat and caught the jar mere inches from its destruction. It was really quite a thing to see, a moment of sublime dramatic tension.

Sadly, neither Elspeth Rose Liberman-Tubbs nor Neferkare-ka-Imsety was there to observe it, as they had both got while the getting was good.

"Neferkare-ka-Imsety," the fellow said, because they hadn't been formally introduced, "but my friends call me Neville."

"Elspeth Rose Lieberman-Tubbs." She held out one gloved hand, and he shook it. "Kind people call me anything but. Elspeth, to you, I think."

And thank goodness they got that out of the way. They both had very long names, and typing them out over and over again was becoming a chore.

They were in the back room of a druggist's of Elspeth's acquaintance, sipping at martinis that still might not contain any gin but which made up for it with generous lashings of bootleg moonshine. The ambiance of the room left something to be desired—they were surrounded on every side by crates and boxes and bottles of horse pills—but at least the lighting was poor enough to suggest an intimate club.

Even here, Egyptian Fever had spread. The password to get into the back room was "Ramses II", and only that because the proprietor felt that the police would too easily be able to guess "Tutankhamen."

For a while they sat drinking in silence, perhaps each of them having their own questions to ponder after the events at the museum. It was Elspeth who broke the ice.

"Poetess," she said, and lifted her chin. Then let it drop again, because for some reason she wanted to tell this fellow the truth. "Well… when I left Radcliffe I intended to be a poetess. I was going to starve in a freezing garret and sit up through sleepless nights, keeping myself warm with the mad fires of inspiration."

"I take it that didn't happen," Neville said.

"No. I discovered something important very early on. That a poetess with no talent can starve all she wants and no one will even notice, whereas a writer of greeting cards with no talent can make twenty-five dollars a month."

"Greeting cards? How delightful. Roses are red, and violets—"

"Oh, please, don't be boring already," Elspeth told him. "Anyway, the game has quite thoroughly moved on from that sort of thing. I was at the museum today looking for inspiration. We're bringing out a new line of Egyptian-themed cards and before Monday morning I need to think of six words that rhyme with 'sarcophagus'. Now. It's your turn, Mr. Neville Imsety. What is it that you do?"

"Oh, me? I'm a mummy."

"You're a madman. Or this is all some kind of practical joke."

"I imagine," Neville said, "you'd prefer the latter, but I'm afraid that—"

"Hardly," she said, interrupting him. "I positively cultivate madmen. At the very least, they're useful for breaking up dull parties. No, let me guess, you're on some kind of wild scavenger hunt, and one of the things you need to recover is a dusty antiquity. Or perhaps you're a Russian spy, that has possibilities."

"Asparagus," Neville said.

"Not exactly a word one finds in many greeting cards. Yes, a Russian spy, and your contact has placed some secret message inside that jar. You couldn't think of a better way to recover it."

"Omnibus."

"Only slightly better. Oh, I've just thought of something. You're a scholar of ancient Egyptian folklore, and you've read a legend of a fabulous gem concealed inside a nondescript clay jar, and only recently one fitting the description was unearthed at Karnak or somewhere. You tracked it across three continents, until it turned up here in America, and..."

"*De Gustibus*," Neville tried.

"*Non est disputandum?*" she finished. "That just gives me an even harder word to rhyme."

Neville stroked his bandaged chin. "For all we strive/the best of us/end up alike/in a sarcophagus."

"There is nothing more hateful to a failed poetess than morbid doggerel. Now, Mr. Imsety. I would like to make you a deal. You will tell me, with complete honesty, why you dressed up like a mummy and tried to steal a no doubt priceless but utterly uninteresting antiquity from the Metropolitan Museum. For my part, I will sit here and listen intently."

"Deal," Neville said, and they clinked glasses to seal the bargain. "Well, the short version is this. Four thousand years ago I was the son of a pharaoh, next in line for succession. Except everyone knew I would be quite terrible at the job. So my sister had me mummified alive, or, if you prefer, mummified to death. So she could be the queen, instead."

"Complete nonsense."

"I spent four thousand years in a dusty tomb, which I did not enjoy at all. In 1920, some kindly British archaeologists came along and dug me up and found me much as you see me now, though not as fashionably dressed. They took me back to the British Museum, where I learned English and table manners and card games."

"If I didn't find you so charming," Elspeth said, "I would hate you *utterly* for being such a liar."

Neville lifted his hands in the air, then let them fall back. By complete happenstance, one of them happened to fall neatly around the stem of his martini glass.

"It was a bit of a surprise even to me," he said, "to find that I was a living mummy. Or alternatively, that the world wasn't completely overrun by living mummies. I seem to be the only one. After some rather diligent research I discovered the secret to my long life. When I was mummified, you see, my internal organs were removed. My lungs, my liver, my stomach and my intestines were all stored in what are called canopic jars. As long as these jars remain intact, I simply cannot die."

"Oh, is that all there is to immortality?"

"My contemporaries took mummification quite seriously, and turned it into a kind of science. I imagine there were incantations and spells and you had to burn the right sort of incense. It was a very long ceremony, and I can't remember all the details—I was a bit distracted while they were stuffing me full of salt and wrapping me up like a Christmas gift."

"I don't believe they had Christmas back during the Old Kingdom," Elspeth pointed out.

"First Intermediate Period, thank you very much. And I was using a simile, something I would expect a professional writer to appreciate."

"My apologies. So you were saying, about these four jars…?"

"After even more diligent research, I discovered that my own four canopic jars had been scattered across the globe. Dug up by various tomb-robbers and archaeologists and packed off to various museums. My liver was still in Cairo. My lungs were in the Kaiser-Friedrich-Museum in Berlin. That jar was a bit tricky to find—it was locked up in a drawer in the back rooms, in a box mislabeled as containing smilodon coproliths. The one containing my intestines turned out to be in the British Museum, right under my nose. And the last of them is here, in New York. I have the other three—I simply need this one, the final resting place of my mortal stomach."

"And so you tried to steal it."

"I'm no criminal," Neville insisted. "I tried to buy it, first. They directed me to their gift shop, where I could purchase a rather nice replica in plaster of Paris. But that won't do. So I was reduced to a more direct method."

"Daylight burglary."

"Admittedly, I am untutored in the more clandestine arts." He shrugged. "Now you've heard my tale. I can see you don't believe a word of it, and that's fine. You got me out of a predicament, and I'm grateful. You introduced me to my new best friend here," he said, lifting his martini, "and for that I am ever in your debt. But I believe I will finish this drink and then head home."

"Not a chance," Elspeth said.

Neville's eyes were covered with linen bandages, which meant that it was quite difficult to know when something had surprised him. He did set his drink down—carefully—and turn to give her his full regard.

"No. You and I are going back to the museum, and we are going to recover that jar," she said. She set her jaw and gave him a determined nod.

"We … are?" Neville asked.

"We are." Elspeth had decided on two possible explanations for Neville's behavior. One was that he was completely insane. The other was that he was under the spell of some prior life as an Egyptian prince (belief in reincarnation being another of her fads). Either way, it was clear he would not rest until he had the jar. "However, we're going to be smart about it, this time. For instance, we're going to wait until midnight, when we're less likely to be caught at it."

"That's still hours away. What shall we do in the meantime?"

Elspeth lifted one hand in the air and snapped her fingers. "Waiter!" she shouted. "Another round!"

A BIT UNSTEADY on her pins, perhaps, but filled with that sort of courage that only the mad and the hopelessly romantic will ever know, Elspeth hailed a taxi just before the stroke of midnight. She bundled Neville inside before she'd even looked at the driver. This man so perfectly fit the image you already have in your head of a New York City taxi driver circa 1920 that no description is necessary, except to point out that he was wearing a gold and blue headcloth in the style of an Egyptian pharaoh.

King Tut fever, again.

"It's called a *nemes*," Neville explained to her, when she remarked upon the unusual headgear. "Good for keeping the sun off your shaved head."

"Is it at all historically accurate?" she whispered, sinking low in the seat next to him.

"We didn't have rayon back then," he said. "What are you doing?"

"Keeping out of sight," she told him. "It's important that we keep a low profile. Isn't it? After we get the jar, the police will ask a lot of questions, and—"

"Ahem." Neville took a twenty-dollar bill from his pocket and passed it forward to the driver. "If anyone asks about us, perhaps you might conveniently forget a few details, my good man? For instance, the fact that you had a passenger who looked like a mummy."

"Mac, for that kind of dough I'll tell 'em you were dressed like the Marquis de Lafayette."

"Splendid," Neville said.

It was not a long drive back to the museum. They pulled up behind the building, in the secluded darkness of Central Park, and hurried through trees and bushes up to the least well-lit of the museum's rear entrances. Elspeth, with a shaking hand, tried the door and found it locked. She tried it again, just to be sure, and found that it was also made of steel and considerably reinforced. Unsurprisingly, perhaps, the designers of a building full of priceless art treasures had chosen to make it difficult to break into. "Perhaps … I can go 'round front and knock on the door and ask to use the telephone," she suggested. "Then once inside I'll make a big show of searching for the number I want, until the guard gets bored of watching me and wanders off, and then I can sneak back here and unlock the door for you, and—"

Neville grasped the doorknob and twisted it until it groaned. Something inside the lock mechanism snapped and the door came open. "This might be easier," he said.

Elspeth stared at the open door for quite a while, wrestling with everything she knew to be true about the nature of reality.

Then she rather meekly (despite herself), agreed with his conclusion, and slipped inside.

It was very dark in the museum. The scant moonlight that made its way in through the building's windows illuminated only a small patch of the floor. Elspeth found herself bumping into things quite often, and had to simply hope she didn't knock any expensive statues off their pediments or ancient curios off their display tables. Her companion seemed far better able to navigate through the gloom. As they wended their way through a long hall full of suits of armor, he offered her his hand.

"If you bump into one of these it'll make a terrible racket when it hits the floor," he whispered.

She took his hand. His grip was delicate and his fingers were cool. The bandages even soaked up the clammy sweat that had broken out on her palm. He led her at a good pace but not too fast toward the lobby of the museum, which abutted on the Egyptian wing. Even after they had passed out of the arms and armor exhibit, he did not release her hand.

Were this a very different kind of story, we might mention that her heart was racing, and not just from fear of being discovered by armed guards. We might speak of how lonely a man can get after forty centuries locked up in a tomb, and how nice it was for Neville to meet a young woman who was even willing to listen to his mad story, much less help him in his quest. But this isn't that sort of story, so you'll just have to imagine what the two of them were feeling as they slipped, as silently as possible into the broad, dark lobby of the Met Museum.

Dark—though not pitch black. The beam of a flashlight was playing across a far wall, and they could hear the echoing beat of hobnailed shoes as a night watchman made his appointed round. Elspeth took the lead and pulled Neville behind the counter of an information desk. Together they crouched in close quarters as they listened to the guard move on, his footsteps eventually fading away into silence.

They ducked inside the Egyptian wing, where the tall shadows took on a whole new sinister aspect. Human forms with jackal heads loomed over

Elspeth on every side. Death masks stared out of deep time into the shadowy room, their golden eyes seeming to glow—and to follow her, as she moved furtively past. Despite having been one of a crowd of museum patrons in this very room not eight hours prior, she felt like she was treading on hallowed and forbidden ground, stepping through the dust of a place no one was ever meant to go. Her mind reeled, just a bit, and she reached out to steady herself. Her hands fell on chilly stone, rough with age. She ran her hand across the surface and felt the chiseled features of a human face, and gasped.

She was leaning on a sarcophagus. She could feel the lid groan and start to shift under her weight.

"Don't do that!" Neville hissed, from farther away than she'd expected. She heard him rushing toward her.

"Why not?" she asked, terrified. "Am I about to awaken some dread magic of the ancients? Am I violating some funerary precept of a long dead religion?"

"No," he said. "That's just a cousin of mine."

Elspeth drew her hands back and lifted them to show she'd meant no harm. "You can see in the dark, can't you? And you're stronger than ten men. I thought, earlier, that when the guard shot you, the bullet must have bounced off of your cigarette case, or something—that you'd been freakishly lucky. But it wasn't that. Was it?"

"Hmm? No," Neville said. He was moving again, headed for the display of canopic jars that was their goal.

"You're ... you're exactly what you said you were," she breathed.

"Blast," he said.

He was not in any way responding to her grand realization. Instead, he was noticing for the first time that there was something missing from the display. Specifically, his canopic jar was gone, absent from the row of them like a broken tooth.

"They've removed it. Perhaps they wanted to check it and make sure it wasn't damaged in today's excitement. Or perhaps they expected me to come back for it, and they've put it someplace more secure."

"The latter," someone said, from behind them.

The lights came on, just then, and dazzled Elspeth's eyes until she could barely see. All around her golden artifacts blazed and shone, and for a moment the world spun around her, a welter of archaic smiles and scarab beetles, a kaleidoscope view of blue and red and green, of old gods and colossal snakes and boats that could carry the sun across the sky—

"I beg your pardon," Neville said. "I don't think we've met."

"Lysander Felixstowe," someone said. "I'm the assistant curator for Egyptian antiquities. And I would suggest you not try anything rash."

Elspeth blinked the ancient history out of her eyes and looked round to see a little man in spectacles and an ill-fitting suit. His hair was slicked back with far too much pomade and his grin was entirely too predatory for her liking.

He was flanked on either side by a guard, big burly men really quite identical to the one who featured earlier in this narrative, down to the fact that both of them had played football in high school. Additionally, both of them were armed with large revolvers, which were pointed at Neville's chest.

"I'm afraid those," Neville said, "aren't much of a threat to me. You see, as hard as it may be to believe, I'm actually—"

"A living mummy," Felixstowe said. "Yes, I've heard all about you from Herr Doktor Gotthard, my colleague in Berlin. He warned me you might be coming. Now, if you'll follow me, we'll head to my office, where we can wait until the police arrive."

"I was going to mention that I can't be harmed by bullets," Neville said.

"Ah. But your mortal friend here can, can't she? You two," Felixstowe said, looking to his guards. "If they try anything funny, shoot her."

"WHAT EXACTLY HAPPENED in Berlin?" Elspeth asked, as the two of them were marched through the—now well-lit—museum.

"I told you, the jar was filed away incorrectly. I had to open quite a few cabinets to find it. I might have made a bit of a mess."

Elspeth frowned. "You said you weren't a criminal."

Neville shrugged, while keeping his hands in the air. "Rather an academic question now, don't you think?"

They passed through a door behind the museum's teashop, and into a series of winding corridors into the offices and laboratories that were forbidden to the public. Elspeth, a woman with a strong sense of adventure, might have been excited to see these hidden halls, if she hadn't been so petrified. She was going to lose her job, she thought, at the very least. She might have to actually move back home to Ohio, and prove to her father that she couldn't make it on her own in New York. She rather feared that outcome more than the other possibility, which was that she would be shot to death.

Felixstowe's office was not large. Much of the space was taken up by his massive mahogany desk and a row of bookcases, so the five of them had trouble all fitting inside at once. The curator sat down behind the desk and steepled his fingers, tapping them together in evident delight. He did not offer them a seat.

"I suppose now that it doesn't matter, I can at least let you see the object in question," he said. He took the jar out of a drawer of his desk and set it carefully on his blotter.

Elspeth could feel Neville tense up in excitement where he stood next to her.

The curator picked up a file card and read from it. "Item Number 1006739. Canopic jar of the royal prince Neferkare-ka-Imsety, First Intermediate Period, circa 2000 BC. Rather an exquisite specimen," Felxistowe said. "Completely intact after all this time. If you shake it, you can actually hear the organic remains rattling around in there."

"I'd prefer you didn't," Neville said. "I had a large dinner."

The curator, however, was on a roll, and ignored the mummy. "A carved alabaster jar with hieroglyphic inscription. Stopper carved in the image of the god Qebehsenuef—"

"You're pronouncing that incorrectly," Neville pointed out.

Felixstowe frowned. "Quay-buh-sen—"

"No, no. Kay-bee-sen-woof."

"Kabe-ess-en-weff," the curator tried.

"Kay-bee-sen-woof."

"Kay-beez-en-wofe—"

"Geseundheit," Elspeth said.

Felixstowe grimaced. "Enough. The important thing here is that this is the museum's property. Your repeated attempts to steal it from us are unacceptable. We're going to have to prosecute you to the full extent of the law."

"How dare you!" Elspeth said.

Both Neville and the curator turned to stare at her.

Well, at least they were paying attention. Men so rarely did. "You say it's your property, well, well, that's just—just applesauce."

Felixstowe raised an eyebrow.

"It's a common American expression meaning 'nonsense'," Neville pointed out. "Popular among the younger set, especially flappers."

Elspeth had never been called a flapper before. Because, she expected, she just didn't have the dress sense. She chose to take it as a compliment. "You can't claim to own it. That's his stomach in there!"

She gave Neville a tiny smile, to acknowledge the fact that she had finally accepted, completely, his wild story. That she believed everything he'd said.

"You can't lay claim to own a man's stomach, that's just not right. I may not know much about the law, but I'm certain there's something in the Constitution about a man having a right to his own internal organs."

This being the entirety of her argument, and as a writer knowing that brevity was the soul of wit, she left it at that.

"You appeal to the Constitution," Felixstowe said, nodding just a little. "Well. I'd like to draw your attention to a much older body of law. One with a great deal of precedent behind it."

"What's that?" she asked.

"Finder's keepers," the curator said. "There's a mania for this sort of thing right now, or didn't you notice? The museum needs all the Egyptian tat it can get its hands on. I'm sorry, but we'll be holding onto this for now."

He picked the jar up off of his desk with both hands. Then, perhaps simply out of spite, he gave it a hearty shake.

Neville sighed. "So it's come down to this. Forgive me, Dr. Felixstowe. I had no intention of allowing things to grow so desperate."

Then he reached out and grasped the jar with one hand. The guards reached for their guns, but Neville had already tilted his head back and was speaking in a language perhaps never heard before in New York City.

A language neither Elspeth nor the guards recognized, though certainly they could make a good guess: it was the tongue of the ancient Nile, the old form of Egyptian Coptic, and every word was pronounced correctly.

For the sake of younger readers or those who slept through their Coptic language lessons in school, we shall provide a translation into English of what Neville said:

> "Who lays a hand upon this jar
> or disturbs its holy contents,
> his mouth shall speak no more.
> His feet will never know rest.

His heart shall grow heavy.
And every time he eats a ham
sandwich, he will spill mustard
upon his tie."

Felixstowe's hands flew away from the jar. Luckily Neville had a good grip on it and did not drop it. The curator's face turned ashen and he sank back in his chair, breathing heavily. The transformation was quite arresting.

"Go," he said. "Get out of here."

The guards looked at each other. "Boss?" one of them said. They were so identical to one another it really doesn't matter which.

"Get them away from me," Felixstowe said. "Show them the door! Quickly, before he does something worse!"

"You ... sure about this?" the second guard asked. "You don't want us to maybe, you know, rough 'em up a little, first?"

"No! And make sure they take the stupid jar with them!"

"YOU PUT A curse on it," Elspeth said, once she'd worked it all out. "You put a curse on the jar, so that he wouldn't want it anymore."

Neville nodded. "When dealing with a bully, the best tactic is often to play on their worst fear. There's nothing an antiquarian is more afraid of than an ancient curse. Occupational hazard, eh?"

After leaving the museum, the two of them had made their way back to Neville's hotel. It was a little scandalous for Elspeth to go unescorted to a man's rooms, but when she heard he was staying in a penthouse suite at the Ritz-Carlton, she decided she would dare society's opprobrium, just this once. The rooms turned out to be exactly as sumptuous and tasteful as she'd expected, and the bottle of champagne the desk sent up to them was the real thing—Prohibition be damned. Anyway, she needed to be with Neville in these, his last moments on Earth.

"So that's something you can do. Put curses on people."

Neville topped off her glass. "No," he said.

Elspeth tilted her head to one side. "No?"

"No. Of course not. I'm a mummy, not a magician. Now. How would you like to come with me and see the view from the balcony?"

"I think I'd like that very much," she said.

The city lay spread out before them like a glittering Cubist jewelry box, a million lights in orange and white. A stiff breeze braced her and made her remember what was coming next, and she bit her lower lip in anticipation. Anticipation, and a little fear.

Neville had the canopic jar in his hands. He strode over to where a carved wooden box sat on a low table by a chaise longue. Already there were three jars in the box, their animal head stoppers facing one another. Neville placed the falcon-headed jar in its place, then balled his hands on his hips and regarded what he'd done.

"So ... that's it," she said. "All you need."

She thought she understood. Elspeth's analyst was a kindly old man with a white beard and a pocket watch. He had explained to her all about what Dr. Freud called the death drive, that inescapable urge toward self-destruction, the need of life to return to the state of inorganic matter. He'd told her it was quite natural, and that it explained why men fought wars, and drove their cars too fast, and why sometimes she didn't feel like brushing her teeth in the morning.

How strong, how irresistible would such an urge be, in the heart of a man who'd lived four thousand years and couldn't die? Unresolved impulses tend to fester. How long had Neville been planning this? How long had he desired to simply end, to cease to be?

"Do you need me to do it?" she asked, because she could tell he was hesitating. "I think I can manage." She bent and picked up the box—it was very heavy—and lurched toward the railing. Intending to cast the four jars down into the street, where they would certainly shatter and release Neville from all mortal concerns.

She would have done it—at least, she believed that she was capable of doing it—if he hadn't gotten there first and snatched the box out of her hands.

"Terribly sorry, but I can't let you do that," he said.

She could only stare at him. "Wasn't this your whole plan? You said you couldn't die until all four jars were destroyed."

"I did say that, yes," he told her.

"But you don't want me to smash them."

"I'd really prefer it if you didn't."

Elspeth shook her head in confusion. "But then I don't understand. Why go to so much trouble to find the jars?"

"Why, so I can put them in a safe deposit box in the most secure bank I can find," Neville told her. "Goodness. Why on earth would I want to die? I spent four millennia buried under the burning sands, sleeping in a golden sarcophagus, with no one but a few disappointed carrion beetles to talk to. Now—now I want to live a little!"

Elspeth covered her mouth with one hand, because she was afraid otherwise he would notice that her jaw was hanging open. Eventually she started to laugh. "Alright," she said. "Alright. Alright! Where do we start?"

"If I remember correctly," he told her, holding out a hand that she took without hesitation, "we left half a bottle back in the room. That's as good a place as any."

THE MUMMY OF RUE DE LA CROIX

LEANNA RENEE HIEBER

THE NIGHT MADAME Alexandria first saw the mummy she was surrounded by shards of canopic jars, moments after she had pulled off a rather stunning Séance calling up the dramatic, tempestuous spirits of Pharaohs long deceased.

Teatre de la Croix was a small venue, a few hundred seats covered in worn red velvet. Intimate. What she loved most about the theatre was its shadows; the generous archways and sharp alcoves of the lobby created distinct chasms, the scalloped ceiling adding breadth above, the pillars of the house, painted to look like marble, cast long black shafts along the orchestra level as gaslight played from sconces on red walls and across the mezzanine from large lanterns meant to bathe the stage in a warm fiery glow. Every dark space became a thrilling abyss.

During her shows Madame kept the audiences small—to create scarcity—and trimmed the gaslamps as low as the flames could go without winking out to maximize the breadth of the beaux arts edifice and its dramatic darknesses.

She chose to host her audience and performances directly on the stage itself, her attendees surrounding her at a great circular table with a secondary crescent of chairs facing her, the great "Wardrobe of Giza" behind her—an old 'spirit cabinet' redone with a few cartouches and distressed to look like a treasure of antiquity. A close audience was good for Madame's routine in that it was hard to hide the theatrics ... and that's exactly what she relied upon. Her tricks, her "prestige" was simple, contained, effective, and yet to be under attack by the likes of Houdini, who was on a present rampage of unveiling charlatan Spiritualists.

Madame chafed at the word charlatan. She was a performer. While she may once have been able to claim some Sensitivities, her gifts weren't quite enough to be considered full Mediumship.

She agreed with Mister Houdini and his friend Mister Conan Doyle, even as they foiled sham acts by describing every trick- rending asunder the code of secrecy sacred to fellow magicians. A *magician* should present a brilliant prestige, and an audience should *know* they are attending a *magic* show.

Charlatan Spiritualists, on the other hand, claimed to actually contact and convey messages from dead relatives, convincing thousands of desperate believers of the ghostly activity of long-lost loved ones while handsomely collecting profits garnered from leading questions, plants in the audience and clever stagecraft. This lot did not present prestige but a direct lie, and while Madame had an ethical standard that varied depending on the circumstances, taking advantage of the grieving had been written off her list of accepted practices. She had turned a new leaf. Her debts, dalliances and name were all left behind in Rochester, New York when she fled to Paris for shelter and a fresh start.

The Egyptology fascination that had gripped France, England and America since the last century gave her plenty of room to contact 'another realm' without personal responsibility. It did occur to her that her routine might be considered sacrilege to anyone actually *practicing* ancient Egyptian worship, so as to not anger Bastet or Thoth, Isis or Osiris, she made up names, rituals and hieroglyphs and crafted items to look like they'd been pilfered from pyramids rather than obtaining actual loot. Grave robbing was terribly rude. Madame was a woman who liked to cover all her bases in this life and the next. She was an open believer in the fact humanity knew precious little about the great beyond and she was rather terrified of retribution from any god so she allowed for the existence of all of them.

Madame left honest mediumship to the less theatrically inclined, the more socially awkward and fiercely driven; poor, unfortunate creatures who Spirits dogged and pestered day and night. Madame preferred to shut her doors and work only when she must. When not performing, she and her young apprentice Ben wandered the great, bohemian metropolis.

Stepping out onto the street for a deep breath of sooty air, one of them would always exclaim; "Ah, Paris. *J'adore*," as they took one another's hand. When away from the stage her illegitimate son could call her "mother", when at work and she became *Madame*, he was an apprentice and she was a consummate lady betrothed to a baron.

They had something good here, on Rue de la Croix, allowed by the theatre's absentee management to rent a dressing room as a flat, and working on the theatre's dark and off-hours was consistent.

But then there was the matter of the mummy.

The mummy threatened all she'd gained.

At least, it would if she didn't play her cards right... At least, if she could keep from screaming in abject terror.

It had appeared twice so far.

The sighting happened when she was holding her small but enthusiastic audience in quite a thrall. Speaking of the long dead, the curses of the entombed, the complicated rituals of death and eternal life, she ended her act with a dramatic bit of Egyptian recitation. (It was not remotely Egyptian but she felt she pulled it off well enough.) Fans fluttered and bosoms were clutched, men leaned in, grasping hands, and someone always fainted.

Just at the moment of ideal swooning, it was then that the shadow was seen in the wings. Unmistakable. Tall, thin, a figure wrapped in cloth.

By God, there is a mummy in the wings ... Madame had thought with wonder, then terror.

A mummy was not a part of her act. She *mentioned* mummies but she didn't *have* one in the show.

Ben couldn't have rigged that up. He was in the spirit cabinet- pardon, the *Wardrobe of Giza*- behind her, knocking out rhythmic responses from across the veil as she granted her audience safe and gracious passage into the night once released from the clutches of ancient curses.

The mummy kept itself safe in the shadows of the blacks, the curtains in the wings, for a long moment. But, as all mummies are purported to do ... it shuffled forward.

A woman who was closely following the direction of Madame's gaze turned. And screamed.

That's how Madame's fortune, and her misery, began.

It returned every night. In the same shadows. With that same dread shuffle. Every time there was some sort of distracting sound, drawing attention away from the mummy after first sight and when the audience returned their gaze to the shadows the mummy was gone.

It was a magnificent prestige, Madame would have to admit, but if pressed she would also have to reveal that it is not *her* prestige; her trick. She had no *idea* what it was. And that would be bad for business.

So she let it be. Terrifying as it was for her every time it appeared. Like clockwork. She prayed it wasn't an angry ancient god and regretted the theatre's distinctly deep shadows.

She had to obtain a larger circular table and expand the perimeter of chairs. Scared to change her routine, all she changed within her text was that the mummy would not appear to them if any of them moved or turned around before it was time, and none were to run after it. None had yet disobeyed, a month in, and the mummy was on cue every time as if a carefully rehearsed part of the act.

On days before a show, if she and Ben were feeling brave, they hunted the prop closets, each dressing room, every rig, walkway and below-stage trap for signs of the creature. Nothing. It was the greatest mystery of the age she could never reveal, for to do so would be to confess the greatest part of her act had nothing to do with her talents.

Sweeping up after a particularly rousing performance from the spirit cabinet, Ben having outdone himself, Madame froze at the sound of a name being called out from across the darkened house.

"Jenny Richards." A loud male voice rang out from the shadows in a distinct American drawl. "Well, well, well," the voice continued, the proximity getting closer down the darkened house aisle, a shadow moving forward. "You didn't make it easy tracking you down here now did you."

Madame sputtered in her French accent, "*Pardon*, I'm sorry, I do not know—"

"Cut the act, Jenny," the voice entered into the ambient light off the center ghost lantern. "You swindled my family out of a great deal of money with one of those acts of yours. My mother nearly lost us everything in your foolishness. I don't suppose you remember your time in Lexington, Kentucky before you reinvented yourself up north, but you were the ruination, or near ruination, to many of those whom you preyed upon and I am here to make you pay for your swindles."

Madame looked up into the wings, the dim backstage lights making out Ben's small profile. She knocked twice upon the table, one of their cues between them, this one meant stay put at all costs. He did not disobey.

The man strode up the stairs to the stage and walked right over to her.

"I don't know who you are," she protested.

She did remember those dark days under the thumb of a terrible man in a down and out place and had wanted to forget about that southern city more than any time in her young life, and never so much as now.

"The name is Drummel and you cheated my mother something fierce with your 'premonitions', she never won a dime at a single horse race and you and that bookie knew it. You'd best have a cash box in this sad excuse for a theatre."

"Everything is locked away," Madame stated. "I'm sure we can have a calm discussion about what troubles you-"

The man reached out and ripped off her auburn wig, tearing strands of her own light brown hair out with it in the pins that kept it attached and she cried out in pain. She could see Ben make a move forward but she held out a hand towards him.

"Stop!" she cried, dropping the French accent and speaking in the neutral American tone she'd left behind on American stages, her old voice again. It sounded more foreign to her ears than the overdone French had become. "You don't understand," she insisted, "this place is cursed, there is something terrible and ungodly in this theatre, we are beholden to it ..."

Drummel laughed and took a menacing step closer, noticing the locket around her neck.

It was really the only treasure she owned. A family heirloom from her mother, may she rest in peace and never know what her daughter had gotten up to. Drummel ripped it off Jenny's neck, the clasp breaking and scratching a piece of flesh away at the back of her neck as she stifled another cry.

She didn't want to betray her son by looking into the wings but she noticed that he had turned away from her, staring back deeper into the wings, where a figure stood in the dim backstage light.

The mummy.

It had something in both hands.

It stepped forward, towards Ben, not a shuffle this time, a preternatural glide forward, something liquid-fast and horrifying.

Jenny wanted to cry out but she didn't dare. Drummel was still chuckling. Out of the corner of her eye she watched Ben's silhouette disappear into the darkness, away from the mummy.

"Cursed," he drawled. "Of course. I'm sure you tell that to all your customers," he sneered. "So that they might pony up more of what precious little they might have to give? You sick vulture."

He put a hand around her throat, the back of his fingers grazing the trickle of blood from the scrape of the broken necklace. "Take from me and mine I will take from you and yours. Only fair." He squeezed his hands, Jenny coughed. "Cash. Where is it?"

There was a shambling sound. A plume of firelight leapt on from the switches in the wings, casting the stage in a sideways shaft of illumination from backstage fixtures, and the mummy now shuffled out onto the stage, closer than she'd ever seen it, all dusty bandages and thin limbs, a distressing rasping sound emanating from its desiccated throat.

"What the hell is that-" he released his hands and stepped back.

"The curse!" Jenny cried, choking.

The mummy threw one of the two palm-sized vases in its hand at Drummel's head. It hit him square in the ear, blood spurting out onto his white collar, dust flying out everywhere.

It was only in that mad moment Jenny realized what the mummy must have thrown; a canopic jar exploding in shards and matter. Organs dried thousands of years ago pulverized upon impact and dispersed into the air in a thick cloud. It might, she thought with shuddering wonder, have even been the mummy's own innards.

Drummel reeled, staring at the mummy, his hand to his bloody ear, and he yelped as the second jar in the mummy's hand was airborne. It hit him square in the back as he leapt off the stage and down back up the center house aisle. There was a sliding sound and an object suddenly at her feet. Ben had, in these moments, run to the dressing room and back to slide her pistol across the floor to her while he stayed hidden in the wings, brilliant boy.

"Now stay out," Jenny shrieked. If I ever see you or hear of you again, you'll find out I have Annie Oakley's aim to punctuate that curse!" She cocked the pistol.

The rear theatre door slammed shut. The silence was deafening save for her heartbeat in her ears.

When she turned back, the mummy was gone.

The only proof that it had been there was the dust and shards of two pots and whatever Ben had witnessed along with her.

"Hello?" Jenny called into the wings. "I ... I want to thank you, whoever you are ... I ... thank you ..."

She looked down at Ben and whispered. "What should I say? Should I tell it to rest in peace?"

Ben shook his head, wiping his brow with his dusty brown shirtsleeve, "No, because if it rests in peace it won't be a part of the act and then where would we be?"

"You've a point ..."

"I think it likes being the star of the show," Ben murmured.

They had a hard time getting to sleep that night. Ben's cot, which was usually across the room from Jenny's, was dragged directly beside and at some point he just crawled into her cot instead. Finally, sleep won them.

JENNY AWOKE TO the sound of a young boy's scream.

Ben.

She called out his name as she jumped to her feet, throwing on a robe and slippers. She had no idea what time it was, her neck still bruised from the night's incident. Having slept with the pistol below her pillow she grabbed it and flung wide the door.

She ran out from the dressing room and out onto the stage, a dim daylight streamed in from the few skylights and barred side windows the theatre sported. It was a Monday, a dark day for the whole theatre, they'd be the only souls in for hours save perhaps for the dotty box cleaner who sometimes brought sweet treats for Ben and never managed to do much cleaning. There was supposed to be a show tonight, if she could even bear it.

He was nowhere in the wings. Not in his crow's nest up in the rails. Not in his spotlight perch in the mezzanine either, none of his haunts. If Drummel had found him- she'd kill him with her bare hands.

"Ben?" she called frantically, weaving through the pillars below the stage and nearly tripping on rolled scrims of pastoral landscapes and coils of rope.

She heard a laugh. A woman's laugh? Ben's laugh?

The sound was coming from ahead of her. A dim light emanated from a small door that was about Ben's height that neither of them had ever noticed before, tucked below a stair to a trap-door in the stage.

She ducked into what was essentially a large wooden closet and her hand went to her mouth at the sight of her son and the mummy.

In dim candlelight cast from a small candle-made hearth and a few glass votives, there was Ben, sitting on the floor in front of a footstool, upon which sat a pot of tea and two cups, across from the mummy, who sat cross-legged on a cushion.

"Ben …" Jenny exclaimed. She shifted, still awkwardly crouching, to the mummy, raising the pistol. "You, I don't know what you are but stay away from my son."

"No! Mom," Ben exclaimed excitedly. "Put the gun down, everything is fine! We just startled each other! Come meet Monique!"

The mummy turned towards Jenny and waved a bandaged hand.

"Monique …" Jenny repeated quietly, moving forward a few steps, hunched over.

"*Bonjour,* Jenny," said a young female voice from a thin part in facial bandages, revealing thin, reddened lips. The gauze around her face was parted slightly at the eyes, revealing deep-set sockets that glimmered in the dim, jaundiced light. She continued in halting English, a thick Parisian accent. "I am sorry to scare you. Ben finally found me. It was a matter of time I suppose."

"Who … what …" Jenny stammered, lowering the gun and bending below a beam to duck forward a few more steps. "What is going on?"

"I used to work here, you see, as a dresser …" Monique continued. "When I was a little girl. My mother was an actress. Like you. When I got older, my skin …" She unwrapped just enough of her forearm to reveal the trauma.

Jenny engaged the safety and set her pistol on the floor paces away from them before coming closer to examine the condition that made her own skin crawl in a shuddering sympathetic response.

In the candlelight shed by a makeshift hearth and one votive between the teacups, Jenny could see redness and irritation on the woman's olive skin, as if veins and blood vessels were too close to the surface, an uneven rash creating angry red patches along the lines of bone.

"You poor dear," Jenny breathed. "Does it hurt?"

"Yes," Monique replied with a shrug. "But there is an herb salve that helps, that's the oily patches," she said gesturing to spots where the gauze was darkened, "and soft bandages hurt so much less than all the layers of clothes a woman must wear …. This, I can manage …"

"Does your mother know——"

"She's dead," Monique continued, undaunted. "She left me enough to survive, here, so long as I'm not outed. I go out at night under a cloak for food. A few of the old actors help me and keep my secret. When I heard your act ... pardon me, I just ... couldn't help myself."

"Isn't it great, mom?" Ben exclaimed. Jenny just stared at this unlikely scene.

"Would you like some tea, Jenny?" Monique asked.

Jenny moved forward and sunk to her knees, smiling, seeing that Monique's eyes were brown and sparkled with warmth and resilience.

"I'd like that very much, Monique. I owe you a hearty thanks and then some."

The young woman slowly turned, her every move deliberate, to procure a chipped cup from an old prop cabinet. Across the top sat various implements and jars and a vase of sand; this was surely the components for the canopic weaponry of the previous night, Jenny thought, glad to see Monique was seemingly in full possession of her organs.

An edge of open bandage caught on the footstool table and Ben jumped forward, unhooking the gauze and gently wrapping the woman's arm back up again, tucking the edge ever so gently under a layer on her palm.

"Thank you, Ben," Monique said, her voice catching, betraying a well of emotion.

"We're meant to help each other," Ben stated excitedly. "We already have. You're a part of our show now. And you saved us from a bully. Now we can protect you too. That's only fair. It balances out. That's …. What do you call it Mom, that foreign word?"

"Karma?" Jenny offered quietly.

"Yes. Karma," Ben exclaimed.

"I don't know about karma, darling," Jenny said to her son affectionately. "We're all just trying to make a living, survive as best we can, we're not perfect, but..."

"Who is?" Monique asked, chuckling as she gently lifted a white porcelain teapot with blue roses off a metal plate set above two lit candles to pour Jenny a cup of tea. "All the world is a stage, we, merely players ..."

"We'll rent another dressing room," Jenny said, "because of you, I can afford it. You shouldn't be confined to a sarcophagus life, Monique, relegated forever to the shadows. I confess I'm relieved you're no longer a holy terror to me."

Monique laughed and lifted her teacup in a toast; "To the Mummy of Rue de la Croix. May her renown spread far and wide ..."

The three unlikely partners each lifted their teacups and toasted to profit, infamy and an unprecedented prestige.

THE HAND OF ANNIE JONES

CASILDA FERRANTE

SYDNEY COVE, AUSTRALIA, 1810

By the light of the Hand we walk unseen and free,
all sleep by the light of The Hand but we.

So sang Annie Jones in her childlike voice as she lit five rotten fingers.

The Hand heard her words and responded, burning with sinister flames.

WHEN I FIRST arrived at Sydney Cove the sky was a shade of blue I had never seen before. Everything was too bright and stark, the landscape looked raw and ruthless.

Women were bundled off the ship at The Rocks, huddled together on the docks while men shouted and whistled. Army men, convict men, free men, all wanting housemaids and wives. Those of us who were not assigned to a master or place of work there and then were taken upriver to the female factory in Parramatta. That's where I met Annie Jones. She told me she was seventeen, but I think she was younger.

The colony at the time looked like a shanty town along the banks, ramshackle cottages cluttered the slopes of the harbour, bustling with progress. The new governor was determined to turn the settlement into a thriving harbour port. Buildings were being constructed, roads and parks were being planned. The bushland and plains that flanked the settlement were inhospitable and unchartered. For the first ten years the colony had starved, struggling to understand the new terrain and lay down foundations in soil that rejected them. By convict labour the colony was taking shape but what it needed to thrive was women. That was the real reason hundreds of us were transported.

The female factory was a labour camp and correction house. Some women and girls obeyed the rules, kept their heads down. They were offered hope of working off their sentence, marrying and beginning a new life in this land. Some women did not obey. I felt sorry for Annie, always subjected to some kind of humiliating punishment for her ungovernable behaviour. I gave her bread I had stashed, after she had starved in solitary for a few days, and we became friends.

Many women who were deported had simply been in the wrong place at the wrong time. But Annie Jones, she was a real felon, a street walker like me, and the best pickpocket and locksmith I've ever met. There was little inside the factory that Annie couldn't get her thieving hands on. A small girl with a frizzy mop of brown hair, sharp, fast and cunning at heart. The kind of girl who shouldn't dabble with black magic but was destined to.

"The true witches mark can't be seen by the eye." My grandmother used to tell me when I was a child. I was never certain if she meant I had the mark or not.

Not all witches had been burned during the times of the trials, many still roamed the gutters of London. It was by the fate of folks like me that the old ways arrived on these new shores.

I performed the working but Annie imagined The Hand into being. She breathed life into it, with her own will and desire, and The Hand became a part of her. Or she became a part of it. I couldn't tell which possessed the other. I envied her natural gift for witchery, her recklessness and ease. I feared The Hand, but Annie courted its malefic power and the disaster it would inevitably bring.

Whenever she lit it she spoke in spontaneous rhyme;

> *By the flames of the Dead Man's Hand*
> *Draw the veil, mask the plan*

Let them sleep, then wake to weep
For all I see is mine to keep
By the flames of the Dead Man's Hand.

"What spell is that?" I asked
"It's my own spell." she said.

AT THE FACTORY we were lined up while convicts or free settlers came to select a woman for work or marriage. Annie and I always lingered at the back, neither of us wanted to be a wife or a maid. A middle-aged woman dressed in a green satin gown attended one of the line ups. The superintendent escorted her in personally and the matron greeted her with a tight smile.

"I need trim lassies. No half-wits or lazy bones."

"Well, I've a factory full of good workers, haven't I ladies?"

The woman in satin scanned the girls. She wore a matching green bonnet on a head of red waves, her pale face was expressionless but scrutinising. She ignored the girls batting eyelashes and smiling demurely, eager for a ticket out of the factory. She waltzed up to Annie and I, parting the rows as she went.

"Pretty face. Under all that dirt. A wash and a bit of rogue would do you good. Name?"

I didn't answer. Annie snarled and wrapped her arm around me.

The woman laughed.

"Come as a pair, do you? That suits me. I need girls of your persuasion." With that she strolled out of the room, the matron at her heels.

The woman told us we could call her Madam Maye. We travelled by cart to the river then down to the harbour by boat, surprised to find ourselves back in the squalor of The Rocks. By the looks of Maye, we assumed she was an upper-class madam and we would be polishing her silver but we soon realised what kind of madam she was.

The Lady Juliana read the hand painted sign in the window of the cottage. Inside it was dark and smelt of woodfire and spices. Simple furnishings were draped with crochet and embroidered linen. The place was a typical convicts shack, with a few small rooms and a kitchen, thin wooden walls and a leaking roof.

A girl with blonde curls lay on a worn settee. "Factory fresh?" she said, "I'm Rebecca."

"Were you on The Lady Juliana?" Annie asked Madam Maye

One of the first ships to transport hundreds of female convicts to the colony, The Lady Juliana was infamously called 'the floating brothel'.

"To be sure, I was. I scrubbed hard for this little place. Keep a solid block on your shoulders and you can become a free woman too. Like me. No master. No mistress. I'll handle all the papers but any grief and back to the factory with you."

"We had another girl working here, Louisa, but she got herself married." said Rebecca.

Annie and I shared a room at the back of the cottage, a curtain between our beds for privacy. At the factory we slept one hundred to a small dorm fit for many less, with little bedding and lived on food scraps after the rats had first dip. The Lady Juliana was luxury by comparison.

I BOUGHT VERY few possessions with me from England, they were stitched into the hem of my petticoat. A crow's foot, a hag stone, a bronze key, a dog's tooth and pages from my grandmother's grimoire. All that was bequeathed to me with the passing of my only family.

My grandmother tried to teach me the traps of the craft but I was too young to take heed. Nevertheless, she had planted the words within me and I recalled them many years later, when The Hand took its hold on the lives of Annie and I.

"Magic will always protect itself, it will seek to thrive, that's why it chooses to work through some and not others. You need to have the *disposition*, you understand, girl. Not good or evil but a living thing it is, moving through a vessel. Always working to its own advantage, not ours, you see. The craft of the cunning is to flow with it, not control it. You think you can control it, well, you'll soon find yourself in a right mess, to be sure."

When I hear her voice, I remember sitting on the floor of our little room, looking up at her, a fire burning in the hearth. Her face obscured by puffs from her pipe, nestled in her rocking chair, wrapped in a black knitted shawl.

She raised me alone and taught me numbers and letters. She taught me how to speak and carry myself like a lady because glamour is the most potent magic of all. She said it was important to learn to live by my wits, to move through the world but not belong to it.

"The laws of men don't protect women like us, so why should we follow them? There are other laws in place, you remember that girl, laws that run through blood and land itself!" she stomped her boot on the loose floorboards, scaring me.

She passed from pneumonia, leaving me alone at fourteen. I kissed her dead body goodbye and slipped out into a cold East London morning. I knew what was in store for an orphan girl so I took my chances.

She had left a small package for me on the mantel, wrapped in black velvet, tied with red ribbon, and a note that said *"Farewell my dear Sarah, For your eyes only, may these charms teach you and guard you."*

Even when I worked the slums of London, I carried them stitched in the hem of my petticoat, so they would never be lost or stolen. Years later when I was rounded up off the street, thrown in goal and then onto a ship to sail to the other side of the world, that ragged petticoat was under my skirts and my treasures came with me. When, after a horrific ten- month voyage, I found myself at the female factory, they came with me, a source of secret strength and comfort.

It wasn't until Annie and I had settled at The Lady Juliana that I dared to take the talismans out. I wanted to see and hold them again, I wanted to show them to Annie. I should have kept them hidden, like gran had warned, for my eyes only.

Annie sat beside me on the bed as I laid out them in a row; crow's foot, hag stone, bronze key, dog tooth. Below them I placed the bundle of pages from my grandmother's grimoire. The crow's foot was long and curled, with short grey talons. The hag stone was a small river pebble, pearly white and smooth in my palm.

"What are these?"

"My grandmother gave them to me. When she died."

"What are they for? "

She picked up the crow's foot then placed it down again.

"Protection, luck, to dispel evil, they do many things."

The dog tooth was sharp and yellow. When I pressed it into my finger it left a deep indent and a pleasant sting. The bronze key was heavy and tarnished, with three square teeth and a heart shaped loop at the top. My grandmother wore the key around her neck.

"These are some of my grandmother's spells." I said picking up the pages of weathered parchment. Faded elegant script detailed strange workings; spells for talking to spirits, bringing a storm, spiting enemies, making one fall obsessively in love. Herbal remedies for common ailments, notes on how to throw bones and read the flight of birds. Rituals for making a Hand of Glory, a black mirror for communicating with the dead, and an ointment for transforming into a fox.

"Spells? You don't say? I knew a witch in Essex who cast a curse on the local priest, he could no longer preach scripture, his tongue swelled and bloated, he choked to death."

"That sounds rather unlikely."

"Not more than a Hand of Glory. A Hand of Glory would be useful."

She took the page from me and peered at the drawing.

"You're a good thief already Annie, you don't need the hand of a murderer."

I reached for the page; she wouldn't return it.

"Your grandmother was quite the witch. Do you think it's real? "

I snatched the paper from her hand. She picked at the talismans like she was inspecting trinkets at a market.

"Girls!" Madam Maye's voice came from the kitchen, "This is not a whore holiday house. There are chores need doing."

I swept my treasures together quickly, glad to take them away from Annie, wrapped them in a shawl, and stashed them in the top drawer of the dresser.

Annie sat on the bed watching me.

"The hand of a murderer." she said smiling

The sly look on her face was disturbing. It occurred to me to hide my things somewhere else later. I knew what a compulsive thief she was, who wouldn't resist taking something she wanted.

PEPPERCORN JACK WAS a regular. A tall Englishman who stumbled in drunk long after curfew with pockets full of coins he won gambling. His face was pockmarked like rotten cheese and his yellow teeth were too big for his small mouth but if a con had the means to pay or barter, they were welcome at The Lady Juliana.

Rebecca, who was his favourite, had named him Peppercorn Jack because his black curls were full of dandruff and when he laboured away it fell upon her like snow and made her sneeze.

I was in the next room freshening up between customers. Annie was in the kitchen chatting up another bloke. I could hear Peppercorn pacing Rebecca's room in a rage over a bet he lost.

"That little Irish bastard cheated me out of me loot then he got his coloured scamp to fight me cause he's a coward 'imself!"

"Settle down Jackie, yer fly knuckler!"

"Don't call me Jackie! Wait till I see that little prig again!"

There was more ranting, then some jostling, then quiet. Peppercorn Jack left in a hurry. It was unusually silent next door but I didn't make anything of it. I was a little tipsy and tired and lay down for a doze.

I was startled by the screams of Madam Maye. She had found Rebecca strewn on the bed, mattress soaked red from the slash at her neck.

Madam Maye was at the military barracks the next morning demanding Peppercorn Jack be punished for his crime. The murder of a young prostitute was not high on the lieutenant's list of concerns but as it happened Peppercorn had also been accused of stealing and eating one of his master's sheep and that *was* a serious offence. He was in custody.

Annie was scrubbing Rebecca's blood from the mattress and I wiped bloody boot prints from the floorboards when Madam Maye came in and told us she had taken care of it.

"He's been boned and will be scragged in the morn. That sharp lush. No girl of mine is going to be done like a rabbit." she said, "These nibblers are costing me. I've lost two girls already. Make me a cup of tea will you, Sarah."

Peppercorn Jack was destined for the noose the next day.

Annie followed me to the kitchen. Our hands were stained red with blood, an early omen, but I wasn't paying attention.

"Only a fool ignores the signs. They come before the magic and tell you which way to work it." My gran had once told me.

Annie lingered around as I filled the pot with water and lit the wood stove.

"We should make a hand," she whispered, "like the one in your papers."

"Pardon?"

"We should score the hand of Peppercorn Jack."

I stared at her. Then I tried to find some clean crockery

"Imagine if we had one, if it does what it says it does."

"It's not easy to make a Hand of Glory. And it's a daft idea anyway."

"Why?"

"I'm not sure the spell would work. I've never tried. I wouldn't know what to do."

"Why do you keep those spells if they don't work?"

"It's not a spell, more of a ritual."

"Doesn't matter what you call it."

"How would we even get his hand?"

"We cut it off. He's going to hang tomorrow. That's what the spell says, the hand of a murderer who's been hanged."

"You're quite mad, Annie. I'm certain they don't let you chop off pieces of dead convicts."

"And you're a bit slow Sarah, course that's what they do! What do you suppose happens to all those bodies on Gallows Hill? They're carted off to Rum Hospital and chopped up by ratbag doctors."

I didn't reply.

"But just imagine if it works Sarah, we would be free. No master, no mistress."

IN THE MORNING Annie tucked a small wood axe in her boot and told Madam Maye we wanted to see Peppercorn Jack hang. I wasn't convinced by Annie's plot to make a Hand of Glory. I told myself I went along to protect her, to make sure she didn't get herself arrested or shot. But really, the idea had taunted me all night. The spells and talismans were mine; they were a family secret; I wasn't going to let Annie try to make a Hand of Glory without me. And the possibility that it might work, that we could be free of servitude, no master, no mistress, was too tempting to ignore.

We scurried through The Rocks to Gallows Hill. We knew we were close when blood ran through the cracks of the cobbled path. The floggings that took place on Gallows Hill were many and merciless.

It was a ghastly place, loud and dirty. A gang of men chained by leg irons hammered at boulders. Others were digging pits in the dusty earth. Two men were stretched wide, strung up for flogging. Two were being cut down from the noose and dropped to the ground in a heap. They were dragged onto a cart by another convict who wheeled the bodies away.

Soldiers strolled around, chatting and joking.

Annie and I hovered out of view but as more people wandered up the hill to watch the proceedings we mingled with the growing crowd.

Two men were taken out of a pen and marched to the gallows, one of them was Peppercorn Jack.

The men didn't protest when the noose was placed around their heads, they had likely been beaten into silence. Without any fanfare a soldier gave the signal and the bodies dropped. Peppercorn Jack twitched and shook, then was still.

"Now what? How will you get the hand?"

Annie didn't answer. She watched and waited. When the bodies were cut down, she took off.

"Annie don't leave me here!"

I stood around anxiously. A convict was being flogged and the crowd jeered as the poor man's back was flayed to shreds. The loud snap of the whip made me flinch with each strike. I had begun to leave when Annie reappeared and took my arm. We walked away as a fight broke out and hurried down the hill.

"You didn't?"

She grinned and opened her jacket to reveal something wrapped in a blood-soaked dirty cloth.

"Good lord, Annie! How did you get it?"

"There's nothing I can't steal, especially from a dead man!"

BACK AT THE Lady Juliana, Annie and I sat on the floor of our bedroom with the bloody parcel between us.

I tugged at the rag and pulled it open, the cloth unravelled to reveal the severed hand. The wrist was roughly hacked, muscle and tendons jutted from the core of it, with a flash of white bone at the joint. Dark hairs on the knuckles and back of the hand stood on end. The flesh was mottled and draining of colour, the fingertips had turned white.

I could see where layer of skin met the muscle beneath it and I thought of peeling the skin off, like a glove. The hand seemed poised and waiting, like it wanted to crawl away.

"Where are the pages from the grimoire?"

I couldn't take my eyes off the flaccid thing, it looked like the hand of a monstrous doll.

"Sarah, get the ritual, what do we do now?"

I got the papers and read them again. "First thing we need to do is press the hand of all the blood then pickle it in an earthen vessel. For fifteen days until dry. Using saltpetre, salt and pepper, fennel seed and verbena."

"Is that all?"

"Hang it in the sun until parched. We also need to make an ointment so we are protected from the hand's magic. With cat urine, sesame oil, beeswax and blood of a black hen, prepared during the dog days."

"Shouldn't be hard to get those things."

"*Whomsoever is present in the house when the Glorious Hand burns will fall into a deep sleep, unable to be awoken. The Hand will burn between sunset and sunrise, those who slumber by the power of its light will have no recollection. Otherwise, it may be extinguished once the wicked deed is done only with fresh goat's milk.*" I read my grandmother's notes, "*It may be used to enter houses at night without fear of being seen. The Hand will open every door, may grant knowledge of hidden treasure, and may light the path of the otherworld. But beware looking directly into the undead lights of The Hand, for madness is sure to follow.*"

Annie and I looked at each other, enthralled, then stared at the dead man's hand, a puddle of blood forming around it.

IT WAS A full house at The Lady Juliana the first night we lit the Hand.

A couple of men were drinking and chatting in the sitting room, Madam Maye was attending to another customer.

We stood the Hand on the dresser. I avoided looking at it directly, with its fingers slightly curled, it looked like it was about to snatch something. Our souls? Our sanity?

"Let's hopes this works, we stink like cat's piss!" said Annie as I rubbed the oily ointment on her temples and chest.

The Hand had been pickled and dried. I brought a candle flame to the tip of the thumb. It sparked and flashed and caught alight.

Annie clapped with excitement.

The noise from the other room was increasing, the men were becoming restless and bored. Maye hadn't replaced Rebecca yet.

"Ladies! We've got company." Madam Maye called out, "I can't keep three men entertained on my own."

"Betcha could, love!"

Rounds of laughter.

"Quick, light the rest!"

Annie began her impromptu incantation as I lit each finger.

By the light of the Hand we walk unseen and free,

all sleep by the light of the Hand but we.

A silence descended on the house, a shift in atmosphere, the noticeable drop in temperature sent a shiver through us. The flames were enchanting, flashing green, yellow, blue.

We crept to the kitchen to see if the Hand had worked its magic. Peeking into the sitting room we saw three men snoozing as if passed out drunk. Maye was snoring on her bed, the man next to her had rolled to the floor.

Annie poked the man with her foot, softly at first, then harder, no response.

We hugged and squealed with glee. Every pocket was picked, the men relieved of their valuables. We left their bodies partly undressed and in compromising positions for a laugh. Rummaging through Madam Maye's things we found a flintlock pistol, vials of opium and labdanum, French perfumes, and a string of real pearls. We took the opium, left the rest. We spent the night drinking rum, chatting and laughing, until the Hand flickered out at sunrise.

"No master, no mistress! No master, no mistress!" chanted Annie as she skipped around the room.

RIPPING OFF MADAM Maye and the lads who frequented The Lady Juliana was easy but soon became tiresome.

They would wake at sunrise, drowsy and heavy headed, thinking they must have had a roaring good time, with their pockets emptied and clothes dishevelled. Annie and I pulled the bedsheets over our heads and muffled our giggles when we heard them rise and stumble out. Madam Maye herself was confused and disorientated, trying keep up her cocky banter. She collected the usual night takings from us and had no reason to suspect foul play on our part.

The Hand offered us a certain freedom; the nights were our own to live as we pleased. No master, no mistress, until daylight. There was nowhere to escape unless you fancied going it alone in the bush, a convict girl wouldn't last a day beyond the confines of the colony. We had no interest or reason to make a run for it, not at first. The Lady Juliana had become our comfortable home. Madam Maye was easy to placate and preoccupied with her own dubious dealings which seemed to involve opiates and gambling rings.

I didn't mind keeping up simple household chores during the day (Annie did as little as possible) but between sunset and sunrise we were free women. I was happy to drink tea, read, go for a midnight walk through The Rocks. Unafraid because I walked under the auspices of The Hand. It became our protector. We had been exiled to a violent and turbulent colony; the light of The Hand was a befitting guide. I was content to have it as an ally, and to err on the side of caution for all magical allies are unpredictable, but that wasn't enough for Annie. She became infatuated with the mysteries of The Hand.

Annie began to venture out with The Hand to rob others. A risky idea but she ignored my concern, of course. Then she lost interest in pillaging altogether. She became obsessed with the things she could see in the phantasmic glow of The Hand, the things it revealed to her.

She no longer went out bubbling with mischief. She drifted into the night, trance like, The Hand tucked in her waistband and under her shirt, off to see sights I couldn't fathom.

One morning I woke to find her sitting at the end of my bed, staring at the wall, The Hand beside her.

"Annie? Did you just get back? Where have you been?"

She began to unlace her boots. I was repulsed by the dead hand. I wanted her to remove it from my bed.

"It's like being in sleeping beauty's castle at first." she said, "All in a magical sleep, so peaceful, nothing can wake them. But the beauty soon changes, ugly things grow on the walls. Pain drips from the ceilings forming puddles on the floors. In dark corners are voices crying, pleading, no bodies just the voices left."

"Is that what The Hand shows you? That sounds horrid, Annie."
"It's always there whether we can see it or not. I still swipe what I can."

She held up her velvet drawstring pouch, full of jewellery and coins and trinkets.

"Last night I walked up to Gallows Hill."
"I hate to think. It's horrible enough in ordinary light."

"This colony is a graveyard, Sarah. The dead dance while the living sleep."

"Stop it, Annie."

"The dead sing while the living weep."

"Get out!"

Annie laughed. I kicked at her and The Hand rolled off the bed and fell to the floor.

"Sarah! Be careful!"

She gave me an angry look, picked up The Hand and cradled it, whispering softly. The Hand was always watching, listening.

BURNING LIKE A macabre candle, yellow flames sprung from each curved fingertip, but the flesh didn't burn. It released a faint smell of leathery moss. Sometimes the flames were tall and leapt high, other times small, almost indistinguishable. The Hand was an unpredictable thing with a mind of its own. When lit it would soften and swell, the stiff leather blushing pink, turning the colour of living skin. Or so it seemed to me.

I sipped a glass of rum, feeling nauseated as I watched The Hand change, while Annie smiled into the flames, their dance reflected in her eyes. They were burning strong, lighting up the small room as if it were day.

Madam Maye and the bloke she was with had dropped to the floor asleep, I heard them fall, there was another bloke snoring in the sitting room. Annie and I with The Hand between us sat at the kitchen table.

Annie muttered under her breath; her lips moved but I couldn't make out words. She and The Hand were communicating, in a private tongue. I felt a prick of envy, why didn't the Hand whisper it's secrets to me? Why had it chosen Annie to bond with?

"I know what's coming Sarah," she said after a while.

I pressed the glass to my mouth. The rum cleared my head but didn't allay the dread I felt whenever The Hand was burning.

"Years and years of slaughter. We shouldn't have come to this land."

"We didn't have a choice, Annie."

"We don't belong here."

"No."

I threw back the rum.

Fingertips flared and Annie leant forward, The Hand drew her closer.

"Royal ships will bring more and more suffering to these shores, unloading disease and disaster. The land will be raped and plundered. More ships will come, ships of iron, carrying desperate people from many lands."

"Ships of iron?"

"In the heart of this land is a great desert, an endless red desert, and it will turn into a sea of blood." Her voice was low and monotone, a seer caught in the visions of those deadly flames.

I didn't want to listen to anymore. I went out the back for a smoke, left her to her rambling. I could smell the sea and meat roasting over open fires. The singing and shouting of revellers down the hill, along the harbour, echoed in the night. It was past curfew, but soldiers were likely drunk themselves in swankier parts of the settlement. They didn't bother to patrol the convict quarter unless they had a bone to pick.

I worried about Annie. I was responsible for unleashing the nightmare magic that had taken hold of her. The Hand had claimed her and together they were changing, leaving me behind.

ANNIE'S BEHAVIOUR BECAME more disturbing and erratic. She spent the days in a stupor, exhausted from lack of sleep, often muttering to herself or to The Hand, even when it was not lit. Madam Maye grew angry with her, but she too suffered a malaise she didn't understand and was plagued by headaches. The Hand was manipulating those around it and infesting our cottage.

My witchcraft had created The Hand. The Hand was as much mine as Annie's. And I had the power to destroy it. Or so I tried to convince myself.

I had never seen The Hand during the day. It slept wrapped in a linen cloth, hidden in a hat box on top of the wardrobe. When I took the box down it was empty. I found The Hand tucked under Annie's mattress. Annie had wandered out and Madam Maye was in bed, feeling unwell. I had a small window of time to get rid of the thing.

I unwrapped the linen, it smelt of sharp, sour rot. In daylight The Hand was gruesome to behold, an ugly shrivelled thing, grey and leathery, tendons bulged, long knotted fingerbones, nails white and cracked. The wrist was a ragged stump, fragments of flesh peeled in stiff curls.

Repulsed, I wrapped it up again, trying not to touch it. I rushed outside and through the alleyways, The Hand tucked in my jacket. It dug into my side and made me sweat. I felt it pointing, wagging a dead finger at me.

Now, now, Sarah, what do you think you're doing? I heard it say and I walked faster, gathered my skirts and began to run, desperate to find somewhere to get rid of it.

A pile of horse manure and vegetable scraps by the back door of a cottage would do. I threw it in the heap, buried it with the toe of my boot, then dashed away.

I felt relieved but as the day wore on I grew concerned and by evening I was quite anxious.

It's not too wise to throw out a tool of black magic. I needn't have worried. That night as I sat at the dresser applying my face Annie slipped into the room. I don't know how long she stood there behind me before she spoke and made me jump.

"How could you, Sarah?" In her hands was the dirty linen parcel. She unwrapped it and nestled The Hand in her arm like a baby.

"It called to me Sarah, told me where to find it."

I opened my mouth but I didn't know what to say.

"Hush now, it's alright." she said "I understand Sarah, you're afraid. Women like us, we're not supposed to have such raw power. But why would you grandmother give you the spell if she didn't want you to use this magic? Maybe your grandmother knew that you would need it."

"Don't speak of my gran! And I'm not afraid!"

Annie shrugged, hugging The Hand to her chest.

UNFORTUNATELY FOR HER, Madam Maye found the pages of the grimoire. Annie had left them on the dresser. We walked into the room one afternoon while Maye was looking at them.

"What's all this? Good heavens, that looks hideous." She began to read the Hand of Glory spell.

Annie snatched the papers from her hands.

Maye glared at her. "Watch your manners. There's a place for girls like you."

"I'm sorry ma'am, it's mine." I said taking the pages from Annie and folding them up tightly. "Just some notes from my diary."

"A diary, you say? Too much free time on your hands?"

I didn't answer.

Madam Maye rubbed her temples and looked frustrated. "I don't have time for your childish nonsense. I have a headache. Clean up this pigsty, I'm sure the factory would love to see you return if you require more household training."

Maye walked out in a huff. She had become aloof and vague.

The Hand shrouded Annie and I with its influence.

Annie brooded for the rest of the day. I worried what she was thinking.

"Madam Maye said we should expect a busy night; a cargo ship docked this afternoon." I told her at supper time, placing a bowl of soup and bread in front of her.

"I need to talk to The Hand."

"I wouldn't mind a trick or two. I need a change from the prim life."

It was meant to be a joke but she didn't respond. I ate my soup while Annie glared into her bowl.

"The Hand is waiting for me." she said and left the table.

She was applying the ointment to herself when I entered the bedroom, so I did the same.

Annie retrieved The Hand from under her pillow. She hid it in different places now to keep it away from me. She set it on the bedside table and began to light the fingertips, chanting under her breath.

I left her to her obsession, put on my coat and went out for a walk.

Later that night I was writing at the kitchen table when I heard Annie's voice, loud and angry.

"You will shut your filthy mouth! You will not speak of things you don't understand!"

She was in Madam Maye's room. I went to check and saw Annie hovering over Maye, asleep in an armchair. Annie held a carving knife in one hand, her other hand was digging into Maye's mouth.

"Annie, what on earth are you doing?"

"She knows the spell. She can't know. No one else must be able to control The Hand. No master. No mistress."   She didn't turn to look at me. She placed the knife in Maye's lap then dug her fingers into her mouth, prying jaws open and pulling out her tongue.

"Annie, stop that!" I took a step forward.

Annie turned on me, the light in her eyes had the same deadly spark of the burning Hand. "The Hand told me what we need to do. Madam Maye will betray us, she must not be able to speak the spell."

Annie gripped Maye's tongue, yanked it up and out, lifting her chin up as she stretched it.

"Annie, no!"

I watched horrified as Annie began to slice away at the roots of the organ. Blood dripped from Maye's open mouth then it began to pour. I took a few steps backward, turned and fled. I sat in the alley behind the cottage, my hands shaking as I fumbled with my pipe.

I heard Annie leave the cottage, singing to herself as she walked down the path. I crept in to spy on Madam Maye. Blood was still trickling from her chin and down her front. It pooled in her lap and seeped down the folds of her dress, dripping from the hem to the floor. The lights of The Hand would go out at sunrise, but Madam Maye would never wake again.

I avoided the house the next day. I roamed the harbour. It was a cold, drizzly day, heavy with fog, the sea was loud and crashed against the docks. Annie had gone completely mad. No one else could know the spell she said. I knew the spell. What else had The Hand instructed her to do? Maybe they were both plotting my murder too.

Before sunset I returned to the cottage determined to stop Annie lighting The Hand, planning to take it and destroy it once and for all. But I was too late.

The house was quiet, the last rays of light filtered through the dirty windows. Madam Maye's body was still in her room. I shut the door.

I went to the bedroom to apply the ointment but found the jar empty. I stared at it in horror, not noticing Annie had entered.

"Hello Sarah."

"Annie!"

She stood holding The Hand and a lit candle, composed and determined, she had been waiting for me.

"Annie?"

"Don't be afraid." She looked at me sadly as she brought the flame to grey fingertips.

I shouldn't have been, but I was stunned that Annie would do such a thing. And terrified that The Hand itself had turned on me. I watched one finger spark after another, bright and eager to destroy me.

With each flame my eyelids grew heavier, I fought to stay awake.

I'm sorry I thought I heard Annie say, or was it The Hand that spoke, or my grandmother? My head spun, darkness fell upon me, heavy and warm. I dropped to the floor and slept.

I woke at sunrise and sat up in panic, expecting to find myself bathed in blood but I was in one piece.

The bedroom was a mess. Annie's things were gone and so were some of mine, she had ransacked my dresser drawers. She had stolen the talismans and pages of the grimoire.

The smell of smoke was building; when I looked through the small cottage I could see flames in Madam Maye's room.

"Goddam you to hell Annie Jones! Crazy little whore! You wretched little thief!"

I fought back angry tears as I tried to salvage a few things in a small vanity case. I had money and valuables tucked in boots and coat pockets that Annie didn't know about.

I ran out the back door and down the alleyway. I didn't shout *fire!* I wanted The Lady Juliana to burn to the ground.

ALMOST TWO YEARS after Annie disappeared, I was walking through The Rocks heading for the fish market and found myself wandering up to Gallows Hill. It was very early in the morning, quiet and deserted. I often thought about the day we went up there, and the hand of Peppercorn Jack, when it was just human flesh and bone, before it became a mummified thing with a will of its own.

Some nights, long after Annie had gone, I could feel the twinge of The Hand at work. I knew it had been lit and was burning bright.

Three bodies were swinging in the wind, three women. They had been left overnight to blacken and blue in the cold and attract the crows. One of the bodies was Annie Jones. She looked like an emaciated child on the noose, her knotted mess of dark hair covered her face, but I knew it was her.

"Magic betrays us all in the end, it changes and consumes us."

Annie had stolen my treasures, but she couldn't take my grandmother's words from me. Or the lineage in my blood that was not dependent on spells or talismans.

When I saw her hanging, I knew what I wanted to do. I no longer felt fear in the face of dark and desperate workings. I understood the price, what stood to be gained and loss. Gran was right. Magic changes you.

I walked away from the gallows with a smile and a small wet hand wrapped tightly in cloth, the hand of both a murderer and a thief, of a child who had walked between worlds.

I knew the hand of Annie Jones would become the most dangerous dead hand of all.

FOG MARSH

RUDI DORNEMANN

THEY KILL ME with seven deaths. I only feel the first.

That death is double. One priestess tightens a loop of braided leather around my neck. Another priestess slits my throat.

At the pain, like a knife of fire, I almost throw up. But the magic won't work without the bitter porridge of chaff and weeds in my stomach, so I clench my whole body, keep it down.

My blood is the last thing I see, gushing away from me through the air, reaching every member of the village, wetting all my family, all my friends. My vision is a red-black cave that narrows to nothing.

The magic, however, has taken hold already and That One Who Walks For Me In Dreams stands among us. I see the rest through her eyes.

My body has fallen forward and a woman I no longer recognize holds me upright. My mother? Sister? One priestess stabs me in the ribs. Although the woman I don't recognize and I are slick with my blood, she holds me tightly, doesn't let me slip. The second priestess cracks my skull with the sacred scepter and shakes it over me in blessing. The metal leaves clank and jingle on its three triple branches.

Then the priestess with the knife slits my belly and my intestines pour out. The other priestess reads omens in their gnarls and twists, and shouts that the sacrifice will succeed, that I'll ensure the world restarts again and again spring after spring.

Everyone I've ever known sighs with a single breath, my blood drying on their skin.

They lower me into a pit carved out of the bog, lay me on my back. A priestess climbs down with a sword and an ax.

"Heal well," she says, and hews me in half at the waist.

Then the priestesses pin me to the dug-out place by driving a forked birch branch over each arm just below my shoulder and laying heavier branches over my chest, hips, legs.

Water seeps in overnight. My body rises against its restraints. This drowning is the final death.

My blood flows sweet into the marsh. The marsh flows bitter into my veins. The alliance is made.

My eyes stare unseeing through the water as days and nights cross the sky, until the moss covers up my face. Moss-water tans my skin like leather, preserves my body so the magic can work its slow work.

A century, and the hole in the bog has filled in, healed up. That One Who Walks For Me In Dreams carries the mist-light and wanders and, when she returns each morning, she can no longer see where I lie and has to find me by instinct. The moss-water dissolves my bones and the weight of gathering peat flattens my body sideways until my face and hips are ovalled.

While I lie under the bog, That One Who Walks For Me goes out. By starlight, by firelight, my dreamself ghostwalks, watches, listens. She hears the bedtime chats of lovers, the midnight deliberations of criminals along the road, the stories travelers bring from elsewhere. She hears the language shift, follows its changes. She watches the land transform as the seasons cycle, watches the people nearby pass from birth to death, from death to decay. The children of our village, and their children, and theirs. She sees the new fashions they wear, the new tools they carry, sees the village grow to a town, sees nations and religions come and go. She recognizes familiar eyes, hears a laugh we once knew, a certain shrugging sigh, echo over generations.

And she knows the bog, finds all the objects placed there as offerings in the times before and after my death. Arm-rings and finger-rings, swords and helmets, dresses and cloaks, food sealed in clay jars and ritual cauldrons shattered to quiet their power. Bodies left here in punishment, lying forever undecayed, between the shore of life and the shore of death. Other bodies, like mine, sacrificed to keep winter from lingering too long.

The spring stirring of seeds in my gut gives the first nudge of spring to the marsh and the land beyond. That porridge contains dozens of plants that aren't normally food, gathered everywhere within a day's journey. They call to their descendants in the world above, the magic of my sacrifice bringing recovery after dead months.

And as the world heals itself of winter, my body heals its wounds. Year by year, the knife-cuts in my heart stitch up.

My intestines draw back into my body like snakes finding a den. Muscles and nerves from my lower body reach like rootlets toward their counterparts in my upper body, pull the pieces of my spine together with the patience of trees overtaking a meadow, of a meadow stealing into a marsh.

My bones grow solid again, learning new substance from the wood that pins me down. My skull pushes out, healing both where it had been crushed by the priestess and flattened by the bog's weight.

My internal organs re-form, their inner workings half-flesh, half-moss. They turn the astringent, airless water to a new kind of blood.

After two thousand years, my throat is whole again and the garroting is no more than a scar-ridge on my skin.

That One Who Walks comes home to my body. One last winter's turn toward spring and my dreamself is bound to me again, the final healing. I wake to the dark under the bog, with all her explorations and discoveries snug as memories in my mind.

I swim up through peat and mud until I can see stars rippled by the water of the bog.

I stand.

I am wet and naked, the air is cold, and colder rain pelts down. Shivers spasm through my body. My blood moves, a bee-sting ache in my arteries. I dig my clothes from the place where they're hidden, rinse them in marsh water. A tunic-dress. A shawl of plaid weaving, once yellow and red, now light brown and dark. Wearing them, I am just as wet, not quite as cold.

I wade toward shore through a slurry that's more mud and less water with every step, until finally the earth holds me up. The bog is smaller than I remember. I climb a bank toward voices and engine-sound, come up into mist lit by silent flashes of blue, yellow, red.

I know the place, a road. Left leads to town; right, a longer distance to the city. That One Who Walks For Me in Dreams has gone each direction many times.

Shattered glass sparkles across the pavement. A smell like pitch. That colored lightning comes from cars with flashing lights. The large metal box of a truck stands in the road, something broken behind it, perhaps another car? Nearby, a metal object made of triangles and circles. The circles are wheels and one is bent. In a place below my mind, That One Who Walks whispers, "Bicycle."

Understanding rushes at me—a traffic accident. That One Who Walks For Me In Dreams has ghostwalked through similar events over the decades. I step onto the road in my bare feet, gently, to avoid the glass. I'd expected to walk a while alone before I'd be among others again.

People move about in blue uniforms or in dark clothes with light-catching yellow stripes—examining the broken machines, talking with or tending to people in ordinary clothes who shiver with shock and cold.

Rain gusts down on us all.

Shouting, maybe at me?

No, not at me—a woman in uniform and a man in a reflective jacket walk past, signaling to a man beside the truck, who kneels beside something.

A body on the ground. A younger woman, cut across the neck, the bones of her jaw and neck exposed. My own throat aches in sympathy as several people lift her onto a stretcher.

"It's clear enough," says the woman in uniform. "All this rain and he didn't see her, or couldn't stop in time if he did. She saw him, but skidded when she tried to stop."

"Her neck—did the bumper do that?" says the man in the reflective jacket. He shakes his head, "A little different luck, she would have slid right under and survived."

I'm uneasy at the way fate has fallen; right when my thread's woven back into the tapestry, hers is snipped.

Another woman sees me, and I startle to see that she sees me.

"Are you OK?" she says. No police uniform or rescue crew jacket, just a worried expression that grows more concerned when I don't answer right away.

"OK," I say. "Yes."

"Terrible night for walking," she says. Although she isn't dressed like them, she seems to know many of the police, and nods a greeting as one passes us.

"A terrible night in many ways," I say.

"Did you see what happened?"

"No," I say. "I only just saw..."

"You weren't in any of the cars involved?" She looks toward a group of people standing near their cars who are talking to a pair of police and gesturing.

"I'm going to Fælleslund," I say. That One Who Walks put the name on my tongue. "A friend lives there."

From the look on her face, she hears the uncertainty in my voice.

Communal gardens, shared meals in a central hall—the Fælleslund community feels a little like my life before. And perhaps not just to me. That One Who Walks has seen someone there she recognized from the former time. It's not likely true, but I need to find out before I do anything else in this new time.

"I had a ride," I say, "but we couldn't get through on the road."

"Well, you're nearly there" says the woman. She waves to the police, and they nod back. "I'll walk with you. My aunt lives there."

"This way," I say.

"Through the woods?" she says. "At night? In this rain? We're better off following the path along the road."

The bog is a patient presence behind the rain and dark and a line of trees. We walk away from its pull. Flat compacted clumps of wet leaves slide underfoot.

I slip and she catches my arm. Under her touch, I can feel that my arm is softer than hers, yields differently, my muscles the density of fresh peat over lighter-than-expected bones. She slides too and laughs but she's observing me, cautious-eyed.

"What's your name?" she said. "I'm Mathilde."

"Tågemose," I say, *fog marsh*. I don't remember the name I had before the bog.

"Do you mean that little swampy area with the pond?" she says. "I never heard it called that. But I was asking about your name—what are you called?"

"Tågemose is what everyone calls me," I say as firmly as I can, to push it more toward true.

Mathilde purses her lips, stifling whatever question she planned to ask next.

"Who was she?" I say. "The woman on the bicycle?" The woman who might have traded her life for mine.

"I don't know," she says. "Lotte and Marius—the first police to arrive, I know them from work—said they didn't recognize her, so she's probably not from the town."

A fork in the path takes us into winter-empty gardens, raised beds turned to square puddles now. That One Who Walks for Me knows the place. Rain veils the playfields to our right while the evergreens along the car park on the left are a wall of more solid shadow. We pass twisted fog-shadows that stand like vague guardians over a children's playground and go up from the gardens into the courtyard between buildings.

Mathilde takes the stairs. I take the ramp. That One Who Walks For Me In Dreams has drifted up and down stairs for centuries, but they're new to me.

The windows of the common house are bright, steamed up against the cool wet night, and full of movement.

In the door, Mathilde takes off her shoes, hangs up her coat. As I wipe my feet on the mat, I kick at the crowd of shoes, hoping Mathilde might think I've kicked off shoes of my own. She probably isn't fooled, but doesn't show it.

There was an offering of shoes in the bog, but I knew they were mostly decayed, so I hadn't looked for them.

I hang my shawl on a hook. I smell cooking, hear conversation and the clink of eating utensils. We've arrived at dinnertime.

A kitchen in one corner of the room. A wall of windows looking out on the rainy dark. A dozen or more small oval tables, groups of people sitting around them. A light fixture hanging over each table. Bright rag rugs here and there on the wood floor. This community of neighbors is like a village within the town. For a moment, I see the faces of the village I once knew, faces red with my blood.

I realize Mathilde is talking, saying we should sit down, that she can get us some food. We find a table near the back.

A woman comes over with two cups and a container of steaming dark liquid that she pours for us.

"You look like you could use something warm," she says. That One Who Walks For Me In Dreams was not wrong—I know her. She was one of the priestesses who'd killed me. The hand that once pulled a knife across my throat holds the chrome and glass coffee pot.

"Welcome to Fælleslund," she says.

I want to shrink back, but I look up. "Thank you."

"Tågemose says she's here to visit a friend in the community," said Mathilde.

"Tågemose," says the priestess, "welcome." She looks at me without blinking. "It is so good to see you again. I'll come back and we can talk."

She moves away to another table. She seems to be acting as hostess. I do not know who she is to these people. That One Who Walks For Me never got this near to her, something like a strong wind always came up, brushed my dreamself away.

An older woman calls Mathilde's name from across the room. Her aunt. Mathilde hurries over.

I sip the coffee and it scalds the top of my mouth. The weight of my dress's sodden fabric pulls on my shoulders. I think I smell like mud. The room smells like food, and I'm hungry, although I'm unsure if my so-long-empty stomach will accept more than a handful of crumbs right now.

Mathilde returns with large bowls of stew. It isn't as hot as the coffee, and I try a few spoonfuls.

While she eats, Mathilde tells me of her work as a dispatcher for the police in the nearby city. Her days pass sitting in a room, listening to things happen. It reminds me of remaining underground and underwater while That One Who Walks returned each morning with new knowledge. Mathilde, however, talks to people in the world, interacts with them in a way I haven't for centuries and centuries.

"Stew's good, isn't it?" she says. "It's an old recipe of Gunnhild's that she wanted us to try."

I don't recognize most of the vegetables, but the flavor of the thick broth is half-familiar. Once I've eaten a bit more, Mathilde seems satisfied that I can be left, and heads back to her aunt.

"Tågemose," says the priestess. I haven't seen her or heard her approach. Without asking first, she leans in to fill my cup. The last time we were this close, I died.

She looks at me and smiles. I don't remember her smiling in the old time, not at me. I twist the cloth of my napkin in my fingers.

Laughter at the next table, and the priestess looks toward them. My coffee is so full I can't lift the cup without spilling into my saucer. One of the men at the next table says something and the priestess laughs in response, goes to join their conversation.

I wonder how long it will be before I'm able to talk so casually, to laugh, to trust and be trusted. I envy the priestess; I envy Mathilde. I see the web of community.

I'm afraid my eyes will be drawn to the priestess if I look at the dining room, so I watch the lamp swaying slightly over my table. I reach toward the bulb, feel the heat on my fingertips. It isn't quite the same heat as fire.

A hand on my shoulder, and I look to my side.

"Tågemose," says the priestess. "You chose your own name?"

I take another spoonful of stew before answering. "Mathilde asked and I needed something to tell her, and that seemed right."

"I was mistaken for an old queen when I came up," says the priestess. "Gunnhild. A mother of kings, a builder of alliances. A woman of power, and beauty, of subtle cunning and keen magics."

"This stew," I say. "Did Mathilde say it was your recipe?"

"My naming shaped who I am in this time," says Gunnhild. "Yours will too."

She resumes her path around the room. The role she plays now is the closest we had to a queen in our time. A woman of influence in the village who wove peace through the room whenever we gathered. A miniature version of the larger peace that was woven throughout the countryside when the effigy of the goddess traveled from village to village at the end of winter. A journey I'd accompanied my last spring, as this priestess' acolyte and her sacrifice.

I recognize the sourness in my stomach, the chalky scratch in the back of my throat. A version of the ancient porridge that had been my last meal, now with a meaty overtone of iron I don't recognize.

This shouldn't be.

When we carried the shrine from village to village, on a cart that rolled only forward, and couldn't be turned, all iron had been hidden at our approach, a proof of the all-peace that greeted the coming of Nerthus and marked the first of the land's greening.

I think the taste is blood, and I think I know whose. I think I know why.

I stand up.

In the kitchen, I place my bowl with the other dirty dishes. A man in an apron nods to me. He's apparently been assigned the cleanup chores tonight just as Gunnhild has been assigned the cooking. I find the priestess talking to three older women of the community and a young man.

"Gunnhild," I say, and then I use the old words to continue: "You take for yourself a power that should be our Great Lady's only."

She smiles at her friends. "Please," she says, "excuse us."

With a firm hand on my arm, she guides me to an empty table, sits me down, and leans close. She speaks quietly, with a smile, pats my forearm. Anyone watching would think she comforts me.

"I've chosen you," she says, "to go into the land again." The women she'd been talking with watch us with concern. "Your strength is restored and you can bring the spring back for many years to come."

"I made my choice long ago and willingly," I say, "but what about Mathilde? Does she know what you plan for her? You gave her the same stew as me."

"You have seen the face of our Great Lady," says the priestess. "Death by drowning takes all who do. If healing from that death is enough to let you rise renewed from the lake, that is a blessing. You should be grateful. If you have the chance to rise a second time, isn't that twice the blessing?"

"I don't think Mathilde has seen Nerthus. Is the goddess even known in this time?"

"Because it is not required, Mathilde's sacrifice becomes still more of a blessing and an extra gift." Gunnhild looks across the room to where Mathilde sits with her aunt. "I'd hoped you'd help me with my duties in this time."

She clasps my hand. I can't look at her.

"But it takes so much more for me to resist the years now," she says, "and I must be sustained. So you'll have to help me in another way. I'm the only one left to ensure the sacrifices. No one else remembers Nerthus or can tend her shrine."

"The shrine was sunk two hundred years after our time," I say. "The holy figure itself was given as the final sacrifice to the goddess."

The priestess nods. "The whole bog is her shrine now," she says, "all this land."

"What about the woman on the bicycle?" I say. "The way she died—I saw her wounds—she was a sacrifice too, but without the ritual and the seeds. She won't heal. Her death is wasted."

The priestess looks at me, as if judging whether to explain or command. "The magic is no longer as focused as when we first lived. Now it's like the surface of the holy lake in this storm—the pattern is hidden among so many ripples. But there is still power. Even in this chaotic time, winters still turn to spring."

"You added your own blood to the ritual meal," I say. "You've turned the spring healing toward yourself."

"Only a small portion," she says. "Only enough."

I remember things That One Who Walks For Me In Dreams has heard. How the winters weaken year by year. How the seasons aren't what they were. I wonder how many she's sacrificed in the centuries she's been back. I wondered if any healing goes to the land from those bodies, how much healing is channeled instead to her. What the land does to try to balance itself again.

The priestess who now wears the name of a queen stands.

"Don't eat or drink anything else," says Gunnhild. "Sit quietly and the magic will be strongest when the time comes. In a little while, I'll return with Mathilde and we'll go out."

I do not answer. I look out at the storm beyond the steamed-up windows, at the reflection of all these people I don't know, at the image of myself among them. None of us should die for her.

The priestess squeezes my hand and goes.

When I see in the reflection that her back is turned, that she's well into conversation with Mathilde and her aunt, I get up and walk quietly, slowly to the door.

I pause a moment before returning to the rain. I'm as dry as I've been in millennia. For a moment, being dry seems like the most important part of being human. Back in the dining area, the man doing the dishes sings quietly in a language I don't know. Neighbors and friends linger at the tables over coffee and talk. I breathe in the light of candles and electric bulbs. Mathilde looks up and sees me.

I'm out the door, into the rain, across the courtyard, and the stairs are raw on my bare feet.

I hear Gunnhild, Mathilde, and others splashing down the path behind me. I race back through the garden towards the bog, the territory I know, that's part of me.

I'm quick through the woods, and their shouts and calls fall further behind. The fog is dark without the flashing lights from the road. But the knowledge of where each offering lies underground is as clear to me as the arrangements of the stars hidden behind the clouds overhead.

Gunnhild shouts, closer, but through the rain I can't tell what she's saying, whether she's calling to me or rallying the others.

I throw myself to the ground, work my hand down through the mud until I feel metal, and pull up a sword. The blade's bent in the shape of a "Z," from that time when an object's use had to be taken from it before it was given in offering.

I wade out, duck into the water, claw down through muck, grasp the hilt of another sword. The sword and I break the water at the same time. I gasp for breath.

Only a hilt, the blade rusted away or melted in the chemical water of the bog. I feel intricate, ancient work under my fingertips. Useless. I throw it down and it disappears with a plunk.

I'm in water up to my shoulders, mud up to my hips. I dive again, and, finally, bring up a complete sword.

A shape comes toward me through the fog, and I splash forward to meet it.

Gunnhild's voice calls out, "She's here!"

I brace my feet as solidly as I can in the yielding mud. The shadow comes closer in the mist and rain. I hold the sword in front of me—a sword that had been dedicated to Nerthus and sacrificed into the bog the same as we were. That should turn Gunnhild back.

But the woman staggering at me is another of our sacrificed sisters, her body still bog-flattened, leathery, boneless, with at least three wounds still unhealed. The priestess' spells have brought her back early.

I pull the sword away, can't add to her injuries, can't lengthen the centuries of recovery she still has left.

I heave the sword from me. It skips and splashes across the water and I taste blood—I've cut my cheek.

The sacrificed woman falls forward, bearing me under the water. We wrestle as we sink, her boneless arms a binding embrace, the pull of the bog heavy like sleep. That One Who Walks For Me In Dreams is restless, ready to resume her wanderings.

My hands find a gnarl of bog-hardened oak root and I strike the sacrificed woman's shoulder. She too knows where the old offerings are hidden and reaches out. I flip us so I'm above her, push the root through her shoulder to pin her into the mud.

She's found a knife. I see its bright edge coming in the bog-murk and push for the surface. The blade slices the sole of my foot, but I'm away, thrashing upwards, gulping air. And my sacrifice-sister can rest secure in the bog again.

"Heal well," I think.

I swim across the pool of open water in the center of the bog. I'm bleeding from my cheek and my foot, a wound I'd given myself and a wound given by another. The flush of healing shivers over my skin—is the priestess feeling it too?

The priestess and the others carry lights. She's halfway around the shore already.

I can't rush my search. I feel through my memories, searching for where each piece of the holy cart lies now. One wheel right below me; the other, several arm-spans to my right. The boards of the cart-bed, separated and piled in a kind of crisscross knotwork, are only slightly twisted by age and waterlogging. The holy cloth, which hid the goddess' form, has dissolved to a handful of scraps.

The goddess herself rests further off, sacrificed in a spot that's now dry land. I wade ashore, tear at the peat of the bank until my hands find something solid.

I don't hear Gunnhild behind me until the braided leather strap tightens around my neck. I push back, pull forward, try to stand. I bring my hands up to try to block the knife that I expect at my throat. My vision goes blank.

Gunnhild pulls my head back and lifts the knife, praying in the old language, beginning the cut below my left ear.

A gust of rain slaps the knife from her hand. I fall into a familiar darkness as That One Who Walks For Me In Dreams pushes between me and the priestess, a human-shaped swirl of wind and storm, marsh-light and mist. That One Who Walks For Me stretches an arm down, clears peat and mud from a wooden shape with quick fingers of rain.

The priestess sees it, dives right through That One Who Walks, scrambles over my body, and grabs the exposed part of the object. Maybe she sees a sword pommel.

She pulls the length of it free.

A twisted branch, carved with a simple face and features. An icon infused with the presence of Nerthus, the holy relic we'd carried from village to village at winter's first waning.

Gunnhild swings it at the storm-shape of That One Who Walks For Me In Dreams.

The goddess explodes in a wind-driven cloud of wet splinters.

Gunnhild cries out at what she's done, falls to her knees. She bleeds from a dozen places where the splinters have hit her, plucks bits of the icon from her skin.

No matter, some fragments of the goddess will always be part of her.

She reaches for her fallen dagger, but can't close her hand around it. When we carried the goddess through the land, her peace banished every iron implement and tool of war. Now Gunnhild carries that peace inside her, traces of Nerthus weaving their journey endlessly through her old priestess' blood.

Perhaps prompted by the goddess' nearness, the seeds in my stomach do their magic and I sit up, sore-throated but breathing. That One Who Walks falls around me, an exhalation of warm spring rain washing the blood from my throat.

The priestess falls back into the dark water, but I catch her, pull her toward me, hold her head above water. Her eyes are closed, as if she would just sink back into the bog and death. With her weight and mine, I scramble but can't climb back up.

Mathilde appears above us, rain streaming from her face and hair. She reaches down, hauls Gunnhild up, then me.

I lean on Mathilde and breathe deep breaths until I can stand on my own again. I am from the bog now, but no longer of it.

"They're here," Mathilde shouts. "They're here!"

IN THE ANCESTOR'S NEW HOUSE

MARISSA LINGEN

THE ANCESTOR WAS in a bad mood again, and he was making Inguill pay for it.

This house is utterly unacceptable, he said for the twentieth time. Tiny. Shabby. One room. Hardly any furniture. No decorations to speak of. We need another building. We need *more*. My status deserves it.

"I couldn't carry you from one building to another anyway, just me," said Inguill, her patience gone. She knew she needed to brush flies from the Ancestor. She carried on preparing their suppers instead. "And you get angry when I drag you."

The Ancestor was silent. Since the Ancestor only spoke in Inguill's mind, this was much the same from an outside perspective, but to Inguill, cooking potatoes, it was far more peaceful. The peace did not last long. It never did. Nor did the complaints vary, on such a day, when the thunder lingered in the distance and the ancestor's bones ached under his wrappings.

I should be carried by the proper tribe of bearers, bred to a smooth gait, said the Ancestor. I should have more women to tend to me, not just you. I should dwell in my halls. Your headband is nasty, said the Ancestor. You have forgotten to put the mask on when you chase the flies from me. Every single time, you forget.

"The mask is gone," said Inguill. "It attracted too much attention.

A woman with such a large bundle was bad enough." She had balled the headband that marked her nobility up in her pack when she and the Ancestor had fled. Her face was pinched and pocked from when everyone else had died and she had lived. But the hairy-faced invaders wanted "princesses," even ugly princesses. Safer to have no status, to toil away anonymously with a bundle.

The Ancestor was silent again. The potatoes were done. Inguill lit the Ancestor's portion for him and ate her own, quickly, quietly. They had a routine, the two of them. She had left behind the bodies of the Ancestor's other descendants, other servants, and with them the grander rhythms of his court. Inguill did not even know who called himself the Inca now, nor whether any power remained to him. No one came to consult the Ancestor now, about the matters of state. There was no order, wherein the Inca would proceed from Ancestor to Ancestor, hearing advice and deciding the best course of action. All was chaos.

But Inguill and the Ancestor had found themselves a place in the high mountains, away from the poxes and the chaos, where they could have a small garden, and Inguill could shoo the flies when she was not tending to the house and garden. The Ancestor grew restive. Inguill rested. Inguill breathed.

Inguill avoided the eyes of the hairy-faced men.

And the Ancestor knew what had befallen some of his descendants. Topa Inca's body had been burned, so that he could only observe his lands from a jar instead of a resplendent body. If no one remained to make the Ancestor his ritual garments but Inguill, no one to cook for him but Inguill, well, no one burned him, no one scattered his remains on the mountainsides, either.

They were safe, for now.

The Ancestor kept saying, for now.

Inguill thought, forever, if we are lucky, if we maintain our new mochadero and placate the spirits correctly. If we do this more successfully than those who came before.

That evening when she went out to draw water from the stream, there was someone else on the mountainside.

The other person was trying, not at all successfully, to hide behind some rocks and be quiet. Inguill thought of hiding also, of going back to the house and hiding, but she decided that someone who wanted to hide from her, who did it that badly, was probably no threat.

"Come out," she said. "You might as well come out now. I know you're there. Come out."

The other person was a woman, a woman who followed the hairy-faced men. Inguill jumped back, and the woman startled back also. Inguill made a placatory gesture.

"What are you doing this far into the mountains away from your menfolk?" Inguill mused aloud.

"My man died, and I did not want to be passed from soldier to soldier," the woman answered, barely above a whisper.

It took a great deal of control for Inguill not to jump again. She had not expected an answer, had expected the woman to speak like an outlander.

"Where did you learn the people's language?" asked Inguill.

"What?" said the woman. "Oh, the language of the valley? I pick up languages easily. I have to. To survive."

Inguill sighed. She drew her water at the stream as she had planned. "Come to my house, then. I cannot turn you out to sleep on the mountain, and there is no one else. What is your name?"

"Lucena."

"Lucena. I am Inguill. I live with my Ancestor here. You may stay with us a night or two."

Lucena bobbed her head. "Thank you."

Inguill acknowledged the courtesy curtly. Perhaps Lucena could do some of the more menial chores for the Ancestor. She seemed to gain a little confidence with each moment that Inguill did not attack her.

Inguill looked Lucena over carefully. Her skin was very close to Lucena's own in color—darker than most of the hairy-faced men, perhaps the women were more like regular people—and she covered her hair not with a headband but with a larger cloth. She was taller than Inguill, almost as broad in the shoulders, clearly not as strong. Her clothing was strangely fastened, with many complicated lacings and pieces that had once been white and were now dingy.

Lucena looked at the sky. The last pink fragments of sunset had slipped behind the next mountain. "I must—before we go to your house, may I—may I speak to the Supreme One?"

Inguill blinked at her. "How could I stop you?"

Lucena's jaw worked visibly, but she shook her head and then bowed away from the direction the sun had set, murmuring words that Inguill could not have heard even if she had been able to understand them.

When Lucena had finished and scrambled back to her feet, Inguill took her back to the house thoughtfully. There had been no mochadero to maintain there by the stream, but the strange woman was clearly diligent in maintaining connections to the spirit world. Perhaps she and the Ancestor would get along well, from a certain reverent distance, taking some of the Ancestor's relentless attention from Inguill. They reached the house in silence.

"Take your shoes off," said Inguill at the door. Lucena hesitated. "The floor is clean, and you must show respect."

Lucena's face smoothed, seeing that Inguill was taking her own shoes off as well. No one, even in their current reduced state, would wear shoes in the presence of an Ancestor. It was unthinkable. But as Lucena's eyes accustomed to the shade of the house, they had a new problem.

"That—" Lucena took a step back, bumping the wall. "What is that?"

She is rude, said the Ancestor.

"She is foreign," Inguill answered the Ancestor, and then turned to Lucena's question. "That is the Ancestor. Atoq, mighty of his name. I care for him. There were many of us once, in his cohort. Now there is just me."

"I cannot—" Lucena's throat worked. "I cannot touch that."

The Ancestor's reply was loud in Inguill's ears. Indeed she cannot!

"No, he will not let you," Inguill agreed, and Lucena relaxed.

"I will help you with the cooking, the cleaning?" Lucena said tentatively. "If I stay?"

"The cooking, the cleaning, if you know how," said Inguill. "But not the care of the Ancestor. That is for me alone."

"Thank the Supreme One," said Lucena fervently.

Rude, repeated the Ancestor, and untaught. Where did you find this beast-woman? Why does she look so strange? The cloth on her head is not a headband, so she is not noble, no cousin of yours. It is cloth. On her head. For no purpose.

"She was by the stream. She needed shelter for the night. She will help me," said Inguill.

Lucena was staring at her. But Lucena was not her main problem.

I do not know her, said the Ancestor. I do not know her people. No one I know in the other world knows her.

This was a problem. The Ancestor and Inguill had their roles very clearly divided. The Ancestor knew things. Inguill did things. The Ancestor could not do things. If Inguill was going to have to both know things and do things, she thought—her life was already very full as it was.

"She talked to the other world," she said. "Before we came in. She talked to Inti, she said."

"I am right here," said Lucena.

"And she is right here," Inguill agreed. "No one else is right here to help me. Only her."

That is so, the Ancestor admitted. She may help you. But she knows not to touch me.

"She will not touch you," said Inguill. She turned to Lucena. "You already know not to touch him. Come, I will get you some food."

Inguill let Lucena sleep between her and the wall, keeping the Ancestor safe from her motions in the night. The other woman's sleep was fitful, and she muttered strange words. In the darkest hour of the night, the Ancestor also muttered something strange, something Inguill did not hear or understand, and there was quiet in the house. Finally, Inguill could sleep.

Lucena learned quickly, how to tend to the garden, how to clean the house, though it was clear that nothing was familiar, nothing was the way she had done it in her own country. She was very quickly too useful to send away. She would not eat most of the kinds of meat, only fish, and she stopped to talk to the spirits too often. And when Inguill tended to the Ancestor, she sighed loudly. These were small things to trade for another set of hands around the house and the garden. Inguill did not want to pry, but the Ancestor had no such compunctions.

Ask her why she has come away from her own people, the Ancestor commanded. And whisk these flies away from me, it grows hot.

Inguill sighed and padded over to wield the whisk. "Why have you left your own people?" she parroted, well used to the Ancestor only speaking to his own kin. The flies buzzed up around her own head. She was not there to tend to her own person. The flies were allowed to alight on her, to creep through her hair, to crawl on her headband.

"The soldier who brought me died," said Lucena, pounding diligently at the corn Inguill had set her to grind. "I did not care to be passed from one hand to another. So I left while they were determining whose I should be. If I had been one of their own women, perhaps they would not treat me so. But we live in the world that is, not the world we wish for."

Inguill peered at her, anticipating the Ancestor's next question. "Aren't you one of their own women, then?"

"Oh no. My people come from further east, further toward the rising sun. I was taken slave. Like yours, but—the other direction."

Not like ours, said the Ancestor, but Inguill had gotten interested despite herself.

"Will they come for you?"

Lucena hesitated. Inguill saw what it was the Ancestor's job to see: that Lucena did not know. She wanted to say no, so that Inguill would keep her and feed her. But she did not know. Inguill turned her head away and did not force an answer.

Instead Lucena turned to the Ancestor, to the work Inguill was doing with the midday flies. She looked at his withered body, at the almost-hidden casket clutched to his chest. Only the essentials. Only the things that Inguill had managed to drag away, when the prince had been captured and the other royal mummies with him, when the plague had taken the rest of the kin group. Only that which kept him together as himself and gave her meaning. None of the pomp, none of the glory. Only that.

"What is in the casket?" asked Lucena.

"The Ancestor's...." Inguill hesitated. Lucena spoke the language of the people quite well, but it would be hard to explain the piece of what the Ancestor had been in a way that would not sound grossly physical to her. His fingernails, his hair, the pieces of his limbs, his teeth: these were sublime, as he had been sublime. They had been carefully preserved.

But Inguill had seen her. She shied away from the Ancestor not in reverence, as he himself assumed, but in disgust. Possibly she had never encountered one so high before, and assumed that his body was as other bodies. "It is his reliquary," she said finally. "Do you know this word, reliquary?"

"No."

"It contains essence," said Inguill.

Lucena did not press her further.

They learned to move around each other in this way, not pressing, not asking. Not discussing the ways in which the Ancestor existed with them, the ways in which Inguill tended to him, the ways in which Lucena shied from him. They began to have a routine. They began to be comfortable together.

Both watched the mountainside. At any time the hairy men might come. Inguill had always watched. But now there was the complication of a recognizable woman as well as the Ancestor to be hidden, and she did not entirely know what she would do with either.

"My people," said Lucena sleepily one night. "My people used to have Ancestors also. But we did not live with them. We died with them."

Inguill nodded. "We live with them until we die."

"We built them special houses."

"Yes. These we have."

"Why is the Ancestor not in his special house? Did the—did the men who brought me take him away from it?"

"Yes."

"Ah," said Lucena. "Now I understand."

Inguill was not sure that she did. But they slept more peacefully that night.

Inguill had begun to think that perhaps she would weave Lucena clothing, that perhaps Lucena would be less conspicuous if she had the clothing of a normal person. Not that anyone who saw her nearby would mistake her for a normal person. But if Inguill could send her up the mountain, into a field perhaps. It might work.

She had nothing to weave.

But with Lucena's work added to her own, the garden flourished. "Do you want me to thin the peppers?" Lucena asked one day.

"It's not what I want, it's what the Ancestor thinks is best," Inguill rebuked her.

Lucena frowned. "You are allowed to want things."

"I serve the Ancestor."

"You eat the peppers."

This was such a nonsensical thing to say that Inguill could not think of an answer. She was not happy, however, to be saved from answering by noise echoing along the streambed. It was a faint noise, hardly more than a frog splashing back into the stream and away, but Lucena froze like a beaten servant hearing her master's footsteps.

"It's them," she whispered.

"I fear so," said Inguill.

They hurried into the house. As they had both known from the start, there was nowhere to hide Lucena. The pile of potatoes was too meager to cover even the Ancestor, much less himself and a living, breathing, full grown woman.

"You must hide on the Ancestor's platform with him," said Inguill.

"What," said Lucena.

This is unacceptable, said the Ancestor.

"So is sending her off with them," snapped Inguill. "I don't have time for the two of you to argue."

"There is no two!" said Lucena.

It is true, said the Ancestor. She is so far beneath me that there is only me.

"That is a sound plan," said Inguill. "She should get beneath you."

"Don't make me do this," cried Lucena.

But her kind and docile benefactress was suddenly implacable. She lifted the mummy.

You know I hate to be dragged, said the Ancestor.

"We are not going anywhere," said Inguill. "Lucena. Lie. Down."

"I will wash and wash," said Lucena through her teeth.

I should say she will, said the Ancestor. My platform is not for the likes of her.

Inguill deposited the Ancestor in Lucena's arms and grated, "Take care of her. I know you can. And you will. For me, for yourself." Then she walked outside, folded her arms, and waited for the hairy-faced men to come.

They did.

Lucena embraced the Ancestor like he was her child, his withered body pressed against her filthy foreign dress. Inguill stood in the door like their sentinel. The foreign men saw her and said many things to her. She stood there until one of them propelled her aside.

There was a man with a hairy face inside the house, and he was paying no attention to the huddling woman and the mummy on the platform.

"What is happening," Lucena whispered.

The Ancestor was silent, not only to Lucena's ears but to Inguill's as well. He was concentrating.

The hairy-faced man said things that Lucena understood. She could have translated them for Inguill, if she had been able to move from the Ancestor's embrace. If she had been able to show herself. But then all would be lost. The hairy-faced man was asking whether Inguill lived alone, who helped her to farm, whether this hovel was all there was on the entire mountain. Whether she had seen a woman of what passed for quality in these parts, a slave, run off when her master died before the others could

MARISSA LINGEN

properly determine who was to inherit her. A Morisca.

Inguill stared at him. She kept her face impassive. She knew that keeping still was the way, that she must walk the line of still being the noblewoman she was and yet not offending the loud stranger. He spread his arms wide in her house. He pointed at things.

He raised his hand as if to hit her. He did not hit her. There was no reason to hit her. But there were potatoes, in a bin; there were many lumpy fine potatoes, and he made loud noises and started poking at the potatoes.

"Those are mine, I grew them," said Inguill. "We—I will eat them. I will need them to eat."

The hairy faced man rested his hand on his weapon, and Inguill went silent. The potatoes were a better loss than the Ancestor or Lucena.

He did not take them all.

Inguill was the one to do things, and the Ancestor was the one to know. But this time Inguill knew. She knew in her heart that things had changed completely between Lucena and the Ancestor, though she would not be able to make the Ancestor say so. Once Lucena had consented to hold him in her arms, thinking that he was nothing, thinking he was a withered lack, it had all changed. So she stood with no expression, and she waited, and the hairy-faced man left her home and took her fear with him.

After he had gone back down the stream, down the hill, she took the Ancestor carefully from Lucena's arms, carefully so as not to spill open the reliquary, and let her rise to her feet. Lucena brushed her dress ineffectually. Inguill set the Ancestor back on his platform.

Horrible creature, said the Ancestor.

"What did he do?" Lucena whispered.

"He went away," said Inguill.

"Not him," said Lucena, dismissing the hairy-faced man she had so feared with a single flick of her hand. "*Him*. The—the Ancestor."

"What did you do?" Inguill asked him.

I have a very good relationship with Mama-kilya in my time between this world and the next, despite the fact that you seem to be permanently opposed to using any of her tears to enhance my current reduced circumstances, said the Ancestor with dignity. I asked her to dazzle the eyes of the beast who searched for our new servant, so that he did not take her from us. And incidentally find *me*.

"He used moonlight on the eyes of the hairy man," Inguill reported.

"You don't happen to have any silver? He won't stop asking about it. Or gold, gold would be even better."

Lucena sat down on the floor with a thump and started to laugh, then to cry.

What is wrong with the servant? asked the Ancestor.

"She is relieved," reported Inguill, who was not entirely sure herself.

You will both stay with me, said the Ancestor.

"No," said Inguill.

The Ancestor was silent. It was not a happy silence.

"I will stay with you *mostly*," said Inguill.

The Ancestor remained silent.

"I will sometimes leave Lucena with you, and I will go to trade with others down the mountain. This will get us finer things for your dwelling. For our lives. And with Lucena here, we can have a second building."

A second building? asked the Ancestor.

"A proper second building," said Inguill firmly. "For your compound. But I must be able to leave sometimes. To trade. I cannot only take care of you."

The Ancestor thought this over.

"He's real," said Lucena. "He really is, he's real."

Inguill shook her head. Lucena was very useful, and it would be a relief to have someone to leave with the Ancestor, someone else to work on a proper second building and tend to the garden, but sometimes it was a great trial to her that that person was a foreign person who said strange things.

Still, her foreign ways did not get in the way of learning to build a proper wall. A few weeks later, Inguill had shown her the right stones, just where she wanted it, and stood in the thin mountain sunlight watching her put down the first stone, with the Ancestor waiting just inside the door of the house.

Tell her it will please Inti the sun god if she builds it further to the north, said the Ancestor. She cares for the goodwill of Inti, this one.

"Lucena knows how to please the Supreme One herself, Ancestor," said Inguill, glancing to Lucena out of the corner of her eye.

"What does he say?" called Lucena. "I am not too proud to learn." She set down the brick, settled back on her haunches, and waited.

LEATHER MAN'S HOLLER

RHODI HAWK

IT WAS A wet year in dry country. Gordon had let his nine-year-old daughter talk him into walking home by way of the gully, she being antsy to check on her soon-to-be swimming hole. That meant it was more practical to go on foot than ATV and that Gordon had to bring the machete. The gully itself was still bone dry and would make for an easy passage, but if a flash flood were to hit, and that would happen any day now, they'd be driven up the banks into the sticker bushes. Gordon wasn't about to do sticker bushes without a machete.

The perimeter of the ranch was lined with barbed wire. Just beyond it lay the highway, the only paved road in the area. It was gleaming and steaming under pewter clouds as they walked along.

"Looks like rain, Sweet Pea. Sure I can't change your mind? We can double back to the house and check on your swimming hole tomorrow."

"Gully."

"It's Leather Man country out there."

"My soul's at ease. It's the restless ones that should worry about the Leather Man."

"I suppose. My fault for telling you campfire tales. You ain't scared?"

"You said yourself, Daddy, I'm too hard-headed."

True. An iron skillet would break in half.

Gordon held her hand and positioned himself on the traffic side of the shoulder, even though there were no cars for miles.

How Gordon managed to hang onto the ranch this long was a mystery. *Why* he did it, an even bigger one. He was born on this land, he'd tell himself, and his father died on it. No outside person could understand the way this land breathed, the years sewn into the bloodline. It carried responsibility. Katy's responsibility one day.

Gordon adjusted his hat. "Responsibility" didn't begin to describe it.

They stepped off the highway onto the embankment just before the guardrail began the bridge. Barbed wire continued down the slope, then hung suspended over the dry gulch—high enough to keep cows in but not so low as to get swept off in a surge.

They stepped down carefully, single file, avoiding soft ledges.

From the highway, the bridge itself was barely noticeable, but from below it became a concrete cathedral where mud swallows nested and golden flats of carved stone spread below. A wonderland of his childhood.

He let go her hand.

Bats chirped, waiting for dusk, from their sleeping nooks along the beams that formed the bridge's underbelly.

Gordon smelled cigarette smoke in the same moment he saw the shape of a car hidden in the shadows.

"Katy—"

From behind them at the wingwall, an arm snatched Katy around the waist. She screamed.

Gordon raised the machete.

A pistol under Katy's chin. A man had her. A drifter. She went still in his grasp.

"Hey man," the drifter said, nodding at Gordon's machete. "You scarin me with that thing. Go on and throw it across the way there."

Gordon looked at the pistol mashed against his little girl's skin, and it made him want to cleave the sonofabitch in two. But he clenched his teeth and tossed. The long blade clattered to the shrub line along the far bank.

The drifter set Katy down but kept a clamp on her shoulder. "That's better."

He had ruddy skin with crude tattoo scratch from arm to neck. Not the kind you get in a shop. Either he'd been practicing the art on himself or he'd done some serious time.

"What do you want," Gordon said. "We don't have any money."

"Money. Shit."

The man laughed, picked his still-burning cigarette from the dust, and stuck it between his lips. "I been watching you two. Saw y'all dam up that gully yesterday. For the cows?"

Gordon frowned. "What do you mean, watching us?"

But Katy said, "It's for a swimmin hole."

Gordon fired her a warning look, but the drifter crouched next to her and pulled a long drag from the cigarette as if he had all the time of the Holy Ghost. "A swimmin hole? In *this* desert?"

"It ain't a desert, it's scrub plain."

"Why don't you take your damn hand off my daughter," Gordon said.

The drifter ignored him and looked back at the golden sand below, then made a point of gesturing at Katy with the pistol. "It don't look like that gully's held water in years. How you gonna get a swimmin hole outta that?"

Katy glanced at her father but not long enough to take in his *shut up* eyes. "It fills all the way in a flood year. We dam up the neck with sticks and just wait for the water to come. It ain't but a wading pool if it's a normal spring. But in a flood year, it'll keep a swimming hole going for weeks even after the gully goes empty again."

The drifter said, "That so? Come to think of it, last time I was out this way it must have been a flood year. That would have been long before you were born. 1987. My friend came here seeking shelter."

He turned to Gordon. "You know anything about that?"

Gordon shook his head.

"Nothing? You don't even gotta scratch your chin a little? We're talkin thirty years ago, man. My friend may not have exactly knocked on the front door."

Gordon said, "I was a kid, but I would have known if anything happened. My parents would have talked about it. We'd get poachers sometimes. Strangers. I remember each one."

The drifter said, "When my friend woulda showed, the gully woulda been dry. But he may have still been around when the gully filled up. He would have had to hole up somewhere around here. Taken shelter in—I don't know, a stable... or a mine shaft or something."

Gordon shook his head. "Not around here."

"We got caves," Katy said. "I heard about that flood, too. That wasn't a regular flood. It was ginormous. That was the year my grandpa died and my grand—"

"Hush," Gordon said through his teeth.

The drifter smiled. "Let the little girl talk."

But she was quiet.

He yanked her arm. "Well?"

"Hey!" Gordon stepped forward.

"You get on back."

The blood leapt in Gordon's veins. But the .38 wavered just under Katy's arm, turning his stomach inside out. He stepped back.

The drifter let the cigarette drop and he rose and stepped on it, waving the pistol. "Go on, kid. You were talking about that flood."

Katy glanced again at her father, eyes sparkling, a gleam that scared Gordon more than losing the machete. She truly didn't know fear, the ornery cuss. Not now, not ever. She had sense enough to sidestep a rattlesnake but couldn't fear it.

She said to the drifter, "That was the year of the humongously big flood. The water come on down the gully, and it made the banks give way so the water backflowed some and kept going. Ate through the brush like a chew line on a corn cob."

Gordon winced. She was retelling it just like she'd heard it. All fun and giggles, roasting weenies around the campfire.

Katy went on. "High scrub one day, and a whole new wishbone gully the next. The old one was just a ditch in comparison. There's a tower of sandstone caves now where the new gully branches off."

The drifter sharpened. "Caves."

"Most too small for a man. But yeah, the flood cleared out all the soft parts and left only sandstone."

She lowered her voice. "Every evening, whenever the breeze blows across the caves, it sounds like groaning. Like from a person. That's why we call it Leather Man's Holler. The wind in the caves'll keep a dead man alive forever so long as he can find a restless soul with skin to wrap around his own."

"Damn it, Katy."

The drifter threw back his head and laughed. "Leather Man's Holler! That is one kick-ass cowpoke name, little girl. Leatherman. That's what, a knife?"

But Katy finally absorbed her father's mien and shut her trap.

"Alright. What about finding something? Buried treasure?" He wiggled his brows.

"Aw, give me a break!" Gordon flung his arm toward the scrub beyond the bridge. "Look at this place. We look like we livin in high cotton?"

The drifter let loose another laugh. "You got me there, mister! I admit, I got here a couple of days ago and couldn't tell one stretch of cow trail from the next. Miles and miles of nothing, nothing, nothing."

He shot Gordon a silver molar smile. "OK. Now I'm gonna tell y'all two a story. Last time I was out in this area? When you got a new gully back in 1987? That was the year my friend disappeared."

The drifter let his laughter peter out, then the smile.

He pointed down the ravine. "Now, it dawned on me that my friend would have probably made his way along a gully. That gully."

But Gordon didn't look where the drifter was pointing. He was looking at the man's ring. Gold, with a red stone.

"What happened was, we'd 'found' something. A *lot* of something worth a *lot* of money, and we put it in a duffel bag and tried to lay low. But then we found ourselves in hot water."

Thunder in the distance.

The drifter said, "That night, it was real dark, no moon, nothing. I'm driving. Pedal to the metal. The cops are right on our ass. We come up over this hill, here."

He pointed beyond the bridge in the direction of the thunder roll. "And my friend gets out with the duffel bag and takes off on foot. I kill the lights and spin the car around, and I punch it. Straight back at the cops. They don't see me, or if they do, it's too late. And they sure as shit never saw my friend get out. Time they turn around, I'm gone."

"They didn't catch you?"

"Not for that anyway." He made for grace at looking sheepish. "I did get picked up for something else a few weeks later. Murder One."

The drifter spat and then wiped his mouth with the pistol hand. "I never saw my friend again. He didn't show at our usual place."

Gordon shrugged. "Take the money and run. Human nature."

"Maybe. Except I don't think so. Anybody else, I'd say that's the case. But he wasn't just my friend. He was my brother. I know him. If he didn't come looking for me, it meant he was dead. I came back here a few days later to find the gully full of water."

"He drowned?"

The drifter pulled out a pack of cigarettes. "Maybe he did, but where's the body? And the duffel? Bodies don't just vanish. Even out here. Place like this, you find some stranger on your property, you could kill him, take what he had, and bury him somewhere out in all that nothing. No one would ever know."

He slapped his pack and took out a smoke.

And Katy seized the opportunity to kick him in the groin.

Neither the drifter nor Gordon could react before she was sprinting up the embankment.

The drifter doubled over with a roar but was aiming the pistol at her dust cloud. Gordon sprang. The gun went off. The bullet flew astray, ricocheted, then kept zipping and clanging under the bridge until there was nothing left but an echo.

Gordon had the drifter flattened on his back. He couldn't reach the .38.

Katy had gotten away, that was what mattered. Gordon hoped to God she'd hightail it to the house and call the police.

Lord, she'd better.

The gun went off again. This time the bullet seared into Gordon's left arm. He tumbled backward.

"You stupid sonofabitch." The drifter leveled the pistol.

Gordon pushed himself up and lifted his hand. "Hold on now—"

The drifter pulled the trigger.

The bullet zipped clean through Gordon's hand and lodged in his shoulder, eight inches from the first wound. Gordon bellowed.

"I'm gonna shoot off both your hands," the drifter said, wild-eyed, one hand on his balls. "And I'm gonna shoot off your feet. Then I'll hunt down that kid and drag her back here so you can watch me shoot her in the head before you die."

"Wait! There was something else!" Gordon clamped a hand over his mangled arm. "You were right. Someone *did* show up here. A stranger. Some transient. It was a long time ago."

Gordon clenched his teeth against tremors that were now rippling from his arm to his jawline. "He—He killed my father."

The drifter kept the pistol aimed at Gordon and waited.

Gordon said, "I'll never forget it. I saw it happen. My dad told me to stay home but I followed him. It was raining. The— Your brother, he came up the gully before the wall of water hit."

Gordon licked his lips. "I guess he managed to hole up in the cave somehow."

The drifter let the pistol sink a hair. "That place the kid was talking about?"

Gordon nodded. "Leather Man's Holler."

"What did he look like? The stranger?"

Gordon rattled in a breath. "I—He—"

The stranger looked a lot like the man standing before him, right down to the pistol. Only back then it was trained on his father.

But also—

A creature with hollow eyes. Hollow mouth. Its own skin an unnatural thickened texture.

Remnants of fabric flagging from its limbs as a pretense of former civility.

A monster.

"Your brother. He wore a ring. Gold. It had a red stone. Just like that." Gordon pointed at the drifter's finger.

Recognition lit the drifter's eyes.

"What was in the cave?"

"I don't know. If there *was* anything, it's still there. I was just a kid."

Your brother shot my father, you sonofabitch.

"I ran for help. By the time we got back, the flood had hit. The whole landscape had changed. The stranger was gone, and my father was dead."

A mile down the flood waters, a bullet in his chest.

"Anything else you want to tell me before I shoot off your feet?"

"Come on, what do you want from me? It's all true. I can show you where the cave is."

"Don't jerk my chain. I came here to find out what happened to my brother. Don't care about no cave he might or might not've holed up in."

"He would have had the duffel bag in there, right? Don't you want to know where it went? What if it all caved in before he could get it out? What if it's still there?"

"What if my ass looks too good for my jeans? What if you're full a shit and your shitkicker family buried my brother out there in all that nothing?"

He spat into the dust. "What if putting you and that kid down slow and hard is the best I got? A little revenge for my brother's sake, thirty years past due, paid in full."

Gordon rocked over his bloody arm. "I think you know I'm telling the truth."

"Don't matter. Maybe I'll go look for the bag, maybe I won't."

"His ring, too. But you'd never find them. I can show you exactly where that cave is."

"You think I can't figure that out on my own? Let me take a guess. You walk up the fucken gully until it branches off at a bunch of fucken sand caves."

"Like I said, the entrance to *this* cave got buried. You'd never see it. My daughter, she'll have run back to call the police by now. I bet they're on the way. But I can take you right to the spot. You can get in and out by the time the police arrive."

The drifter gave him a hard stare down the barrel. "You lyin to me, I'll come back and kill you and your whole family in your sleep."

But he lowered the .38. "Get your ass up, then. I got a shovel."

THE LEDGE STOOD two-thirds up a vertical embankment of the smaller, older gully. Katy's dam lay further upcreek. The western skyline had already gone purple beneath charcoal clouds.

Gordon leaned on the shovel, sweating, fighting a swoon. His wounded hand was puffed and ashen.

Several feet above, the bluff dipped to mark the old cave-in. Beneath them, a twenty-foot drop to the gully.

"Keep digging," the drifter said.

"Give me a second. I got this far with one hand. Just need to catch my breath."

"You ain't worked that hard. The sand's brittle."

"It'd be a hell of a lot easier if you hadn't shot me."

The cliff face was honeycombed with sandstone caves. Some large enough for mountain lions to den, some so small they could harbor only bees. None large enough for a man, though, not anymore. Not *yet*.

From the south, the wind carried the scent of petrichor. Rain now minutes away.

Gordon hoisted the shovel and gave another one-armed shove. The sand broke to a small avalanche. It spilled all the way down to the gully.

A twelve-inch gap now showed at the top of the dig. The drifter pulled out a pen light and pressed it to the opening. They both leaned forward. The walls of the old cave reflected vertical red striations in the flashlight. The drifter angled the beam down to the floor.

There in the dust, a shoe.

About two feet from the shoe, a gray lump of something curled into itself.

"What the hell's that?" the drifter said.

Gordon squinted, and could barely make out dusty hair, whiskers, and a tail. "Dead possum."

The drifter frowned. "*Just* died? Shouldn't it be bones by now? Trapped in a cave thirty years?"

Gordon shook his head. "Things don't rot up here. Not in these caves. It's just the right balance of temperature and moisture, like a humidor."

Gordon nodded at the caves. "Enough wormholes in the sandstone to keep air circulating without letting water in. Too deep and convoluted for ants or flies to take the scent."

The drifter waved his pistol. "Keep digging."

Gordon grit his teeth. He swept out an armful of dirt. Then another. Pain sparked from his gunshot wounds. Then sand gave way and streamed out on its own. The gap widened four feet and kept going.

The drifter shone his pen light into the cave again. "Go on, get in there."

Gordon shoved two more armfuls out of the way and eased inside, bent over, shouldering in to allow the flashlight's beam.

The breeze picked up and the cave filled with a low, keening wind.

The shoe.

The possum.

A snake, too, glinting near the wall.

Deeper in.

A figure lying on its back across the dust.

"What do you see?"

"It's—"

Gordon tried again. "I think it's—"

But his breath held in his throat. If this was the person who'd killed his father thirty years ago, there was no recognition. It looked like a skinned animal, only shaped like a man.

The cast from the penlight swept over the body and Gordon realized the drifter had entered the cave and was now beside him on his knees, mumbling something. A prayer.

The flies were quick to join the assemblage. Gordon had to turn away.

This death did not look quick. And it seemed the opposite of easy. But it also did not look like it had happened thirty years ago, when Gordon had watched this man disappear into the cave. What lay before him looked more like a medical student's specimen of human anatomy without the skin.

Sure, there was the preservation factor.

But there were also tales of the Leather Man walking the gully at night. Transforming himself to dust and back to leather, searching...

The penlight swept to a curve of the cave. Gordon could make out an old wooden box, a duffel bag, and a ring: Golden. Red stone.

The cave felt cramped and airless.

The drifter crab-walked toward his brother's ring.

"No, don't touch anything. You can't touch it. This place is cursed. We treated it like a campfire tale for Katy's sake. But it's all true."

From beyond the opening came the call of a bird. A specific call. *Katy.*

Gordon's heart jumped. He scrabbled backward.

The drifter turned. "Where you think you're going?"

"You can't touch it. Don't even venture beyond that point."

"Don't you fucken move."

But Gordon was already at the ledge, clinging to the cliff face with his good hand. The drifter now had the penlight in his mouth and was reaching for the ring and the duffel.

The idiot had been warned.

Gordon dared a glance up the bluff and saw Katy leaning over the ledge directly overhead. She was lowering a cable toward him. The headlights from the ATV shone above. The cable was still well beyond Gordon's reach. He waved his daughter off, new streaks of pain shooting from his wounds.

The evening breeze soughed through the cave. With it came an impossibly deep lowing.

From within the cave he saw the drifter raise the .38 and point it at him. Gordon flung his body sideways just as the bullet nicked the cave entrance and whine into the dusk.

"Daddy!"

"Get back!" Gordon called to her.

From inside the cave came a rattling vocalization, vast and bottomless

---

as though coming from the belly of the earth itself. And then the sound of something snapping.

The drifter leaned out, pistol first. Gordon grabbed for it. With his one…good…tired from digging…uninjured hand.

"Good. There's the kid," the drifter said, and fired up the cliff as he and Gordon struggled.

Gordon jerked his head up and saw that either the bullet hadn't struck Katy or it had bounced off her hard-headedness to go worry the sky.

From inside the cave came a sound Gordon hadn't heard since 1987. And suddenly the drifter's fingers loosened, allowing Gordon to pry the pistol free.

The drifter roared, doubling back, and then his voice ratcheted to a shriek.

Gordon scaled the cliff face like a field mouse, reaching one-armed for a rock and a toehold, only to jettison a small rock slide on a long drop to the gully before he himself fell back to the ledge.

Easy, Gordon told himself. *It has what it needs now. Stupid to come this far only to fall to my death.*

The drifter let out a howl that echoed through the tower of caves. Gordon squeezed his eyes shut.

The ATV's cable bumped his shoulder. Relief washed through him.

He managed to close his fingers over it and look up at his daughter. "Got it, Sweet Pea! Now go on put the ATV in reverse and move back real slow."

But from the top of the bluff: "Daddy, please don't leave him like that."

"What?"

"You know what the Leather Man is gonna do. It could go on and on for—"

Gordon blinked at her. He could see only her silhouette, her ponytail against the flashing silver sky.

The family legends. A man made of leather, seen in the gully under moonlight. Bringing back food and water to the restless soul he kept locked away, because skin can rejuvenate. It just takes time. It could go on for years, is what they say.

Gordon tore off his hat and cursed, shoved it back on his head, and dared a look into the cave.

Thirty years is a long time. The creature looked hollow. A gaping hole where its belly should be. Empty eyes. Sunken mouth. Its skin was

---

thickened, albeit supple, as though cured by a tanner's hand. The drifter's fresh skin would help with that. The creature would wrap itself as though with strips of field dressing. It might tear strips of the drifter's clothes to bind it all together.

And it would have another pretty gold ring to add to its treasures.

Gordon hefted the .38.

The drifter's penlight had gone out, but amid flashes of lightning, Gordon saw his kicking feet, a glimpse of leather skin enfolding him. He heard breaking bone. A sound like no other.

Gordon primed the action and peered down the sight. But it was already too late. The creature had dragged the drifter so deep inside that Gordon couldn't get a bead.

"Alright, listen to me in there," Gordon said, wiping sweat from his brow. "I am going to toss you your pistol. But hear me. It ain't for you to try and kill that thing. You can't kill it. The pistol is for you. Understand what I'm saying?"

There came no reply, but Gordon had no choice but to assume the drifter understood.

He continued, "They say it prefers to keep a body alive as long as it can. I don't know how many shots you have left. You already fired off a few."

Gordon stepped inside the cave as close as he dared and slid the .38 toward where the drifter was struggling with the Leather Man. It looked like the drifter was already missing a strip of skin from his left arm.

Gordon swallowed. "You look a little indisposed right now, mister. Didn't catch your name because you didn't give it. I know you can't reach your gun right now. That may change when the Leather Man goes to seal off the cave again. When that happens..." Gordon licked his lips, "Well, that'll be your chance. Just get it over with, is my advice."

THUNDER AND LIGHTNING split the sky, leaving Gordon momentarily blinded as he clutched the cable. Katy was backing the ATV to help ease Gordon up the cliff face.

"Watch out for this last—"

But Katy continued on, pulling him one-armed and stumbling, through the last outcropping of thorny weesatch that now clung to his dungarees. But he was so glad to finally be up and staggering onto the high ground that he'd happily kiss the dirt and spit out the fire ants.

He saw Katy's dusty pink cowgirl boots approaching. "Don't act fretful, Dad. Night like this, with the Banshee walkin the wind? The last thing you wanna do is show yourself as a restless soul."

Gordon picked himself up onto his knees and she continued past him to where the bluff made a deep curve. "Look."

He stepped over to where she pointed. Around and below, they could see the creature was scraping at the sand surrounding the cave. Filling it back in. Once a cave. Now becoming a sealed chamber.

The light had faded to violet. At the ledge, the creature already had half the cave mouth closed off.

There came a loud crack. It could have been thunder. More likely, a gunshot. Gordon wondered whether the drifter had pointed the .38 in the right direction.

"You're bleeding," Katy said.

"We need to get back."

The bluff gave a tremor. From beyond the bend came a rumble, then a mighty crash. Gordon felt the ground shake under his boots.

"The flood! Can we stay and watch?"

"No, dammit. I been shot. Twice!"

"But my swimming hole...?"

Gordon dragged his forearm across his filthy, sweaty brow. "Sweet Pea, you'll be some kinda hard woman when you grow up."

But then he took her hand and waited just a few minutes more because a flood of this size wasn't liable to happen for another thirty years.

The wave that came didn't seem like much. It moseyed down the gully and then snuggled Katy's dam. But then another wave three times its size barreled through and smashed Katy's dam apart like a pile of match sticks.

Katy whooped.

"I'm sorry, Sweet Pea."

"Are you kidding? That was great!"

Satisfied, they walked back to the ATV. They had just climbed inside when hard rain began pelting the ranch, and they finally set off in the direction of the house—

Driving away from Leather Man's Holler and the split gullies—

Bouncing past Witch's Dram and the swarm at Dead Man's Tree—

Making a very, very wide berth around Devil's Switch—

Passing the old family graveyard where Gordon's own father lay buried—

Rolling through the hundred-year oaks, the firefly meadows; and passing before the eyes of a hundred beasts and beings as they made their way across this ranch they called home. A stretch of land that the drifter had called miles and miles of nothing, nothing, nothing.

THEIR SILENT FACES

MICHAEL CISCO

Kirtan Bhowmick and I were not close friends, but we knew each other for quite a long time. We would encounter each other at journalistic functions a few times every year, have a few drinks, commiserate, exchange contact information again, and vanish back into our lives. Seeing him at intervals like that made the development of his alcoholism particularly stark and plain to me. Eventually he disappeared, becoming exclusively an online presence, emitting flurries of messages with ever longer gaps in between. Each posting was denser than the last, more impenetrable, filled with untraceable allusions, but also laced with keen insights and sharp characterizations. Everyone knew his wife had finally left him, and I had heard from a mutual friend that she had approached him about helping Kirtan, since she was simply unable to go on with him. In the last nine months or so, his messages became more regular and more condensed. They were gnomic sayings about current events, which seemed to have been exuded under pressure. We thought he must be drying himself out.

I ran into Kirtan in New York City, and I realized we were only kidding ourselves about him. He was still as nattily dressed and princely as ever, but glassy eyed, stumbling, clumsy. His gestures were stiff and flailing, and he chattered over the din of the bar, his eyes fixed and remote over his working mouth. His knees folded under him repeatedly and I once had to take hold of him and set him back on his bar stool; his body was as light as a child's. Once again we made the ritual exchange of contact information, but this time he really did contact me. We began an exchange of correspondence that eventually led to his writing out a fuller document, although I did not receive the entire thing until after his death.

Of all people, Kirtan chose me to be the last person he would ever speak to. He called me out of the blue one morning and asked if he could see me; I invited him over. He came by around three o'clock and told me in person much of what follows. I hadn't seen him in months, and his condition was shocking; his hands trembled in his lap, he spoke to me tilted back in a chair with a spine as stiff as a rod, and he was panting, as if it were an effort to breathe. His voice rose and fell, sometimes booming out so loud I wondered if the neighbors would hear it, other times dwindling to a low murmur, but always the same surprising command of language and that punctilious pronunciation he had had drummed into him as a boy. His eyes rolled incessantly around the room, returning again and again to my face with a wordless, almost impersonal, plea in them. I could not, in good conscience, offer him a drink, but he had a bottle of his own with him, and would from time to time take a frighteningly mechanical pull at it. I had a crazy impulse to time those drinks, they came so regularly.

He told me all about his mummies. I sat there as I guess anyone who thought they were in the presence of a lunatic would sit there, nodding and listening, rended with pity and wishing desperately that he would leave. I had a reprieve for about an hour when he went to buy another bottle; he still had enough self-respect not to ask me for a drink, for which I was grateful. Eventually he staggered into the two AM street outside, still waving his empty bottle, although he had since switched to a flask. I watched from my window, and raced down after him when I saw him stumble and fall on his face. He was already gone by the time I reached the street. Two days later I heard he was dead. He had killed himself less than twelve hours after he left me.

There was no note, but he did send me this a few hours before his suicide. His reason for sending this to me is a mystery; I can only assume he wanted to be understood. Considering that far more of what he told me was true than I had believed at the time, I can see why he would have both wanted to explain himself, and have wanted to avoid explaining himself. His compromise, I guess, was to transfer the job in part to me, as a sympathetic friend. Kirtan spent most of his adult life destroying himself for reasons I can't fathom, and which I suspect he himself did not know. He caused his wife and those around him immeasurable anguish on his behalf, and perhaps he needed to. Given the circumstances, presenting his own account of himself is the only real way to avoid sensational and opportunistic speculation, and therefore, more pain to his loved ones. So, here it is.

LOOKING BACK, IT seems I always had an imaginary retinue. I would animate stuffed animals and dolls, salt shakers, staplers, whatever came to hand. It wasn't hard to give something a face, an attitude.

My dummy was an ordinary Charlie McCarthy replica my parents bought for me when I was in fifth grade. I was a spoiled child. The head and hands were made of cheap plastic that gave off such an eye-watering chemical stink at first that I used to get woozy handling the thing. The smell made me think of narrow stone passages in forsaken religious buildings, like the cell the anchorite is walled up in. In time the smell weakened, but it was always there, bringing with it the same vague impression of premature burial. I tried to teach myself to throw my voice, but I lacked any real aptitude for it. So, I simply talked and worked the jaw, turned the head, the fixed, staring eyes, to and fro.

I was a spoiled child, as I've said, and from time to time I had fits of vapid, causeless rage. One day, furious at having been balked somehow, I forget what it was although I'm sure it was frightfully trivial, the dummy fatefully met my eyes, the vacancy of its stare seeming to dare me somehow. Grabbing it by the legs, I battered the doll against the heavy desk, the wall, the floor, then dropped it, panting, momentarily exhausted. It was then that I noticed the crack in the side of its hand, and the fibrous, tobacco-colored stuffing that the crack exposed. Prising the crack apart a bit more to see inside, I encountered again that ferocious chemical smell, so intense it stung my nostrils and made my eyes water. Inside the arm I found the slender, tea-colored ulna nested in ragged bandages. It moved slightly, and I couldn't be sure it was only my handling of the doll that moved it. The thin bone seemed to turn almost coquettishly in my direction.

It seemed obvious that I had to examine the head. Using a pair of scissors, I bored through the center of one of the large pupils and the caustic stink of plastic came whistling through the hole, playing uncleanly over my face, filling my nostrils with a biting, snarling aroma of dark, rancid confines inside a plastic head. All its color fled, the room vibrated before my eyes like the skin of a snare drum, the dead grey plastic smell knotted and tensed in my sinuses and swam tingling like death through my head. My grip slackened and the dummy's mouth fell open. I didn't have to check to know there was a slender brown mandible inside it, and yellowed, half-melted teeth fitted inside the inanely neat smile. Mindlessness boiled in the wrinkled crease at the back of the mouth, behind the painted pink tongue.

I spent countless hours in base communion with the doll. I wondered if perhaps all the ventriloquist dummies I'd ever seen had had miniature skeletons inside, and I concluded that they did, although they weren't exactly part of the manufacturing process. The hollow shape was a kind of housing that called prospective tenants in out of the ether to materialize inside the stinking, lightless, child-shaped vessel, and preserve themselves, sealed in with the fumes, untouched by the indignities and stupidities of the doll itself. The dummy is always more canny than the struggling, sweating puppeteer. The dummy had such a presence for me, it was like living with a vampire coffined up in the basement. An exhilarating sense of darkness and doom clung to it, like the smell. I wanted to smell like that, to be frightening in that passive, ungregarious way, without gestures or threats. An innocuousness so total and perfect it becomes inexplicably terrifying; nothing could possibly be as harmless as that, it must be the opposite, it must be so harmful it doesn't need to come at you. Just seeing it, just knowing it's there with you in your town, is enough; the dummy is terrifying merely because it exists. Or that was how it seemed to me.

The mummy inside was not the mummy of someone, I decided. It had always existed, it had been born a mummy, into the outlines of my Charlie McCarthy doll. Its memories and knowledge were not the memories and knowledge of life. Nor of death, either. It had never died because it had never lived. It remembered unliving, and related those memories to me in a soundless whisper, dry as cinders and reeking of cheap plastic, the stink of ancient swamps, of dinosaur muck and the putrescence of colossal early earth insects, distilled and concentrated, transformed into this sterile preservative mace, stinging and hallucinogenic not with the cornucopia of an superstimulated imagination, but with the ignis fatuus of a rotting imagination deliquescing in acrid diesel rainbows, like the iridescent lesions that erupt on oil-soaked asphalt after it rains. It told me about the analogs to darkness and silence that exist for those creatures who have never had sight or hearing, their analogs to pain and pleasure, at the same time abstract and miserably corporeal. Pleasure like the very, very gradual subsidence of a piece of cigarette ash, as it flakes off the top of a little cylinder of discarded powder, lying upright by chance among the cobwebs and dust on the windowsill in the back of a gas station. The thump that piece of ash makes when it lands on the sill is so unimportant it achieves a special kind of perfection, escaping the universe by being beneath its notice. The vilest and the most minor, the least. The dummy was silent, stinking, but the vision sang to me. I was still a child. I struggled to express, to understand what I was learning. In retrospect it's clear to me that I could not put that song into words because it was already in its own words, so exactly in its own words that there was nothing I could do with them, they could not possibly be made any more clear. What I remember is a vision of lightless and silent corners, dim light from windows, the dust and silence by the edge of the wall where the moulding parts from the withering floorboards. The song of corners where emptiness teemed like drafts and became positive, a singing voice crooned out from the warp and woof of houses, streets, rugs, hours after school. I heard the song in school too, where I plotted assassinations. I loved school. I loved learning. I wanted to kill all my favorite teachers and keep them with me, so that I could continue to learn from them even after the end of the semester. I would learn how, and mummify them. Mrs. Donoso I would keep secreted in the attic, since she didn't like basements and confining places. Mrs. Teusel, with her magnificent cushion of platinum blonde hair, I would stretch out from floor to ceiling in the corner of my closet. I would be the only boy in school with his own cabinet. In time, I would have a whole collegium. Brittle, bundled wasps' nests trembling with countless voices from outside, hived up within hollows breasts, bellowed words heard across incalculable distances, the words themselves conjugated and declined by the distance, smoothed by their interminable resonation ...

Puberty, the exigencies of life, drew me out of this phase. The dummy was left to sit in silence at the back of a closet, and at some point or other it must have been thrown away. Perhaps I threw it away myself. I forgot everything, apparently instantly. From time to time, as I recall, there were moments when the old dark seemed to look in on me from the lightless end of a cul de sac, or the spacious abandonedness of a building, things and places with a specious barrenness about them, but I never really remembered until later. How much more stark that song was, and how much much richer it was. There came a time in my thirties when I tried again to write it down, but I always forgot everything between episodes. Only when I recognized the song did it all come devastatingly back to me. I tried using a tape recorder, but on playback found I'd captured only my own snivelling, disgracefully feeble.

Nobody goes around inserting mummies into ventriloquist's dolls, let alone mannikins or statues. The mummy is already a mannikin. My childhood ideas were ideas only and what I saw weren't bones but wooden dowels. Stiffen the arm up. Make the motion more natural. But do all dummies sing that song of empty hallways in gleaming black apartments, whose lyrics are an ominous breathing, the suspense of the floorboards, tables and chairs, the plaster and wires, all already different and still changing at a molecular level, simmering invisibly in the dark where already unheard of shapes and transformations were nursing? The mummy is a preserved body, but what is preserved exactly? The mummy looks nothing like the living person. The preservation is a transformation, it's all I want, a paper body lighter and lighter. So I drank. Alcohol is a preservative, clean and dry, sterile, chemical, pure ... my mummification potion.

The effect of the withdrawal was postponed by my growing, or perhaps my growth was a misleading aspect of it, that darkness I mean. This withdrawal did not gather intensity quickly, but it did not fade, not one iota. It gathered itself patiently, grain by grain. An ache, a feeling of being always too hot or too cold that made me yearn for tepidness. Everyday events confronted me and there I was, there I was, there I was, helpless without my sweet consolation, the stench of decomposition and improperly cured plastic. Countless mummies were ground up into powder and sold as medicine, guzzled down in possets. Extract cadaverine from the powder, concentrate it thousands of times, then shoot it into me. I had no idea what I was yearning for; I could not then connect what I was going through with what had come before. All I knew was present suffering, when my sensitivity to temperature would suddenly burgeon out into attacks of fever or chills and often both, heat pounding in my temples heated up orange like hot glass, chills rinsing my body cavity with ice water. My flesh quivering in the slightest motion of the air, weak, melting, almost liquefying, my joints grating together agonizingly and my thoughts too swift and massless to follow; sights and sounds and smells shooting like comets through me, and gone. But always leaving a scar. Then, after an eternity of this sleepless, restless impotence, the spell would lift away in minutes and there I would be, normal again. Normal clicked all my outlines. But in the interval, between the subsidence of the nightmare and that click, I could feel the blue and powdered sugar skies of my childhood running out through my fingers, too fast. All of nature is moving too fast and my life can't keep up; so it was with something like resignation that I clicked back into my normal outline. It was a surrender. Drinking didn't actually ease the pain at all, in fact, it made that pain easier to distinguish from the ordinary, everyday pains of my miserably failed journalistic career, my ill-fated marriage. Drinking, for me, became a pathway that allowed withdrawal to find me wherever I went; I wanted to feel the need for a drink I didn't have in front of me, overlaid on that other yearning.

I found an actual mummy in the men's room of a cafe. This must have been almost a year ago. I had gone to meet with an editor and I was sober, outwardly. Inwardly I was in an achingly jumbled condition that had no simple name. You can't have a drink yet, not yet, not yet, when is yet, not yet, not quite yet. I drank coffee although I didn't want to. The mummy was propped in the corner of the bathroom by the door, so I didn't see it coming in. Only when I went to wash my hands did I notice an oblong brown form there behind me, with candle flames burning in each of its upturned eye sockets. Was it a real mummy? A corpse? The manager didn't know, but she hadn't been there for more than a few days. I brought the mummy home with me and put it into the corner of the room that had been my wife's. There are sixteen mummies in that room now. One I noticed half hidden in the weeds of a vacant lot beside a laundromat. It was still adorned in its golden regalia. Another I discovered bundled into an alcove toward the back of a hotel lobby, behind an enormous potted plant. There are mummies hidden inside the walls of houses, airplane fuselages, abstract sculptures in public places, furniture, subway cars, perhaps household appliances. The police have inspected my collection, questioned me, taken photographs. None of the bodies have been identified. There are no matching dental records, or fingerprints. I believe their forensic examiners know how old the bodies are, but they refuse to tell me. In the end, however, despite my alcoholism, their interference ended after a preliminary investigation. No mummies like mine were reported missing anywhere.

"You can have 'em," was the last word, so far.

The mummies had all been *candied*, though, that was the thing. Embalmed by candying. They all had the musty smell of powdered honey.

Like hot hay. While they weren't sticky, they glistened and sparkled as you turned them to and fro, the light playing over the flesh crinkly, the whole body like hard candy, dry as dust.

I sleep with the mummies standing all around my bed, smelling them in total darkness as I sink into unconsciousness, numb with drink. When my eyes shut, the darkness curdles and ferments. I keep thinking a fly has landed on me. I brush my face, my hands, even my body under the covers. The darkness in my room becomes curly. It forms phosphorescent muscles with sharp fibers, in constant motion within itself. I can feel my own muscles wanting to move too, as if my muscles were making gestures inside my fixed body. I felt like a city at night. All my senses open, I see a river with big clacking stone and glass chimes suspended in it, rolling in a steep trench through a garden, surrounded by a city whose high buildings stood black against an orange sky like a glass kiln. Vinegary sweat trickles in my hair, under my arms, soaking into the sheets I'm wrapped in. Everywhere figures sat facing the river, stiffly erect on their benches, flesh like old vellum, spotted brown and shrunken, skinny necks and hands, or rounded forms of saponified remains, all gazing blindly and silently on the scene, piebald, with infinite repose, but their fingernails are sprouting long parentheses, their hair grows down to the ground and plaits itself into the grass, the wood of the benches is sprouting suckers and so is the metal, their garments are fruiting out in new layers and folds and antlers. Flies keep landing on them. Flies with seven wings and nine eyes swim heavily through the smothering air and under it the city turns to candy, my body candies inside, the veins and arteries take on the curious pastel colors, the bright reds and blues and yellows, of candy, my flesh becomes taffy flesh, hardening within a coating of transparent sugar, my breath and circulation are the tricklings of sugar grains through a fog of fragrant alcohol, expelling all my grosser materials in streams of toxic sweat. This is the dream of the mummies, another version of their song as heard through a brain slowly candying itself in alcohol.

THE SONG HAS stopped. The mummies have stopped speaking to me. What I have I done? Or not done? Why have they stopped? Their silence felt like talking, singing a song right out of an absence that was a getting out of the way or an unblocking of a pathway to a paradise of infinitely proliferating being, and now their silence feels like an amputation. I've been cut off. I enter the room but I am not actually getting in. I'm frantic, like an alcoholic on a desert island, but I have no reason to believe this need will ever weaken. What happened? Why won't they talk to me? Why leave me trapped in these outlines and this horrible ordinariness?

I am nothing without them. Have they, knowing that, withdrawn from me in order to make me nothing? But then why collect around me, if only to abandon me? The solemnly drawn candy faces of my mummies are silent now in a hostile, ostracizing way — but not even that, not even that. I don't know how to describe it, the impersonal refusal at once utterly indifferent to me and yet focussed directly on me in a way that it doesn't seem possible to ascribe to accident. The universe spoke to me through these mummies, gave them to me, and now the universe torments me with this ban that falls on me without noticing me.

I was sitting among the mummies, forlornly, when I looked up at the wall, and saw the blade of light reflected from a car door in the street. It swung suddenly across the wall and shuddered there by the corner. The door of the car had been opened. Then it swung back to where I had first seen it. The door of the car having closed again. Then again, it sailed over to the corner, and again, back to where I had first seen it. This happened several times, and every time the resemblance this streak of light had to a knife blade became more and more marked. I realized now that this could be a sign, an indication that I might have to do what I had after all been entertaining I might do. It could be nothing more than the motion of a reflection. If it moved again, I would take it as a sign, I told myself. It didn't. I fell asleep, and the reflection was gone when I woke up.

Was it a sign? Or was it something I chose to see as a sign? The mummies confirmed nothing. They denied nothing.

Then a new thought came to me, one that was so striking and solid, after so much groping and murkiness, that it was like a message, a direct order. Perhaps they had fallen silent because they had reached the limit of what could be communicated to me in my current state. In that case, the only way to restore communication with them would be to join them, and it was this for which they waited. Now suddenly the image of my exile was transformed into a pathway for my salvation. The possibility, the idea, had been introduced to me, deliberately or not, when I was a boy, so that, by chance or design, I should have had all these years to wean myself of its terrors, to prepare myself for its realization without knowing what I was doing.

Now mindlessness boils in the wrinkled crease beneath my eyes, a foul odor billows from my toothless gums, and oozes from the corners of my eyes. My head and hands tremble, my bald pate peels and sheds its skin. My whole body palpitates to that rhythm. The surgings and plummetings of oceanic space and time. The spurt and crinkle of the grain in the wood, the threadiness of tobacco smoke tangling up with soundwaves and lightwaves. I see now only in a confused and all too deliberate memory the shapefulness of all things, the warm, unravelling bath of decay that sets our forms free. That unlocks our bodies inside our forms. Infinite energy minutely coiled into the springs that drive those outlines to thin, curl, lengthen, spiral or straighten in forms all tightly ground in together, right down into my brown bones, my sagging, colorless skin and gnarled, hardened muscles. Knotted into my muscles and joints I can feel the feral symmetry, ecstatic and profuse, that scribbles itself everywhere, and I know — dying, drunken old idiot that I am — that hideousness is a living thing.

BIRTHRIGHT

INNA EFFRESS

ALEX WADED THROUGH a sea of Blue Paradise. Their fragrant petals bedecked the Colonial, set back on a respectable Chappaqua street. They sprawled lavishly, their red mouths, the mouths of sirens. The bathroom window had been left open just enough to insert leather fingers the color of Brazil nuts. Eggshell paint flaked to the floor as the window screeched higher and Alex squeezed through, careful to set her boots astride the toilet seat. By the milky light of the moon, the discolored bowl wallowed like a dish of blood pudding. Its smell mixed with marijuana and Febreze. Her ski mask provided little relief.

Inside, the house was lifeless. Bill and Barb Byrd had pulled out of the garage twenty minutes before. Bill had escorted his wife to the passenger side, his left hand moored to her rear. Bound in taffeta that clung like a vine, her dewy breasts cleaved together. A wrinkled infant slept, swaddled, in her arms.

On the marble countertop of serpentine green, a bottle of Boss cologne squatted, a bloated sphere on a tarnished silver tray. The mirror had three faces, multiplying the presidential squint of Bill Byrd's portrait. From that angle, at the sink, it seemed he was squeezing in, like cliff walls at the bottom of a ravine. Alex removed the gloves, revealing stubs where her fingertips should have been, the result of what she was told was a rare disorder, an inexplicable compulsion to devour oneself. In the semi-darkness, the empty gloves looked like sodden, detached skin. Hooking a mutilated thumb against the neck of the mask, Alex peeled if off and glared into the glass, her lips tight under Bill Byrd's beefy head. There was no denying the rage in her eyes, the heat in them, and the fear.

From inside of her shirt she drew out a tiny notebook dangling on a suede strap around her neck. With red ink she scribbled:

"Because it is so clear, the realization takes longer."

She tore off the sheet and tucked a corner under an ashtray. Swimming in the ashes was a roach, its tip still wet with what she guessed was the man's spit.

Alex sparked the blackened joint. She was convinced that people's magic entered things they'd used. She considered their power transferrable.

A long, whistling pull. Lips still forming a compact "O," she removed the joint, lifted her chin, and without exhaling, sucked in again. Smoke needled her lungs. It scraped her insides and obliterated all other sensation. Her eyes rolled back, then came the combustive violence of a coughing fit. Doubled over, hands gripping knees, involuntary urine dribbled on her underwear. She had to keep moving.

Elaborate rails curved down the staircase. Steps flared at the bottom like a hooded cobra. When she reached the landing, she halted. There it was. The antique Turkish dagger glinted on its wall mount, its double-edged blade of Damascus steel protruding cruelly from an elegant handle of walrus. Her heart kicked. Her mouth quivered. She'd read that the secrets of the ancient world were forged into the artifact. That the armorers, for centuries, had concealed their mysterious practices. To abruptly cool the red-hot blades, medieval smiths did peculiar tricks. The quenching, as it was called, had to be performed covertly, using the urine of redheaded boys, or baby goats, or, as in the case of the finest specimens such as this one gleaming on the wall, the blade was heated until it glowed, as it was written in the ancient accounts, red as the skies of the mosque at sundown, then quelled to a royal shade of violet and plunged, hissing, into the fierce body of a captive warrior, his bold blood cooking, and his vigor siphoned to the sword. This was Bill Byrd's prized possession. He had gone to great lengths to locate and obtain this very piece. For an instant, she paused and looked around her.

Two portraits presided from above. To the left and right of the dagger, they hung in gilded frames. In one, his three-quarter profile like a tomahawk, the backdrop, a rippling American flag. The other, a bold silkscreen, in screaming fields of color, his jaw and chin confronting, as if to say, "What do you think you're looking at?"

With her pen, Alex scrawled atop his smug lips "Man = Pig." She freed the dagger from its brackets.

On the nightstand in the master, a quart of wildflower honey and a glass of tea magnified a glittering crown. Encased and pristine, it perched on velvet. The engraving was visible on a plaque affixed to its base: Miss New Jersey 1998. At the tearful end of Barb's reign, Bill had commissioned a seventy-carat replica so she would always have a crown to keep. Now its stones trapped the light, slowing and bending it, revealing the mysteries of the universe with its flashes of brilliance.

"I'M STARVED," THOUGHT Alex. "I'd better fill up before they get back." She stuck her head inside the cavernous fridge. Breathing hard, she inspected a jar of pickled tripe. With her mangled fingers, she plunged into the clear gel inside the jar and shoved the rubbery honeycomb pieces in her mouth, chewing. She tore into the cheese, the olives, and the duck pate studded with cherries. A wound reopened on her hand, and she sunk it into the freezer's ice reservoir. Pink ichor smeared the cubes.

ALEX WAITED IN the closet, at Barbara Byrd's cluttered makeup table. An hour passed, then another. High-pitched wailing, like a cat in heat, pierced her as Bill and Barb ascended the stairs with the screeching baby. Her ears throbbed.

Alex unscrewed a vial of Barb's silver pigment and frosted a mask around her eyes. With onyx paste she blacked out her jaw and swept more around her lashes, in two big circles. The effect was a skull, grinning widely.

In wine-drenched syllables, Bill Byrd slurred. "That shrieking can drive a person crazy. Can't you do something?"

"He's just hungry," said the wife, her laughter bright, the clinking of glass. "There was nowhere to nurse at the theater." From the closet Alex watched the baby's frail arms unfurl like batwings as the triangle of blanket fell away.

"Next time, we're leaving that gargoyle at home. Why would you let Rosa take the weekend off? Not too smart, was it? We pay her way too much."

"I'll feed him now, and we can all get some sleep." The woman pulled her skirt above her Spanx. She liberated a breast, engorged and marbled blue. Plunking her behind on the bed, she kicked off her heels and lay facing her baby, skin-to-skin. His bowlegs burrowed into her soft abdomen. His immaculate feet grazed her pubic bone. With swinish grunts he rooted for her nipple, the color of liver. Streaks of mascara marred Barb's doll face as the infant drained the right side, then the left. The baby's lips softened and the struggle lifted up and out of him, like a soul from a deathbed. His mother's body went slack.

BILL BYRD UNBUTTONED his shirt. From the dark closet, under racks of dry cleaning like ancient lava stalactites, Alex stewed in silence, in shame and in lust. Through an open sliver, she watched as he pushed the woman's face into Egyptian cotton, the gleaming cutlery of his teeth, his body clenched and shuddering, while the former beauty queen held her breath. The baby stayed sleeping beside her, his sated mouth hung open in bliss. From her lookout, Alex admired those breasts, swaying over the sheets, the clouded crystals of bluish milk suspended from slick cracks of skin, shimmering droplets, rough as diamonds on a panner's brown, exploited palm. She swallowed, but her mouth was a tidal pool, filling and filling from every crevice. Waves of hunger rocked her.

With a final rattle, Bill disengaged, re-zipped his pants, and headed down the stairs, slapping out a drum beat on his chest.

"Barbie, did you leave this idiotic note in my private bathroom?" Bill's voice, now a rolling barrel, shook the closet, which was directly above where he stood. Gripping the dagger's creamy hilt, Alex rose, sweating with excitement as his volume increased. "The realization takes longer? Do you have any clue what this is all about?"

Barb hid a smile, "No, Bill, it's not mine."

"Someone's been here," he said from the master doorway. 'They've left menacing notes. They've defaced my painting." His growl twanged low in his throat. "My Turkish dagger." A quiet panic seeped into his lament. "It's gone."

Panting, he entered. Alex stepped out from the darkness and into their marital sanctuary. Barb calmly kissed her sleeping son and moved him to his bassinet.

Alex's war paint caked and cracked, parching her skin, stretching it taut, like raw canvas. It was as though her original face had merged into the paint. Alex motioned for him to stand by his wife and child.

"Do you have any idea who I am?" His shirt flapped open, airing a soft gut and a tangle of dark hair. He stepped toward her and swiped at her outstretched arm. "That's my property. Hand it over now, and we won't press charges."

The blade broke skin, like the initial incision of the surgeon's scalpel. Blood stained his clothes. Bill Byrd bared his teeth.

Alex held up the notepad. "I am your firstborn," it said.

For a moment, Bill's impressive forehead softened in a question mark, like a schoolboy puzzling over a math equation. Avoiding his eyes, his wife signaled Alex with a slight shake of her head. But it was too late.

Alex arched her back, thrusting the blade into him, just under his ribs. The tip nicked bone and her slight arm wobbled. On the second try, the length of the blade sank into his belly. She twisted in both directions. An inhuman lowing escaped him. This time, Barb looked directly at his face, which had contorted into something unnatural, like an animal that had grown too big for its cage.

"There's no reason," Barb said, "for a father not to sacrifice. You know, the way a mother would. It's every child's birthright." Then, with regret and shyness – as if reacquainting with an old lover, or an ally, long-lost, who returns shining with unspoken forgiveness – Barb smiled at Alex.

Bill's wet amphibian mouth opened and closed.

When Alex dislodged the dagger from his gash, hot blood bubbled through his fingers. It matted his coarse body hair. Bill Byrd could only gurgle. The baby sighed in its sleep.

Lowering himself to the bed, the injured man spread his legs. The space between them was a triangle. To the four bedposts, Alex tied his limbs, and in the stench of blood and cologne, of feces and jewels, her heart flowered. At the foot of the bed stood the beauty queen. A shiny film of dried milk clung to her nipples.

Together, the women waited for the man's forehead to relax, for his eyes to surrender, for his mouth to freeze. Then Alex thrust the knife into his throat, under his Adam's apple. Finally, his body relaxed. When she cut his wrists and ankles loose, they thumped against the mattress. It was time to dismantle him. She made a deep slit from his anus to his neck, through one side of his trunk to his armpit, across the collarbone, and down the other side. Blood soaked the bedding, her gloves, clotted on her arms, and spattered her legs. Sliding one arm between the duvet and his chin, she jerked his head backwards, repeatedly. Crack, went his vertebrae. Around and around, she turned the lifeless head until finally, the spinal column gave, and the head tumbled to the floor. Only then, she exhaled.

Gazing down into his bulging eyes, Alex pulled his lids closed. "Let's preserve his head. As a memento," she said.

Tenderly, Barb nodded. "If we steep him long enough, you know, he'll make the perfect medicine. A confection, for your sickness, darling."

The honey transformed his countenance. It seeped over, warped and amplified his tortured brows, dribbled into his gaping mouth, liquefied him, the swells and canyons of his final resting face, greenish as oxidized copper, into something entirely repulsive and not quite human. Potent, larvae-like, sheets of honey wrapped him in its viscosity, a primordial sludge that both snuffed and enshrined him, like the plaster casts of the victims of Vesuvius, petrified, and eternalized in ash.

"I can't look at him that way." Shivering, Barb carried the sticky head, dripping, to the downstairs bathroom. Next to his cologne, on the tray, she set his head down.

FIRST TO COME out was the liver, then the stomach, lungs and intestines. Most shocking was the small size of his heart, like a boy's, Alex imagined. On his outer left thigh, there was a scar. Alex made an "X" with her pen. On the chest, she drew a dark line and the word "Ham." She removed his windpipe and the horseshoe of his hyoid bone. Separating the skin and muscles from the arm, she carved it up. The innards went into a stainless steel bowl.

Aching from their exertion, the women finally lay down to sleep before dawn, in the other bed.

IT WAS MORNING when the first bee flew in to the bathroom window. By the time Rosa had let herself in, the head was transformed into a teeming mass. The bees crawled through every orifice, into his nostrils, ear pathways, and in the hollow left by his missing tongue. The horde smothered him. No trace of skin was exposed. Hundreds of them pulsed and expanded, together, as one, united being, their sound a jet engine, swooping low to the ground.

Rosa shut the window.

As the two women slept, Rosa tied the apron around her enormous stomach. She rubbed the cuts of meat with extra virgin olive oil. To keep it from curling in the heat, she wedged a stick into the large intestine. Her hands were slippery with fat. Nicely charred, the intestine shrunk to a third of its size. She dressed it with sesame seeds, garlic and chiles, humming sweetly and seductively, with a young girl's voice. Tender slices of tongue from the middle section, with the rough outer layer removed, she flambéed on one side to a moist jerky. But when they sat for the feast, it was the taste of the heart, with its deep and vibrant color, that surprised them. It was like beef, Barb said, but with a little more crunch. The rest of him, the cutlets from his chest and thighs, were nearly identical to pork, but tougher, more bitter, like the burned end of a roast.

Afterwards, the baby boy sucked greedily on Alex's finger stubs, which she had dipped into her father's fat. For dessert, Rosa served her grandmother's strawberry tarts. Their secret was rosewater, which she infused into the custard topped by small strawberries – not in rows of refined formation, but scattered loosely, without a care. With their cherry-red glaze, the tarts shimmered like perfumed jewels, then crumbled, as the women lifted them, one by one, into their hungry, chewing mouths.

In their post-feast torpor, mother and daughter lounged on their bed, their arms and legs entwined. Filling and hardening with surplus milk, Barb's breasts pushed against Alex's cheek. Alex seized one breast with both hands and slurped, not bothering to wipe the warm liquid running in cloudy streams down to her collar.

"There's a spider," Barb began, "called the Black Lace-Weaver. For three weeks in late spring and early summer, the mother spider sits with her egg sac until a hundred spiderlings emerge. A few days later, they molt. Then the mother drums her legs against the web, a kind of dinner bell. Within a half hour, the hatchlings swarm over her body and begin to feed. Her body will start to liquefy, giving her hatchlings plenty, until she disappears. She does nothing to fend off their attack."

Alex traced her mother's cheekbone and fought to stay awake. Then she pressed her face, smeared with paint and milk, into the other breast.

INTO SOMETHING RICH AND STRANGE

THANA NIVEAU

THE *FOREVER YOUNG* slid through the cold blackness of space, her destination a tiny speck on the ship's scanner. She had crossed the notorious Chandelier Nebula with minimal disruption to the instruments. The computers were just finishing their assessment when Kim Cavens took her seat at the nav station. Down below on the Andromeda deck, the rest of the crew was still being revived, having slept for most of the starship's sixteen-year voyage. The 400 colonists would remain asleep until they could safely be woken.

It was one of the best things about being a pilot – being first on the flight deck after a long spell in cryo. Kim loved being the first one to see where the ship had brought them, the first to set eyes on a new void, a new starscape. Until the captain joined her, the ship – and the world – was hers alone.

She switched the navigation system to manual and dropped the *Forever Young* out of hyperdrive. The lightscape melted around her, congealing into individual stars. It was a sight that never got old. The astonishing, terrifying beauty of space.

Among the stars emerging from the pinpoints of light was the sun Zeta Carinae. It swelled into orange brilliance as Kim piloted the ship into her system and set a course for the fourth planet, the one that was their ultimate goal. They would be the second ship ever to visit it.

150-ULEY was about the size of Saturn and the same pure blue as

Neptune. A much larger version of Earth, but without a single continent. There were no land masses at all across the vast watery surface and the crew of the *Valentina Tereshkova* had nicknamed it "Aquarius".

Kim could still recall the initial excitement over the discovery. The planet wasn't only an immense source of water but a potential second Earth. Back home the floating cities had begun to cover the rising oceans, spreading like the terrestrial cities had done across the land. Soon the whole of Earth would be a single sprawling metropolis, with nothing to distinguish where any boundaries or borders used to be.

There was nowhere left to build, no way to expand. The space stations could only be temporary homes. Earth's moon was a dead world. Worst of all, the Martian colonies had failed. Nothing would grow on the red planet, and the bleak and barren landscape had driven one entire community to mass suicide. Since then, it had been officially declared a dead planet, a destination only for morbidly inclined tourists.

Aquarius was their only hope for a fresh start.

The planet hove into view, a pale dot that bloomed into a vast cobalt ball as the ship drew nearer. There wasn't even a single cloud to mar the pristine surface. Kim put the *Forever Young* into orbit and gazed at the new world before her. It was as beautiful as any unspoilt place could ever be. Zeta Carinae was a relatively young star, only a few million years old, and the planets were likewise in their infancy. If there was any life on Aquarius it would probably be of the same type found on Europa in the previous century. Microbes and fungi. Creatures that might, millions of evolutionary years later, become space explorers themselves.

The initial reports sent back from the *Valentina* had compared its all-encompassing ocean to the Dead Sea. The extra buoyancy created by the salinity might help to counteract the gravity, which was considerably greater than Earth's. But that was for the scientists and terraformers to sort out. Kim's job was to get them here, which she had done.

There was another job to do, of course. A far less pleasant one. They had to find the missing *Valentina*.

The doors to the flight deck whooshed open and Kim waved from her seat. "Morning, Captain!"

Yasuko Shimizu managed a bleary-eyed smile as she sank into her chair. "Morning? Feels like I just went to sleep."

"It *was* a long one," Kim agreed. That was another good thing about being the first one awake. No one had to see her stumbling around, cranky and dishevelled, until she got her bearings.

Yasuko peered at the image on the screen. "So that's Aquarius. It does look beautiful."

"Yeah. Hard to believe there isn't even a single island anywhere on it."

The sheer volume of water was almost inconceivable. At the poles were ice caps and glaciers, but if they were to build a new Earth, they would have to start by constructing artificial continents. Once the planet checked out, they could send back word to Earth and start waking their colonists. Then the human race could breathe a sigh of relief as it expanded further into the galaxy.

Both women gazed at the vast ocean, neither wanting to voice the thought that haunted every person on board, and back on Earth. Finally, Yasuko spoke.

"Any sign of a distress beacon?"

Kim shook her head sadly. "No. The computers haven't picked up so much as a whisper."

But Yasuko didn't look worried. "It's okay. When Redfern gets up here, he can try a few tricks. If anyone can find the ship, he can."

One by one the rest of the shift crew began to arrive on the flight deck, each marvelling at the beautiful blue planet. Four of her seven moons were visible. None of the images they'd seen of it back on Earth could have prepared them for the sight of the actual place.

"It's like a massive droplet of water floating in space," Ray Palmer said, sounding enraptured. "I can't wait to get down there."

But even the lead diver's excitement was tinged with dread. "Down there" was probably the final resting place of the *Valentina*. When the transmissions had stopped coming, everyone on Earth had feared the worst. Of course, it was always possible that the subspace messages simply weren't getting through. Even so, the galactic scanners should have been able to at least pinpoint the location of the ship. But there was nothing. *Valentina Tereshkova* had vanished, along with her crew and colonists.

"Anything on the scanners yet, Redfern?" Yasuko asked.

He frowned, deep in concentration. "I'm not sure. There's something.... Wait a minute. It's almost..."

Everyone was silent and Kim realized she was holding her breath, straining her ears for electronic signals – tones, blips, beeps, alarms. The air suddenly seemed full of synthetic voices, like a robot choir. Was there a distress beacon in amongst those discordant notes?

When Redfern began to smile, Kim knew he'd isolated the signal from the rest of the noise. The flight crew breathed a collective sigh of relief.

"Have you got it?" the captain asked. "Where is it?"

Redfern made some adjustments at his station, tapping and swiping his fingers across the console until only a solitary pulse was audible. He listened intently for a few moments as he waited for his display to provide him with more information.

"Yes," he said triumphantly, "I've found her." Then his face darkened as he read what was on the screen. "But I'm afraid it's not good news."

They all knew what that meant. And as they stared at the massive spherical ocean, no one needed to explain.

Eventually Yasuko broke the silence. "How deep?"

"Seventy-one meters." He pulled off his headset and pinched the bridge of his nose. "Damn it!"

Kim stared down at her own console, the lights blurring as tears filled her eyes. So their worst fears were realized. The *Valentina*'s captain must have sent out a distress call as soon as disaster struck – whatever that disaster was. Now the ship lay at the bottom of an alien sea. Life support might have sustained them for a year or two, but the *Forever Young* had set sail for the Zeta Carinae system one year post radio silence and it had taken sixteen more years just to get here.

Ray spoke then, his voice barely a whisper. "Full fathom five thy father lies."

Kim thought she recognized the quote. It was from an ancient play about a shipwreck. She didn't want to give voice to the dark thoughts that hovered on the outskirts of her mind, didn't want to imagine what the worst might mean. She thought of the Martian colonies and pushed the memory away.

"What do we do now?" she asked.

"We go down there and find out what happened," Ray said. "And then we retrieve the bodies."

Kim flinched at the word but Yasuko nodded.

"Yes. We have to find out what happened. We have to know whether the planet is safe. We've got 400 colonists depending on us."

The *Valentina*'s fate could have been the result of equipment failure.

All the data she had sent back to Earth before she disappeared had been checked and re-checked. There were no dangerous chemicals or bacteria, no freakish weather conditions, nothing at all to suggest that it wasn't perfect for a fresh start for the people of Earth. The galactic scanners back home hadn't been able to find the *Valentina*, but neither had they picked up any meteor showers or other dangerous astronomical events that could have disrupted the ship's orbit.

Yasuko got to her feet, her normally casual demeanor vanishing in an instant. "Right, then. Ray, assemble your diving team. Let's keep it to six of us until we know it's safe down there. Redfern, tell the Harbour deck to prep a shuttle for us. Kim, you're in charge here."

Not trusting herself to speak, Kim merely nodded. A lump filled her throat as she watched her friend and captain turn to leave. Ray was right behind her, looking every bit as purposeful as Yasuko. Kim wished she could share their confidence. But the truth was, she was afraid. She wasn't a diver herself, but she remembered Ray telling her once that, in the ocean, the most dangerous things gave you warning by being either very ugly or very beautiful. And Aquarius was certainly very beautiful.

DESPITE THE GRIMNESS of the mission, Ray couldn't entirely suppress his exhilaration over where they were going. He'd explored every ocean back on Earth, never able to get enough of the world beneath the waves. He had applied for an expedition to Europa, to dive beneath the ice crust of the Jovian moon. Unfortunately, his expertise had been required as a search and rescue diver in the Pacific when the floating village of Little Honolulu sank beneath the force of undersea volcanic eruptions. He and his team had recovered hundreds of bodies in those weeks.

When the *Valentina* had first discovered Aquarius, he had been sick with envy at the thought of not being the first to dive in its waters. Would the planet-wide ocean contain wonders to compete with the coral reefs of Earth and the incredible diversity of life there? Or would it be like the reports he heard of Europa—cold and colorless and utterly alien?

Vibrant azure filled the viewscreen as the shuttle entered the planet's atmosphere and descended, homing in on the *Valentina*'s coordinates. There was nothing but water in every direction. The planet had a solid core, but no violent seismic activity for creating continents. The thought of having to build their own to support life was almost as exciting as seeing what was beneath the sea. The craft came to rest gently on the calm surface of the water in the southern hemisphere.

The instrument readings were all encouraging, and confirmed what they had already learned from the *Valentina*. The outside air temperature was breathable and temperate, 24 degrees Celsius. And the water looked no different from that of Earth's clearest seas.

The shuttle was buzzing with both excitement and trepidation. This was to be everyone's first dive on another world. And while their present job was regrettable, it was impossible not to feel like they were embarking on an adventure.

Ray zipped himself into his vivid green N-suit and vacuum-sealed it against his skin before fitting the mask and mouth gill. Years of innovation had done away with traditional diving equipment. Gone were the cumbersome air tanks, hoses and regulators. A Nitrogen suit did most of the work now. The tiny fibers of the suit penetrated the outermost layer of a person's skin, siphoning nitrogen bubbles from the body, eliminating the need for tiresome decompression stops before surfacing. "The Bends" were a thing of the past.

But no amount of scientific advancement could change the fact that divers still needed to equalize the pressure in the body's air spaces – the ears and sinuses. And human eyes still needed a lens to correct for the visual distortion under water. A mask with a rubber nose guard was essential, but it incorporated a dive computer with a digital display showing the depth and the remaining time in one's gill.

The gill was the most ingenious device of all, replacing the hose and regulator with a simple mouthpiece that filtered oxygen directly from the water into the diver's mouth. A chemical reaction took place inside the gill which injected nitrogen and helium into the mix, in whatever quantity the body required.

"I think we're ready to go," Ray said, looking around at his team.

Yasuko tied her hair back and slipped her mask into place. "Okay then," she said. "Ray and I will go in through the main airlock and head for the flight deck. Finch and Taborska, you two find the Harbour deck and see if they launched any shuttles."

Finch nodded and looked to his partner, who was adjusting her mask. "Understood," they both said.

"Gascoigne and McMahon," Yasuko continued, "you guys head for the engine room and see if you can find out what happened to the ship."

"What if we find any survivors?" Gascoigne asked.

Yasuko exchanged a glance with Ray. They both knew there wouldn't— *couldn't*—be any.

"Don't get your hopes up," was all the captain had to offer.

"Keep in touch," Ray said, changing the subject. He didn't want them any more apprehensive than they already were. "Report back anything unusual."

"And the bodies?" Taborska ventured.

Ray looked to Yasuko. She was silent for a few moments. "Leave them where they are. We're just going to investigate for now. Once we know what happened we'll put together a retrieval team."

The crew nodded agreement as they fitted their mouth gills and ran through brief equipment checks with their diving partner.

When they were ready, Gascoigne opened the hatch and extended the short ladder down into the water. Waves lapped softly, invitingly, at the hull. Yasuko gave Ray a wistful smile and motioned for him to lead the way. He appreciated the gesture. Although the crew of the *Valentina* had technically got there first, he would be the first man to step into the ocean of this planet. Yasuko and the rest of the team followed.

The water was pleasantly warm, like a bath. The high salt content meant that they'd all needed to fit their N-suits with extra weights to get them beneath the surface. Once in the water, Ray deflated the buoyancy layer of his suit, and he and Yasuko descended together, kicking their fins as they swam straight down into the Aquarian sea.

The readout appeared in the upper left corner of his mask. It showed his rate of descent, which was slow and gentle. All the other readings looked fine. Around them there was nothing to see but water. No fish, no coral reefs, no plant life. It was eerie. Even the air mixture tasted strange. It wasn't unpleasant, just – alien. Yasuko met his eyes and frowned slightly, pointing to her mouth gill.

Ray raised his arm and tapped a message to her on his wristband.

YOU OK?

She read it in her own mask and signalled with a thumbs-up before replying.

JUST TASTES WEIRD.

He agreed. He wondered what exactly the gill was filtering to give the air such a peculiar flavor. What if they were drinking in microscopic life forms they couldn't see? Suddenly the water felt chilly.

Of his bones are coral made. Those are pearls that were his eyes.

In spite of the sunshine on the surface, the water beneath was dense and dark. Visibility was very poor and soon all six of them had turned their masklights on. The beams swept through the dark currents, illuminating only each other.

As they reached a depth of fifty meters, then sixty, then seventy, the hulking shadow of the starship came into view, growing like a stain in the water until its identity was unmistakable. A shudder went through Ray's limbs as he drifted down past the name proudly emblazoned across the ship's prow. *Valentina Tereshkova*. The first woman in space.

Ray glanced uneasily over at Yasuko. The captain hung suspended in the water for a moment before kissing her fingers and touching them to the huge capital V. In her green diving suit she looked suddenly vulnerable, like a leaf about to be swept away in a current.

The other dive pairs began making their separate ways around the shipwreck and Ray watched until they were out of sight. Then he swam with Yasuko to the main airlock. It was covered in rust and tangled in something limp and pale, like thin ribbons.

SAFE TO TOUCH? he typed.

Yasuko shrugged. Gascoigne knew more about this sort of thing than either of them did, but he was on his way to the engine room. The ribbons certainly didn't look dangerous. They didn't seem to be corroding the hull of the ship. Possibly they were some type of seaweed. Ray decided not to take any chances. He unsheathed his dive knife and used it gently to untangle the flimsy threads, trying not to cut them.

The ribbons drifted away, undulating in the water like tendrils of seaweed at the mercy of ocean currents. He watched for a few moments, but they exhibited no sign of life.

He and Yasuko had to work together to prise open the door. Inside it looked just like the *Forever Young*, only flooded and rusty. The ship had only been on the seabed for seventeen years, not long enough for the water to eat through the hull. But the water had still gotten in somehow. Ray had dived many shipwrecks before, back on Earth, but this was disconcerting. He couldn't shake the feeling that they were exploring a future version of their own ship.

They made their way to the flight deck, where they had to force open the doors to get inside. Following the thin beam cast by her masklight, Yasuko swam to the main computer station and touched her wristband to the panel. There was a slow blink of sallow light, briefly illuminating their surroundings. Ray gave a watery cry and leapt back. All around them, huge white shapes drifted, silent and motionless.

Yasuko swam to him instantly and took his arms, peering through his mask at him to make eye contact. She removed her gill for a moment. *Okay?* she mouthed.

Still shaken, Ray collected his wits enough to nod. The figures were freakishly bloated.

Yasuko looked around, sweeping her masklight over the drifting figures. Tears shone in her eyes.

HORRIBLE, she typed.

All Ray could do was agree. It was worse than he could have imagined. He'd seen drowning victims before. He knew how awful dead bodies could look. That wasn't what had startled him. No, there was something else. Something was very wrong about this.

Nothing of him that doth fade...

He took a few slow, deep breaths through his gill until he felt calm enough to look again. Twelve members of the *Valentina*'s crew floated around them, their bodies pale and swollen to many times their size. They bumped gently into the walls and one another before spinning off in other directions. They might be drifting in space.

Yasuko swam back to the computer station and, after a few more attempts, managed to get the emergency lights on. The watery yellow glow was enough to illuminate the room, but Ray suspected the power wouldn't last long.

But doth suffer a sea-change...

The words of the poem were haunting him. He pushed his feelings aside and forced himself to confront the nearest body. And he had to stifle another cry as he understood what he was seeing. The body wasn't bleached and swollen from the water. It was wrapped in bandages. They all were.

Into something rich and strange.

He turned to see Yasuko staring in horror as she made the same discovery. Ray searched his mind, but he couldn't think of any emergency protocol that would involve something like this. Had one of the crew gone insane and killed everyone, then wrapped them up? How? Why?

His mask vibrated softly and he glanced up into the corner to see the message. It was Finch.

NO SHUTTLES MISSING. H-DECK FINE.

Yasuko was reading the same message as Ray. So no one had left the ship. No one had been in the water. Whatever happened had taken place on the ship itself. And Finch and Taborska obviously hadn't encountered any bodies or they'd have said something.

Yasuko tapped a response into her wristband.

STAY THERE. DON'T TOUCH ANYTHING.

Her next message included Gascoigne and McMahon.

ENGINE ROOM?

A few moments later McMahon replied.

DOOR JAMMED. STILL TRYI

Yasuko's eyes flicked to Ray as the message cut off.

The silence was monstrous. Ray could only stare at the bandaged bodies floating past like giant grubs. Loose ends of the wrappings trailed behind them like hair and he realized what had been coiled around the airlock door. His blood turned to icewater.

Then the light around them began to dim. In the awful silence they watched as the yellow glow wavered and then winked out like a candle. Was it his imagination or had the bodies begun to glow?

Ray turned his head to shine his masklight on Yasuko, suddenly afraid of losing sight of her. She seemed to have had the same idea, as she swam closer to him. The gentle kicking of her fins stirred the current and one of the bandaged crew nudged up against him. He shoved it away in revulsion, not wanting to touch the ribbons.

MCMAHON? GASCOIGNE?

But there was no response to Yasuko's message. Were they hurt? Or merely cut off? He was about to ask Yasuko what they should do. Then he saw the expression on her face. She looked utterly terrified, her eyes wide with shock and disbelief. He reached for her, intending to reassure her. But then he realized she wasn't looking at him, but at something behind him. He didn't want to turn around, but he sensed something gathering at his back. His skin prickled.

He turned around slowly. Behind him were two of the *Valentina's* mummified crew. They hovered in the water, glowing. There was something horribly purposeful about the way they hung there. They were looking right at him.

Ray flailed in the water, pushing himself away and crashing into Yasuko. She grabbed his arm and they clung to each other as the dead were joined by others. The bandaged bodies looked as though they were trying to walk, like old-time astronauts on the moon. As one, the dead crew reached for them.

A chaotic jumble of dark thoughts raced through Ray's mind. Thoughts about strange and ancient practices back on Earth. Bizarre religious rituals. Cults. Madness. Murder. Suicide. Were these people alive or dead? Or something else, something *worse?*

Yasuko was yanking at him, urging him to move. She clasped his hand as she swam for the doors, kicking violently to stir the current as they passed. Ray did the same, hoping to knock the grasping corpses away.

But as they made for the doors, he felt something grab his ankle with a viselike grip. He sensed a cold and terrible presence behind the touch, a brutal intelligence. It was burning through his suit. He kicked furiously at the bloated hand but it wouldn't let go. The pain was worse than any jellyfish sting he'd ever suffered and it was all he could do not to scream.

Yasuko saw what was happening. In one fluid motion, she spun round in the water and drew both her legs up to her chest before punching them out and into the face of Ray's captor. The force of the kick sent the figure slamming against the bulkhead, where it came apart, shattering like plaster. The ribbons collapsed as whatever was inside dissolved into a cloud of gray powder in the flooded compartment.

For a moment both Ray and Yasuko were transfixed by the awful sight. Then they turned and swam hard for the corridor. Trying to ignore the pain in his leg, Ray helped steer them both as Yasuko jabbed at her wristband, sending a frantic message to the other divers.

ABORT!

The gray cloud engulfed the corridor, making it even harder to see. Yasuko swam ahead while Ray followed the light from her mask. He could hear the echoing bump of things moving around behind them, the watery thuds of their mummified pursuers. Ribbons of light billowed in the water all around them, waving like long, boneless fingers. They were everywhere, glowing with hypnotic luminescence. Seductive. Ray could feel the spell they were trying to cast, could feel himself almost succumbing to their vicious, spellbinding beauty. He forced himself to focus on the burning pain in his ankle as he drew his knife and slashed at them as he passed.

The engine room was at the opposite end of the ship, and without power, there was no way to reach it from inside. They'd have to leave the way they'd come in and swim around the ship to get to the rear airlock. No one had replied to Yasuko's abort message and he could only hope that the others were busy fleeing the ship themselves. But Ray and Yasuko couldn't leave that to chance. They had to go and see if the others were all right.

Ray was so busy hacking at the drifting tendrils around him that he didn't notice at first that Yasuko had stopped swimming. She was clawing at her right leg. Something pale and writhing had attached itself there. The ribbon was glowing, pulsing with savage life. It gave off a sickly green light as it coiled tighter and tighter around her calf, slithering up to spiral around her thigh. In seconds it had engulfed her whole leg. His own leg throbbed in sympathy.

Ray swam to her as fast as he could, but the thing had clearly penetrated her suit. A dark liquid spilled like smoke into the water and Yasuko screamed, losing her gill. Ray grabbed it and pressed it firmly against her mouth as he reached for the thing constricting her leg. It was too tightly wrapped to get his gloved fingers underneath and he didn't dare use the knife.

Yasuko clutched at him, jerking her head from side to side in agony. She knocked her head against the bulkhead, hard, and Ray winced at the sickening crack. Her mask came off, trailing its thin beam as it fell. It illuminated even more of the writhing ribbons, which were now snaking towards Yasuko. They were no longer drifting aimlessly, at the mercy of the current. They had tasted blood. They were awake.

With no other option left to him, Ray aimed the point of the knife at the creature on Yasuko's leg and jabbed. But if he caused it any pain, that only made it tighten its grip. It squeezed tighter and tighter, drawing in like a tourniquet made of acid until it cut through the bone. Her leg dangled at a hideous angle, twirling in the water and turning it black with blood. Yasuko screamed again, releasing torrents of bubbles as she spat out her mouth gill.

"*Go!*" she cried, her underwater voice chilling in its acceptance of her fate. Then she deliberately sucked in a breath, inhaling the alien water, hastening the end.

Ray edged away, watching helplessly as what looked like hundreds of the ribbons gathered, as if for a feast. They too began to glow as they coiled and constricted around Yasuko, wrapping her entirely, like a spider wraps a fly. Her body jerked and convulsed as she drowned before him, unable to fight off her attackers. Blood pooled in the water around her and was absorbed by the creatures just as quickly.

He had to go now, while they were occupied. His eyes were blurred with tears he couldn't scrub away and he swam through the unfocused haze of the corridor, kicking as hard as he could to reach the airlock before his pursuers did.

When he got there he was relieved to find it still open. There didn't seem to be any of the creatures waiting for him. He swam out and followed the curve of the sunken starship, heading for the engine room.

CAPTAIN DEAD, he typed. SURFACE NOW.

There was no response.

The airlock was open and he knew at once from the greenish glow emanating from there that he wouldn't find Gascoigne or McMahon alive. Tendrils waved from inside, as though beckoning him in. Ray swam close enough to shine his masklight on two bloated forms floating within. The ribbons were wrapped so thickly it looked like the men were wearing hundreds of layers of winter clothes.

Ray swam away before the creatures noticed him. He sent a message to the last two divers, with little hope of a reply.

The Harbour doors were open and he could see the domes of four shuttlecraft inside. He ventured inside and swept his masklight around, searching for Finch and Taborska, desperately hoping they had gotten away in time. But then his beam fell on a bulky, glowing shape beneath the nearest shuttle. His heart sank and even as he swam to it, he could see the waving ribbons of the creatures that had wrapped it up, claimed it. And then he saw the head. It was bobbing in the water, trailing long hair and glowing tendrils. Taborska. The things had clung so tightly to her neck they had severed her head entirely, just as they had pulled off Yasuko's leg.

There was nothing more to do here. Numb with shock and horror, he fled. But as he reached the open doors, he drew up short. He wasn't alone. A ranked series of humanoid shapes was waiting, their numbers extending far into the distance. The *Valentina*'s crew and colonists. All the hundreds who had been frozen for the voyage, who were to be revived once they found a habitable planet. They had all been cocooned. Now they stood on the floor of the ocean, staring at Ray. The figure in front was misshapen. Its right leg dangled, held loosely in place by the pale wrappings that covered the rest of the body.

And all around them, loose ribbons danced in the water, a billowing wave of light, radiant and mesmerizing. He could see them coiling upwards, beyond the surface of the ocean, rippling into and across the sky like a visual siren song. It must have looked so beautiful and inviting to the *Valentina*. Just as it must look to the crew of his own ship far above.

All the strength went out of him and he sank to his knees on the seabed. There was nowhere to go. Coiling ribbons trailed from each of the wrapped bodies, pulsing with light and hunger as they reached for him.

As they began to embrace him, Ray wondered how much of him would fade, how much would change, and how rich and strange would be his new form.

OSCAR RETURNS FROM THE DEAD, PROPHESIZING

JOHN LANGAN

To DISTRACT MY son after his first breakup, I told him a story. It was the only thing I could think to do.

—Do you remember Oscar? I said. We were in the car, heading north on the Thruway. We were going to Albany International Airport, to meet my wife's return flight from Seattle.

—You mean Dylan's lizard? Jordan said. He was staring out the window at the fields rushing by.

—Leopard gecko, I said. You know he died, right?

Jordan sighed. In the fire, he said.

—No, before that. When we were watching him.

—What? Jordan said. No, he didn't.

—Yes, he did.

—That's bull—that isn't true, Jordan said.

—It is, I said. You were gone, at a sleepover. At Owen's, I think. The weather had turned incredibly hot. I had the idea that Oscar would appreciate a little time in the sun. His tank wasn't heavy, so I moved the heat lamp off it and carried it out to the porch. I set the tank down next to the doorway, away from the direct sunlight. Then I went back inside, and forgot about Oscar.

—How long did you leave him there?

—Too long. I wasn't the one who noticed he was gone. After Mom got home and had dinner, she said, Where's Oscar? And I said, Oh no. Actually, that isn't what I said, but you understand. I raced onto the porch. The sun was down, but the wood still burned my feet. I hefted the tank and ran into the kitchen. Almost dropped the tank on the kitchen table. Not that Oscar would have minded.

—He was dead, wasn't he?

—Yeah. During the afternoon, the sun had moved, and the tank had turned into a little oven. Oscar had ... shriveled, dried out.

—Mom must've been upset.

—To put it mildly. Which was fair enough. Although it was an accident, I had cost Dylan his pet.

—What did you do?

—Mom called around to the local pet stores until she found another leopard gecko. The next morning, I drove up to Wiltwyck and purchased Oscar 2.0. Cost me forty dollars.

—How about the first Oscar?

—We removed him from his tank, wrapped him in a couple of dish towels, put him in an empty chocolate box, and buried him in the backyard.

—Where?

—Under the pine tree next to the fire pit. It was the only place the soil was deep enough, and which was sufficiently out of the way for you not to notice. I had a couple of pieces of slate left over from when you and I had dug the pond at the side of the house. I laid them on top of the box before I filled in the hole, to keep any animals from digging Oscar up. The whole thing was done—new lizard bought and housed, old lizard interred—by the time you returned from Owen's.

—I can't believe I never noticed.

—You had lost interest in Oscar by then. At first, you were fascinated by him. Do you remember watching him chase the crickets we fed him for dinner?

—Yeah.

—We were supposed to be able to handle him, but the first time you stuck your hand in the tank, he snapped at you, and that was that. Which worked out for us, in the long run. It meant you didn't notice when we swapped him for his replacement.

—Did Dylan know?

—He didn't, but that's a little complicated.

—How so?

—The pet we returned to him was the first Oscar.

—What do you mean?

—Four or five days after Operation: Fresh Gecko, I heard a noise from Oscar 2.0's tank. This was around noon; I was sitting in my office, catching up on e-mail. I walked into the kitchen. I heard the sound again. It took me a minute to figure out it was gravel, spraying against the tank's sides. I crossed to it, and was just in time to watch the original Oscar swallowing the last of the other gecko's tail.

—Where was Oscar 2.0?

—I couldn't find him. I knew leopard geckos could drop their tails in stressful situations, which is what I assumed was the case, here. But there was no trace of the other Oscar. There wasn't any place in the tank he could have hidden that completely, so I concluded he had been eaten, too.

—Wait.

—What is it?

—You're making this up.

—I am not.

—You're a horror writer. This is what you do for a living.

—I am not making this up.

—Dylan's lizard died, came back to life, and ate the lizard you bought to take his place.

—Granted, when you put it that way, it sounds like something I might have written. Although, a leopard gecko?

—You always say you're open to new ideas.

—True, but an undead pet?

—Invent from what you know: isn't that another one of your sayings?

—You really are your mother's son. You have an answer for everything.

—I take that as a compliment.

—Do you want to hear the rest of the story or not?

Jordan shrugged. If you feel like telling it.

I was sufficiently irritated to want to spend the remainder of the drive in silence. Jordan's effort to discredit it, however, was evidence that the story was fulfilling its purpose of shifting his attention from the breakup. I sighed and said, I hate to leave a story unfinished, especially when it's true.

—Or true-ish.

—Very funny. All right. I was pretty freaked out. I could not understand what had taken place. Because I wasn't prepared to believe that Oscar had returned from death to consume his successor. It was—there are moments of strangeness, instances when some feature of your surroundings doesn't make sense, and it puts a strain on everything else. You hear a voice in another room in a house you know is empty. You get out of bed in the middle of the night to have a pee, and there's a shape moving on top of the dresser. You're out walking the dogs, and you see a figure in the woods, watching you. Most of the time, these moments resolve. The voice you heard was a clock radio whose alarm turned on the radio. The shape in the bedroom is your reflection in the dresser mirror. The figure in the woods is the trunk of a tree in whose bark your brain picked out a face. You realize what's actually happening—what was always happening—and the strain you felt relaxes.

—Sometimes, though, it doesn't resolve. This was how I felt after your grandfather died. The world had been wrenched into a new configuration, and the sensation of it was terrible. Granted, it was on a much smaller scale, but seeing Oscar in the tank, I experienced something like this. There was a case of Gatorade sitting unopened on the kitchen table. I grabbed it and lifted it on top of the tank, then backed away, in case it wasn't enough to contain Oscar.

—What did you think he was going to do? Jordan said.

—I had no idea. Just the fact that he was there was bad enough. Not to mention, the whole cannibalism thing. He looked awful. His skin was shrunken right to the bone. There was no sign whatsoever that he'd eaten the other gecko's tail, let alone the rest of him. His claws were yellow, most of the ones on his forelegs cracked and broken. His eyes had a white film over them.

—How did I not notice a zombie gecko?

—You were a lot shorter, then. You had to stand on one of the kitchen chairs if you wanted a good look into the tank. Which, as I've said, you no longer did. And Oscar didn't make me think of a zombie so much as he did a mummy. He had that white, pebbled skin, and it had shrunken and bunched around his skeleton in a way that reminded me of a mummy's wrappings.

—Not to mention, you had buried him in his own tomb, in a kind of sarcophagus.

—Right. I'm sure you can guess what I did next.

—You called Mom.

—I called Mom. She was in her office.

—What did she say?

—Pretty much the same thing you did.

—She thought you were pranking her?

—In a particularly tasteless way. It took me what felt like forever to convince her I was serious. Of course, she didn't believe Oscar had come back from the dead, or that he had eaten Oscar 2.0. As she saw it, Oscar must not have been dead when we put him into the ground. He had clawed his way out of the grave and made his way to his home, where he had discovered the other gecko and chased him away. In the process, Oscar 2.0 had dropped his tail, which the original Oscar, in need of sustenance after his interment, had gobbled up. It was all very reasonable—or, not as unreasonable as my version of events—though it meant there was a second leopard gecko hiding somewhere in the house, and we should find him before you came home from school and were confronted with the evidence of our deception. And in a house with three dogs and three cats, a solitary lizard's chances of survival were not good.

—So while I was certain I would find no trace of him, I spent the next hour and a half conducting an exhaustive search for Oscar 2.0. I went through cabinets; I opened drawers; I looked under tables and chairs. I shifted the refrigerator; I pulled out the stove; I removed the cushions on the couch. I went through the laundry hamper. I sifted the recycling tubs. I lifted the garbage bag out of the garbage can. The entire time, I could feel the original Oscar behind me. I had the craziest impression he was … not watching me, but *aware* of me, of the search I was conducting. It was as if he'd returned from the grave accompanied by a presence he hadn't possessed before.

—Well. I turned up no trace of the second Oscar. I tidied the house as best I could and was left with forty-five minutes 'til I had to meet you at the bus stop. I decided I had better check the spot where we had buried Oscar.

—What did you find?

—The grave was open. Obviously. The earth at the spot had mounded, pushed up by the pieces of slate I'd laid over the chocolate box. They had been shoved away from the coffin with considerable force. There was a hole at one end of the mound, through which Oscar had escaped his tomb. I dug with my hands until I could see the edges of the pieces of slate. They were hot. Not warmed-by-the-sun: these things might have come out of a baking oven two seconds before. I couldn't touch them. There was a gap between them, through which Oscar's coffin was visible. The heat from the slate had caused it to blacken and shrivel. Nevertheless, I saw the hole Oscar had clawed through its top. The box was beginning to smolder. I pushed earth over it, filling the grave, tamping down the mound. Once I was finished, there was barely enough time for me to run into the house, wash my hands, and run down to the bus stop.

—Why didn't you leave it open?

—I didn't want you poking around in it. Unfortunately, this meant that, when Mom came home, she had to take my word about what I'd found.

—Did she?

—Let's just say that your mother is possessed of a healthy skepticism. She could credit Oscar tunneling to the surface—she had to: he was sitting in his tank in the kitchen—but she was less convinced about the shifted pieces of rock that were also burning hot. It sounded to her as if a larger animal had scented Oscar and attempted to get to him. Maybe Oscar had been moving in the box and a racoon or a bear heard him. The animal dug until it reached the pieces of slate, which it levered up, allowing Oscar to escape.

—That sounds reasonable.

—Of course it does. I had witnessed Oscar's grave, which in no way looked as if it had been excavated by a hungry predator, and I half-believed her explanation. She couldn't account for the temperature of the slate, said it was probably from the sun. Which, as we had learned in the recent past, could be plenty hot.

—What did she say when she saw Oscar?

—Oh, she agreed he looked pretty horrible. We would, too, if we had been buried alive, with no food and water, for almost a week. A lizard's metabolism was much faster than a human being's, especially if he was tearing through the box, tunneling to the surface. It was a wonder there was anything left of him.

—Makes sense.

—Except it doesn't. The math didn't compute, so to speak. As I saw it, if his metabolism was that amped up, then Oscar should have run out of gas long before he dug his way to freedom. Not to mention, there was the problem of how and why he had found his way from his grave to his tank. Wouldn't it have made more sense for him to flee into the woods? Instead, you have to imagine he scrambles across the lawn, around the porch to the stairs, climbs the stairs, leaps through the doggy door into the mudroom, traverses the mudroom, leaps through the doggy door into the kitchen, races across the kitchen, and scales the cabinet to his tank. There, to confront and devour the interloper. It's like a twisted version of one of those Disney movies about the loyal dog who follows his family cross-country, only with undeath and cannibalism. Even if I could accept that we had mistakenly buried Oscar alive, the rest of the situation defied sense.

—Okay.

—I'm just saying.

—I know. What happened next?

—Nothing, really. Mom and I had a brief, somewhat contentious debate over what to do with Oscar. I thought we should remove him from the tank and destroy him. Dylan's family weren't going to move into their new home until the end of the summer. That left us plenty of time to find another leopard gecko. Mom wasn't having any of it. As far as she was concerned, Oscar's miraculous return, after we had almost killed him twice, obligated us to ensure his safety until we could reunite him with Dylan. She won the argument, though I succeeded in persuading her that we needed to replace the pack of Gatorade I'd set on top of the tank with a heavy board.

—Did Oscar try to escape?

—Nope. In fact, he didn't do much of anything. Just squatted in the middle of the tank and stared out at the kitchen. Half the time, I was sure he had died. Again. That I could tell, he didn't eat, either. I continued to tip a few crickets in with him every couple of days, and they evoked no response. They hopped all over the place—they hopped onto Oscar, and he remained motionless.

—Maybe he was hunting them when you weren't watching him.

—It's possible he might have eaten one or two, but from what I could see, the overall population stayed the same. Finally, I stopped adding crickets to the tank. It had reached the point that, if I was up late writing, I could hear them chirping.

—Oscar number one ate the other lizard's tail.

—He ate the other lizard.

—Either way, maybe that gave him the nourishment he needed.

—For a week or two, I could believe. But this lasted two months. I had left off feeding Oscar and turned my attention to the insects, making sure they had food and water. And then they all died at once.

—All of them?

—Every last one. I was working on a story that was well past its deadline, and I realized that the house was quiet. I had the impression that the crickets had been singing not that long before, but I couldn't say when they had stopped. It was strange enough to cause me to walk into the kitchen and flip on the light. The crickets were motionless. Some were on their sides, some on their backs, some upright. I want to say I wasn't sure what was going on, but that isn't true, not exactly. Right away, I knew they were dead. I could feel it, as if their lives were water that had rushed down a drain, and the pipes were still gurgling. Oscar sat in their midst, his lower jaw hanging open. There was a sound coming out of him, so soft and low I almost missed it. I had to lean in close to the tank—much closer than I liked—to make out what it was.

—What was it?

—A word. A single word was broadcasting from his mouth, in a creaking, raspy voice that might have belonged to an old, old man—an ancient man.

—Seriously?

—Yes.

Jordan sighed, but said, What word?

—Life.

—That's...odd.

—You're telling me. I went to the butcher block, withdrew the butcher knife. I was halfway to the tank when I hesitated. Already, Oscar had come back from being baked. Who could say if a knife would work any better? I needed fire, to incinerate the lizard and scatter his ashes. I couldn't figure out how to accomplish this without making so much noise I'd wake Mom and you. That was not a conversation I wanted to have. Honey, what are you doing? I'm setting the gecko on fire because he talked to me.

Jordan snorted.

—And besides, Oscar's mouth had closed, and the voice had stopped. I slotted the knife back into the block. That night, I slept on the living room couch. I told myself I was guarding Mom and you from Oscar. I don't know what I thought he was going to do. I don't know what I thought I was going to do to stop him. But I felt better positioned there. Surprisingly, I fell asleep. When I checked the tank the next morning, the crickets were gone.

—Oscar ate them?

—Presumably. You still wouldn't know it to look at him. He was as shriveled as ever—desiccated, is the word I want. I didn't know what to do. Things that seem obvious to you at night become less certain during the day, and vice-versa. I tried to do research. I went to Oscar's grave and carefully opened it. I was hoping to unearth some clue to the cause of his return. I wore heavy gloves, in case the pieces of slate remained hot. Which would have been weird—at this point, Oscar had been back in his tank for a solid couple of months. It was almost time for us to hand him over to Dylan. But the whole situation was so bizarre, I wouldn't have been surprised if the rock had retained its heat. It hadn't, though. It had crumbled to pieces, to sand, as had the box and towel beneath it. I dug down another foot and a half, in case whatever was responsible for re-animating lay deeper. I didn't find anything.

—Next, I tried the internet. Most of the hits for mummified animals led to sites concerned with ancient Egyptian burial practices. They were informative, but not helpful. There was one pharaoh whose tomb's contents included a mummified crocodile, which seemed as if it might be relevant, but it wasn't. In the end, I knew no more than I had at the beginning.

—What did you do?

—Nothing, really. For the remainder of Oscar's stay with us, I slept on the couch. I told Mom I was having trouble sleeping, which was not as much a lie as it was an incomplete truth. I listened for that old man's voice, but I didn't hear it—although there were a couple of times I woke up certain it had just been speaking.

—In the end, we returned Oscar to Dylan. We loaded him in his tank into the car, and drove him to the Lucases' new house.

—I remember that, Jordan said. Kind of. Dylan showed me his room. There was a secret passage to the stairway.

—It was an old house. It had lots of peculiarities like that.

—Wait: what did Dylan do when he saw Oscar?

—He didn't say much of anything. Nor did his parents, for the matter. For the week leading up to it, I had rehearsed my responses to Dylan and his folks reacting to Oscar—to what Oscar had become. I was prepared, I thought, for tears, for shouting, for angry recriminations. But they barely paid attention to him. They were too caught up in unpacking. I swear, I had to stop myself from pointing to the tank and asking them if they noticed anything different about their pet.

—No one said anything?

—John, Dylan's little brother, wrinkled his nose at Oscar, but that was it. And that could have been an expression of distaste at a lizard. I left the house like someone backing away from a bomb. The minute the Lucases paused and took a good look at Oscar, I was sure they would be on the phone. They never did, though, and then when the house burned down a few months later, Oscar was the sole casualty.

—Was that after Dylan's parents got divorced?

—During, but it didn't help matters.

—Huh, Jordan said. You know, it's been a while since I've seen Dylan. Maybe after we pick up Mom—when we're home—I'll call him and ask if he wants to come over. If that's okay.

—Sure. I don't think we're doing anything tomorrow.

—Cool. Do you mind if I put on some music?

—Go ahead.

Jordan tapped the screen of his smart phone a couple of times, and soon was singing along with Bon Scott about the dirty deeds they would do dirt cheap. I had expected him to comment on the end of the story, ask me if I was certain Oscar had met his end along with the Lucases' house, maybe press me again on inventing the entire thing. He might later. My own teenage years lay long enough in the past for me to have lost touch with the peculiar schedule of their mental processes. Should he question the veracity of the narrative, I was prepared to answer honestly and say that everything I had told him was true. Should he question the story's close, I was prepared to lie and say that it had concluded with me setting Oscar's tank on the Lucases' kitchen table.

Because there had been more. Not much, but enough to make its omission a dishonesty. It began with a phone call three months after I returned Oscar. Van Lucas, Dylan's dad, was on the other end. Despite the time that had passed, I flinched when I heard him, trying to remember the lies I had prepared for his discovery of Oscar's state. I needn't have worried. Since we had deposited Oscar with them, we hadn't heard anything from the Lucases, which was unusual, as we saw them for dinner every few weeks. I speculated their silence had something to do with the lizard; my wife chalked it up to the move. I decided her explanation was more likely. As Van started talking, I learned that there was a third reason for their silence. Their marriage had collapsed, and they were getting a divorce.

I was shocked. Van and Polly Lucas had been together longer than

Denise and I, and theirs had seemed to me one of those unions of opposites that proves the cliché. Of course, there's a great deal in every marriage that remains hidden to those outside it. Polly's mother, I knew, had died suddenly as the Lucases were closing on the new house, which was more than they could afford, except its previous owners had defaulted on their mortgage, and the bank had put the place up at a price that was a steal. My experience with buying and moving into our house had taught me how stressful the process could be, and this was on its own, with no concomitant tragedies. Van refused to say any more over the phone, so I met him at the Starbucks in Huguenot. There, he told me the reason for his and Polly's split. While up late one night, Polly had heard her mother speaking to her. Her message was simple: you and your husband don't love one another. It's time for you to leave this loveless marriage and find a better life for yourself. Crazy, but Polly believed the voice that had spoken to her immediately and without reservation. You didn't have to be much of a psychologist to know that she was using this supposed incident as a way to lever herself out of a relationship she had grown tired of. Van wanted her to see a doctor to ensure she wasn't suffering from some affliction physical or mental, a brain tumor or psychosis, but Polly found a lawyer who said there was no requirement for her to do so, and from there, their split had been accomplished with frightening speed. She had moved out, found a new place in Joppenburgh. Really, the only major thing that hadn't been settled between them was the house.

—I swear, Van said, some nights, I stand in the kitchen, hoping that I'll hear someone telling me what to do, my father or grandfather, you know? But it's just me and the gecko, me and old Oscar.

I must have blanched, but Van didn't notice. I said, Is that where you keep him?

—The lizard? Yeah. Dylan didn't want him in his room, any more, so we left him in the kitchen.

—And that was where Polly said she heard her mother?

—Yeah. Pity we can't question Oscar about Polly's voice, get him to tell us what really happened, right?

—Yeah.

Two weeks after that, I was breaking into the Lucases' former home. Technically, I wasn't breaking in, since the back door was unlocked. There was no one there. Polly was at her new place with Dylan and John. Van had gone up to Lake George for the weekend to visit his mother and step-father.

The house looked much as it had my previous visit, full of boxes of clothes, books, and toys. In the kitchen, Oscar's tank was on the counter near the stove. According to Van, he and Polly couldn't agree about custody of the gecko, either. Oscar was in his familiar position, surveying the room. He did not register my presence.

Although it was late, past one in the morning, I had parked several streets over and crept through a number of backyards and a stand of trees to reach the house. The night was quiet, but I didn't want to take any chances of being seen, which was why I was wearing a black turtleneck, black slacks, and black shoes. Prior to entering the house, I had pulled on a pair of rubber dish gloves I brought with me in a small rucksack. I was still carrying the rucksack with my left hand. When I saw Oscar, I opened the top of the bag and withdrew the butcher knife I'd stowed in it. The knife was old, from the junk box in my basement. I'd sharpened the blade and wiped the whole thing down for fingerprints. I moved to Oscar's tank. I had returned the tank with the heavy board I'd kept over its wire top at our house, but the wooden lid had been removed. This made it easier for me to lift the screen. I was ready for Oscar to attempt an escape, but he stayed put, didn't acknowledge the exit I'd provided him. If it was possible, he looked worse than he had the last time I'd seen him. His skin had contracted around his bones to the point he appeared more skeleton than flesh. Had I been told he'd been found in some minor pharaoh's tomb, I would have believed it.

I thought I was prepared for Oscar's jaw to drop open, for that ancient voice I'd heard to claw its way out of his throat. I was wrong. What emerged from the gecko was neither the old man's voice I had heard the night of the great cricket massacre, nor the old woman's voice that had encouraged Polly to end her marriage. This was another old man speaking, one whose low tones could have belonged to my father, dead the past decade. It was mixed with a hissing noise, like sand pouring over stone. I froze as it said my name, then continued speaking.

What my father uttered in slow, halting syllables was horrible. The kitchen tilted, as if I had been punched in the head. On trembling legs, I stepped forward and stabbed the knife down into the tank. It struck Oscar at an angle, cleaving his head and right foreleg from the rest of his body, and stuck in the glass under him. His mouth snapped shut, and the voice ceased. I had intended to remove the butcher knife once it served its purpose, but the prospect of touching something that had touched this *thing* made my stomach churn. From the rucksack, I slid a small can of lighter fluid and a box of matches. The pungent odor of the liquid stung my nostrils as I soaked Oscar's remains. I replaced the lighter fluid in the rucksack and reached for the matches.

After all this time, I still wasn't sure exactly what went wrong. I hadn't used that much lighter fluid, yet when I dropped the lit match into the tank, the air inside ignited in a swirl of blue that leapt straight to the ceiling. I looked for a fire extinguisher, but already, the ceiling had caught, flames racing across it. The glass of Oscar's tank cracked, then burst outward, spraying flaming shards around the kitchen. Ten, twelve struck boxes, setting them alight. In no time whatsoever, the situation was out of control, the ceiling rippling with fire, the boxes flaring like torches. Soon, the flames would find the gas line snaking into the stove, and the house would be lost. I had left my cell in the car, and could see no sign of a house phone. I chose the only option left to me, and fled out the back door. Panicked as I was, I had enough sense to retrace my route through the woods and backyards. I was almost to my car when a distant WHUMP announced the propane tank's detonation. As I drove home, I heard the first sirens.

Needless to say, the destruction of their house and about fifty percent of their material possessions did not help the Lucases' divorce. Apparently, it was obvious to the investigators that the fire had been deliberately set, but Van's alibi of being with his mother was rock solid, nor was there evidence of any suspicious activity in his phone or internet histories. For a short time, a good deal of interest focused on Polly, a consequence of some intemperate threats she had made to Van within earshot of their respective lawyers and their aides, but that didn't lead anywhere, either. I spent a month in near constant dread of the knock on the door that would herald my discovery, but the door remained silent; though it was another year until I felt I could truly relax. But the guilt I felt at having destroyed my friend's home, however accidentally, continued to surge in me at unexpected moments, sometimes with such force I had my phone in hand and was halfway to entering Van's number before I gained control of myself. Of course, there was no way he would believe my explanation, and he was well on his way to a new life, so I felt justified in continuing to conceal my responsibility for the blaze. The gas explosion had been severe enough that the evidence of my dispatch of Oscar had been obliterated; Van would likely take my attempt to explain events as nothing more than a sign of mental illness.

But if the lizard was gone, and my part in his demise a secret, the words that had been delivered to me through him had lodged in my memory. I had done my best to forget them and, failing that, to ignore them. Every time Denise flew to another conference, though, I heard the voice I did not want to accept had been my father's saying, *The landing gear will fail. The plane will split, catch fire. Your wife will survive, but the two of you will wish she hadn't. Your son will suffer the most. It will be the end of your family.*

There had been no way to convey the prediction to Denise, not without revealing my role in the destruction of the Lucases' house. She wouldn't have believed it, any more than she could accept that a dead gecko had returned to life (or, had I told her, that it had channeled the voices of the dead). So every time she flew, I was there to see her off and to greet her, in hopes that my presence would act in some way as a good luck charm. I didn't like to bring Jordan, but he had asked, and with the bad breakup, I hadn't wanted to say no.

There wasn't much further to go. Traffic was heavy; we were going to be late. Call Mom, I said to Jordan, tell her were almost there.

After a moment, he said, She isn't answering.

In the rearview mirror, I saw the flashing lights, racing towards us.

FLOWERS FOR BITSY

LEE THOMAS

IN THE FALL of 1982, Ollie Burton lay in a hospital bed very near the end of his life. Morphine dripped euphoria, delivering numb weightlessness and the attendant muddled thoughts. The white walls swelled and deflated, demonstrating a steadier respiration than Ollie's own, though he struggled to breathe in unison with the illusion. On the small, gritty television screen suspended in the corner, an elderly Spencer Tracy chatted with Sidney Poitier. Ollie loved the movie. He'd seen it a dozen times, the first time upon its release while he was still in college. He couldn't remember the name of the movie, not just then, and several scenes appeared to have been cut. The story skipped around in a bizarre tangle of conversations and confrontations, some of which struck his jumbled memory as out of order, and before he knew it, the end credits appeared, followed by a commercial for the Pocket Fisherman.

Ollie's ex, Mitch, came to mind. Mitch had been a dead ringer for Spencer Tracy. Tall. Muscular. Thick chestnut hair. With…but…

No. Wait. That wasn't right. Mitch was Rod Taylor from *The Birds*, not Spencer Tracy from– Why couldn't he remember the name of the film? And who was he thinking of?

If Bitsy were there, he could ask her. She'd notch her head to the side and then look around the dismal room as if he'd asked her to fetch an invisible stick. She was his best girl, and she knew how to manage his nonsense.

Where was she?

He turned his head and caught sight of her tearing across the lawn, carrying a blue ball triumphantly between her jaws. Chocolate colored with a line of white like a smudge of chalk running the length of her muzzle, Bitsy had the narrow body and pointed face of an animal built for speed.

A souped-up lowboy Deuce coupe whipped around the corner. All black and chopped, the Deuce screamed down the street. Ollie's belly knotted. He knelt in the grass of a suburban front yard, certain of a horrible event he was incapable of stopping. He groaned in panic, fear icing his neck and chest, until he realized the grass in which he knelt had turned brown more than twenty years ago.

As the panic receded, a kind face emerged to soothe him.

"Hello, Mr. Petrie," Ollie whispered.

And this was the man that had reminded him of the actor from the film. Mr. Petrie, a kind if distant neighbor, was the spitting image of Spencer Tracy, not the white haired and haggard Tracy from the movie he'd just watched, but the more energetic Tracy from the 1940s. He shared Tracy's blocky torso and the sincere, blunt features, except Petrie's voice was rough, all gravel, made unthreatening by a reserved delivery and a thick British accent that further attested to his misplacement among the rigid, Texas folks with whom he shared a neighborhood.

Ollie smiled at seeing his old friend, and then frowned as Mr. Petrie's face faded into the wall of the hospital room. On the television, a somber anchorman sat behind his desk. His mouth formed a perfect O, and the moaning cry of whale song poured over his lips.

Ollie tried to focus on this oddity, but after blinking to bring clarity to the grainy screen, the news had been replaced by a game show, and the bright colors hurt his eyes.

His friends, Morris and Gene, were there. He couldn't remember them coming in. They sat in molded plastic chairs. Morris, a balding set designer whose round belly tested the limits of a navy blue polo shirt, read the newspaper. Gene, who was wiry and small, maintained the rictus of a fabricated smile; the lesion on his neck was still the size of a dime.

"Where's Bitsy?" Ollie mumbled, feeling the looseness of a back molar against his tongue.

"The hospital doesn't allow dogs," Morris said, not looking up from his paper.

"They won't let us bring her in," Gene added.

Ollie nodded and the motion caused his thoughts to scatter. The hospital walls turned to dust and blew away, and he was nineteen, enduring a scratchy visit home to see his parents. He sat on the sofa in the living room with Bitsy curled up at his feet. His mother seemed afraid of the dog, who remained of a sweet disposition. After two hours of pained, forced conversation and tea so sweet it made his pancreas cringe, Ollie excused himself, saying he needed to walk his best girl. It was a lie. She never needed to be walked.

He strolled down the block with no destination in mind. Going somewhere wasn't the point; he was getting away. His mother's friends, many of whom still fashioned themselves after late-1950s television stars, observed from their porches as he led his pet to the intersection.

"Do you want some juice?"

Ollie blinked away the Texas sunshine and returned to the gloom of a New York hospital. Gene stood over him, holding a glass. Ollie shook his head and the sun returned.

Bitsy stayed close to his heels. At Mr. Petrie's house Ollie stopped to note its disrepair. The place had lost shingles, and the robin's egg blue paint flaked. A section of the eaves hung from below a gutter. Rot blackened the exposed wood.

The front door opened and Mr. Petrie emerged. Unlike the house, Petrie looked hardly different. His face appeared fuller, and his hair was cut tight to his scalp.

He owed him so much, but he hadn't intended to visit. Still, he waved and felt a tremble of warmth in seeing Mr. Petrie's smile. Because of his aging neighbor, he hadn't lost Bitsy. No matter how hard his dirt-stupid neighbors attempted to slander the man, Mr. Petrie would always mean the world to Ollie.

The suburban tribunal, his mother's clucking friends all of whom swept about, draped in pastels and wearing their bouffants like helmets, impenetrable to ideas not authorized by their husbands, had passed judgment on the middle-aged gentleman. They commented on his status as a "confirmed bachelor." Sneers bolstered the scorn in their voices, lest their peers think they felt anything but contempt for the appellation.

Ollie felt as if he hadn't seen the man in more than a decade, though their paths had crossed briefly at the grocery story only a week before he'd left for college.

"Hello, Ollie," Petrie said. "How are you, and how is our good girl?"

Morris rattled the newspaper as he turned a page.

The lights dimmed on the sunbaked sidewalk until the hospital room returned from the dust. He focused on the television screen, which someone had turned off.

Ollie shifted on the bed because his back felt wrong.

"They're calling it AIDS, now," Morris said, face deep in the tent of his newspaper.

"Calling what AIDS?" Gene asked

"This!" Morris said with agitation. He shook his newspaper violently as if trying to remove a spider from the page. Then he folded it up roughly and swept it back and forth to indicate all the corners of the room. "All of this. That's what they're calling it now."

"Oh," Gene replied. "Let's talk about it later."

"Fine," Morris replied, placing the newspaper on his lap. "Yes. You're right."

Gene turned to Ollie. "Can I get you some water?"

"I slept with Mr. Petrie," Ollie said.

"Really?" Gene asked. "Who's that?"

"He thought I was paying a bill," Ollie continued. "But I might have loved him if he'd have let me."

"If only they'd let us," Morris said, still occupied by bad spirits.

Silence returned to the room. Ollie's thoughts tumbled.

This time, when the light bathed him, it came from expertly positioned PAR cans, their illumination tinged with colored plastic gels. He stood on a stage, accepting an award. He stood on another stage, pretending to be the husband of a harried young woman, played by an actress who would go on to be a movie star. He'd stood on so many stages, small and large. How many people had watched him over the years?

At the edge of one stage he bowed. The lights went out.

He picked at the edge of his sheet. His tongue worried the inadequately anchored molar in the back of his mouth.

Though he tried to remember the stages, the colleagues, the accomplishments, he only managed to conjure himself standing in the living room of a grungy and compact apartment in The Village. It was his favorite apartment. He stood on the tattered rug, reading a script. Excited about the role, he'd spent hours that afternoon memorizing lines for a supporting part in *Romeo and Moskowiz*, a comedic bastardization of Shakespeare. He'd played the role of Mercutio before (the character Shakespeare had written) in college, and despite the awkward anti-Semitic jabs the contemporary playwright had woven into the dialogue, the rhythms of the piece came easily to him.

Bitsy watched from the sofa, eyeing him expectantly as if waiting for a familiar command to let her know what was expected of her.

Then he sat at a dinette table in a larger apartment on the Upper East Side. Bitsy stood on the tabletop, still expectant as Ollie ran lines from a far better play. Ollie's boyfriend, Mitch, stomped around the living room in a huff.

A former chorus boy who had thrived in theatre management, Mitch was muscular and decisive and impatient. Stomping about was as common for him as brushing his teeth.

"I do not want to stay cooped up all night," he said.

A souped-up Deuce coup.

"Let's go to 54." He shot a finger out, pointing at Bitsy. "And get that animal off the furniture."

Bitsy sank low on the tabletop. Ollie set down his script and scratched her behind the ear before lifting her and placing her on the parquet floor.

"You go," Ollie said. "I have to work."

"The damned show doesn't open for another three months, and it's not that big of a part."

"You go," Ollie repeated. "I have..."

"Broadway," Ollie announced from his hospital bed, hoping Mitch would understand how important this part was for him. But he hadn't seen Mitch in two years. Hadn't heard from him in six months, not since the call.

The dreary room was empty. Morris and Gene were gone and the window was dark. Alan Alda's face floated like a ghost, trapped in the suspended box in the corner.

"Where'd you go?" Ollie asked. "Where's Bitsy?"

The chocolate-colored dog emerged from the shadow of the front porch, walking across the grass with a blue ball clamped in her jaws. Her tail wagged furiously, though her paws moved at a slow, sleepy pace.

"My best girl."

Pain stabbed along his spine, sending blades deep into his back and hips. Ollie moaned. His bowels loosened.

He pressed the nurse's call button. All of his strength went into grinding his thumb against the plastic nub. But no angel of mercy raced to his side. He wasn't even certain the button actually triggered anything, and wouldn't that be a fine joke? Alan Alda's ghost grinned playfully down on him. The hospital staff would let him lie there in his stinking, cooling filth for an hour, maybe two. He'd almost gotten used to the smell of his own shit.

Bitsy smelled of wine and spices and honey and flowers.

KNEELING IN THE middle of the street, Ollie sobbed. He was a little boy, who'd been playing tug of war with his best girl. But she'd won the game.

Resting on his lap, Bitsy panted fiercely. Blood bubbled at her nose. The bubbles popped, splashing his jeans and the brown and white striped shirt. Her eyes darted as if seeking an explanation, but Ollie could only explain with a wash of tears.

He lifted his head, spotting his mother's friend Mrs. Landry on her porch. Through the blur of wet eyes, he was unable to read the expression on her face, and what did that expression matter?

"Help her," Ollie cried. "Please. She's hurt."

"I'm not sure how I feel about having that thing in the apartment," Mitch said.

Ollie closed his eyes, blinding himself to his source of grief. From over his shoulder a gravely baritone voice said, "Oh now, isn't this a terrible thing?"

On the television, lights flashed and mechanical music began to play.

"New from K-Tel…"

He stood in a field of wildflowers. Though his hand was already full of autumn flourishing blossoms, he continued to gather. His bouquet of butterfly milkweed, partridge pea, and purple coneflower grew. He stuffed stems in his pockets and down his shirt.

The processed voices and synthesized keyboards from the television hit Ollie's ear, and he winced. Despite the low volume, the songs rang shrill and painful, a rhythmic interpretation of computer screams from a sci-fi film.

Flowers spilled out of his shirt, and his hand ached from holding such a large bouquet. Ollie looked around the field, and though he saw more blossoms at its edges, he knew he held all he could manage.

"She deserves something nice," Mr. Petrie said, taking the bundle of flowers from Ollie's trembling hands. "I can't make any promises, but I'll see what I can do."

OLLIE WOKE WHEN Gene entered. He carried a brown, cloth suitcase across the room and set the luggage beside a chair. Then he returned to the door. He peeked into the hall and then rushed back to the chair.

"Is Morris yelling at the nurses again?" Ollie asked.

"Morris doesn't yell at the nurses, sweetheart. *I* yell at the nurses. But Morris isn't here. He was afraid of getting in trouble."

"Why would he get..." Static followed, and Ollie knelt in the sunbaked street of a small Texas suburb, cradling his best girl as blood bubbled from her nose. "Help her," he said.

"I can't make any promises, but I'll see what I can do."

"This might make things better," Gene told him. He reached down and unzipped the suitcase.

Bitsy lifted her head and searched the room. Then her brown eyes found Ollie. She waddled out of the suitcase, and Gene lifted her, placing the dog on the sheet next to him. Her warm nose pressed close to his cheek, and her dry tongue lapped at his jaw.

Ollie laughed. The dizziness, the static, the horrible alien qualities of his body receded. He lifted his arm and scratched Bitsy's back as she settled into his armpit and rested her head on his shoulder.

"Who's my best girl?" Ollie asked.

Bitsy's tail thumped on the cheap, abrasive linens.

"Now you can see why Morris wouldn't come."

"Just let me know if Mitch shows up. He gets furious when he sees Bitsy on the furniture."

Gene fixed the grimace to his face and stepped to the edge of the bed. "Mitch won't come, Ollie. You don't have to worry about that."

Because Mitch died nine weeks ago, Ollie thought.

Mitchell Kramer, Longtime Manager of Lovitz Theatre, Dead at 56.

Bitsy wriggled against him. Gene stood at the bedside scratching her ear, occasionally rubbing a palm along Ollie's forearm. Gray light poured through the dirty window. The rain would start soon.

In the bed next to him Mr. Petrie said, "You should probably get back to your parents' house."

"Probably," Ollie said. "But I can come back later."

"That's not necessary. You didn't owe me this, and you don't owe me anything more."

Ollie didn't understand what Mr. Petrie was saying. What did "owing" have to do with anything?

"How about a little consideration?" Mitch asked, throwing back the sheets and storming from the bed. "I mean, you weren't exactly burning up Broadway when we met. Besides, relationships require some level of compromise."

"I've had her since I was a kid," Ollie said.

"Then maybe it's time to put away childish things. She smells like a wino, and it gets all over the furniture. Gene adores her. Keep her at his place."

"She's my dog." My best girl.

A nurse wearing latex gloves, a surgical mask, and goggles stormed into the bedroom. Blonde chicken wings of hair flared away from the mask. The goggles magnified her eyes and the dense paste of blue eye shadow above them. She looked hilarious and horrifying. The finely papered walls of Mitch's bedroom peeled away behind her as if painted on a scrim now drawn back to reveal a grimmer set. She stomped to a halt and pointed a bony finger at the bed.

"What the fuck?" she cried. The surgical mask deadened her tone. "You can't have that thing in here."

"Just a minute," Gene said tersely, rising from his chair.

"No," the nurse said, shaking her head so furiously, Ollie thought she might take flight. "Who knows what kind of germs are crawling on that thing?"

"I've had her since I was a kid," Ollie said, not certain if he was repeating himself or not.

Mitch glared at him from the foot of the bed. He flexed his chest out of habit and then bent down to grab a pair of blue running shorts. "I think we both have to make some decisions here. Hard decisions."

The nurse stalked toward Gene. "You get that thing out of here right now, or I'm calling security."

"She's my dog," Ollie muttered. "I can't give her up."

"Haven't you made enough bad decisions for one lifetime?" the nurse asked.

Bitsy wriggled fiercely, pushing as close to him as she could manage.

Then Gene was yelling at the nurse, and the nurse was yelling back. Mitch threw a tantrum as he tried to get into his shorts, unable to believe that his companionship was being weighed against that of a dog.

Ollie released the ball.

Bitsy rocketed away, headed for the far side of the yard and then for the road. She was too enthralled with her victory to notice the souped-up lowboy Deuce whipping around the near corner. All black and chopped, the Deuce screamed down the street like a demon freshly loosed from Hell.

HIS MOTHER SAID, "That's a shame," as if he'd just informed her he'd missed the ice cream truck on Palmer Avenue.

His father said, "Bury her in the field. I don't want coyotes tearing up my backyard to get at her."

Mr. Petrie said, "Gather up all of the wildflowers you can carry. We'll do something nice for her. She deserves that."

THE CHOCOLATE-COLORED DOG emerged from the shadow of the front porch, walking across the grass with her ball. Her tail wagged, but otherwise she seemed sapped of energy. When she drew close, Ollie smelled the wine, the honey, and the spices. Behind these odors was the fragrant accumulation of wildflower blossoms. He knelt and scratched her ears and ran his hand over her muzzle to confirm she was real.

Bitsy released the ball and rolled on her side, inviting him to scratch her belly. His fingers noticed the sutures before his eyes found them. A straight line of finely sewn threads ran like railroad ties across the soft skin of her shaved stomach.

Mr. Petrie had operated on her, saved her life. Ollie had gathered flowers for her weeks ago, and now she was back. His best girl. Home where she belonged.

Static sent him into the future. Into the present.

Gene and the nurse were gone. Ollie hadn't witnessed the climax of their argument, but he assumed the nurse had won, because Bitsy wasn't beside him. He rolled his head on the pillow and searched in case she'd taken refuge in the corner beneath the television set, but he was alone.

His tongue found the loose molar and nudged it free. It sat on his tongue, and then he rolled it back and forth and wondered if he should swallow it. Instead, he spit it out, spraying the sheets with a spatter of blood as the tooth bounced off the edge of the bed and hit the sidewalk.

The traffic on Second Avenue slithered in a shimmering blur. He crossed Sixty-Second Street and entered an apartment building on the corner. He fished keys from his pocket as he rode the elevator to the Twelfth Floor. A density of Chanel N$^{\circ}$. 5 scratched at his nostrils like a possessing spirit seeking entrance.

Gene would be at the theatre, but he'd promised Ollie that he could visit Bitsy anytime. "Anytime at all."

He'd done as Mitch had asked and hated himself for it.

Ollie unlocked the door to Gene's apartment, and Bitsy jumped on him. He bent down to receive her affectionate tongue. He didn't know how she could forgive him, how she could bear the sight of her betrayer, but she welcomed him enthusiastically, the way she had every time he'd visited over the past four months.

Even so, this visit would be his last. Bitsy belonged with him in *his* home. If Mitch gave Ollie any shit, he'd find a new home.

The nurse with the Farah-Fawcett hair rushed into the apartment. She made a wide circle around where Ollie knelt, hugging his dog. Then Ollie lay back on the floor and pulled the scratchy sheets up to his chin.

Clad in her familiar horror drag of mask and gloves and goggles, the nurse stood as far away as possible as she held out a thermometer for him to place under his tongue. Three minutes later, she happily announced that his fever was worse, "A hundred and one. That's what happens when you let a germy mutt lick your face. You're lucky she didn't kill you."

"She saved my life," Ollie muttered.

"You saved her life," Ollie said to Mr. Petrie. "I thought she was…"

"Some life," the nurse said, shaking the thermometer between latex-sheathed fingers. She shook her head as well. "The things I've seen."

Mitch scowled at him from across the room.

Mr. Petrie smiled lightly and patted Ollie on the shoulder. "Working in a museum introduces you to a million interesting things. I picked up a few."

The nurse continued berating him for allowing Bitsy in the bed, until Gene pushed open the door and interrupted her rant. They glared at one another. Neither said a word until the nurse had escaped into the corridor.

Then Gene turned to Ollie. His smile seemed more sincere this visit, infused with genuine happiness.

"I'm getting you out of here," he said.

Ollie stood on the threshold of Gene's apartment, holding a gym bag in one hand and Bitsy in the other. "I need a place to stay," he said through a split lip.

THE HOME HEALTHCARE provider Gene had hired, a woman named Dana who looked like Anne Margaret playing the role of Janis Joplin, turned sideways and scooted along the side of the bed, the only way to traverse the tight spaces in Gene's modified, guestroom. She kissed Ollie on the forehead and gave Bitsy a light pat before saying, "How are my two favorite creatures?"

Bitsy's tail swatted the quilt. Ollie said, "Just fine."

"Cool," Dana replied, checking the IV bag before reaching for the garden of pill bottles on the nightstand. "You all dry and comfy around your business?"

"Yes. Thank you."

"Cool. Then it's snack time," she announced. "Who's got the munchies?"

"Snacks" was Dana's code for medication. Ollie had snacks eight times per day. The morphine came more frequently than that, delivered under his tongue with an eyedropper. Morphine was "Sippies." He spent his whole day going from sippies to snacks to sippies again, but he didn't mind.

The three days he'd spent in Gene's apartment, three days away from the hospital, had revived him. He still lost himself to memories as he had little else left, but his lucid periods were more frequent, and his discomfort was abated. And he had Bitsy, who stayed close to him, next to him, part of him.

"How about a story?" Dana asked.

"Sure," he said, though what he really wanted was to close his eyes.

Dana scooted sideways to the end of the bed and went to a broad wicker basket, sitting on the chest of drawers that filled the space between the entrance to the room and the closet door. She dug through the contents of the basket and lifted a *Playbill* into view. Giving it a cursory inspection, she shrugged, and returned to Ollie's side.

"Is this you on the cover?" she asked, turning the small book for him to observe.

He recognized the name of the play but not himself. The man with the angry expression and the muscular arms, one emphasized by the handle of a crutch, bore little resemblance to the way Ollie perceived himself now.

"*Cat on a Hot Tin Roof*," he said.

"God, that's a tired tale," Mitch whispered in his ear. "They're only mounting it because Tom is in such dreadful shape these days."

"Written by Tennessee Williams," Ollie said, ignoring the ghost's voice and trying to remain in the present. "Everyone called him, 'Tom.'"

"Did you get to meet him?"

"Yes."

"Far out."

"Yes."

"Who were your costars?" Dana asked.

Static tickled at Ollie's temples. Dana's "story time" had nothing to do with the narratives of the plays he'd done, but was centered on his experiences while preparing for the plays and performing them. She believed that talking about his life would help him fight for it, would remind him that there was a person in the bed and not a collection of miseries and infections.

But reliving those moments from the past came with the possibility of flowing into that past and losing coherence. Ink in water.

"Mitch didn't want me to do the play," he said. "He thought doing a revival was the wrong move for my career, which was starting to take off."

"Who were your costars?" Dana repeated.

"I brought Bitsy back to the apartment," he said, all but certain he was answering the question she'd asked.

Ollie sat at the dining table, reading the letter his mother had sent him aloud. Bitsy stood on the tabletop, rapt by the sound of his voice.

"We didn't know him well," Ollie read, "but you'd mentioned him a few times, so I figured I should let you know that James Petrie passed away last week. Rebecca Landry said they found all kinds of artifacts and papers in his house. Said the stuff was worth a fortune. It seems obvious to all of us that he stole a treasure from that museum in England before he came here. Why else would he be hiding out in the middle of Texas?"

Ollie set the letter down. He breathed deeply against the grief.

Mitch stormed into the apartment as Ollie prepared to continue with the letter. "I thought you got rid of that thing," he said.

"She's my dog," Ollie said. "She stays with me."

Bitsy jumped off the table and stood between the two. She didn't growl. She hadn't produced a sound—not a bark, not a whimper—since returning to him nearly twenty years before.

"Well she can't stay here," Mitch said.

"Then neither can I."

"I can't believe you care more about this fucking mutt than you care about us."

Ollie pushed the letter away and stood. "Then let me do everything in my power to convince you."

The line was from a play. It was a bad play, but he'd appreciated this particular snippet of dialogue. He reached for his best girl, but his fingers never touched her.

Mitch drove his foot into Bitsy's side, sending her skittering across the parquet floor. The violence so shocked Ollie that he froze, unable to process what had just happened. But the violence didn't end there.

Mitch ranted in grinding hysterics. He drove his fist into Ollie's lip and followed up with a punch to the back of his head.

"Ollie?" Dana asked.

Light flashed. Colors popped.

Ollie cowered against the radiator, arms covering his face against further attacks. Mitch continued to rage, but a startling crash sounded, and the tone of his fury changed. Ollie lowered his arms to find Mitch on his back. Bitsy stood on his chest with Mitch's throat in her jaws.

A warm palm touched his cheek.

"Ollie?" Dana asked.

He swam away from the fugue and into the spare bedroom of his friend Gene's apartment. The nurse stood at his side. At first, he didn't understand the expression on her face, and then he remembered they'd been having a conversation.

"She was just waiting for me to tell her what to do," Ollie explained. "She would have killed him if I'd asked, and I was so angry, I might have given the command, but I didn't."

"Was this in the play, honey?" Dana asked.

"I told her to let him go," Ollie said. "He kept yelling and threatening, but he didn't touch us again."

"In the play?" Dana asked more insistently.

He sat against the radiator with Bitsy cradled in his lap.

"Oh well, isn't this a terrible thing?" Mr. Petrie asked, gazing down on the scene, his eyes full of intelligence and warmth and understanding.

"It's okay," Ollie replied. Though he cried and his lips stung horribly, he felt a comfort in the world he hadn't felt in many years.

"And then I came here," he told Dana. "Gene let us stay until we found a new place."

The nurse smiled and nodded and carried the *Playbill* back to the basket.

OLLIE DRIFTED INTO the murk of the room from a liquid sleep. Bitsy had curled up against his hip. Pain flared across his stomach and then shot to his hips. A moment later the same pain erupted in his chest. Ollie wheezed.

The sound of a car's revving engine from the street below delivered cold panic.

From her place at his hip, Bitsy stood and turned several anxious circles on the bed. Then she lay down and began scratching at her belly. Ollie watched this as the pain spread around his ribcage and shot along his arms.

Tires squealed on the nighttime pavement. Light flashed over a sunbaked street as a murderous coupe roared around the corner like a metallic terror seeking blood and meat and bone. His best girl darted off the lawn and into the street, giving the demon its due.

"Bitsy," Ollie said with a gasp.

Then she was by his side, in a comfortable bed.

Bitsy licked at her stomach. Her tongue drew down the line where Mr. Petrie's stitches had held her together. Her back paw scratched the area. After half a dozen licks, her lips curled into a mute snarl, and sharp teeth ripped into dry flesh. She grazed the skin with her paw, scratching her muzzle in the process. She appeared desperate to tear herself open, and Ollie slapped the quilt, though his hand landed with hardly a tap.

"Don't," he whispered.

Bitsy pulled away a flap of skin and brown stems and petals showered the bed. Her jaws worked the wound and clamped down on the edges of her own flesh. She yanked as if trying to tear a ball from a child's grasp. Her head whipped back and forth, and with a final effort, she opened her stomach entirely.

"Bitsy," Ollie said.

The desiccated husks of a dozen wildflowers spilled along the quilt. A trail of them followed as she crawled up the bed. She dragged herself into the pit of his arm and rested her muzzle on his shoulder. Her warm nose pressed to his jaw.

The warmth spread across him like late afternoon sunshine.

Ollie and his best girl played tug of war with a blue ball on a lawn of cooling grass. Bitsy growled playfully, digging her paws into the ground for leverage. Ollie pulled and taunted.

These few seconds engulfed him. A boy. His dog. A late summer afternoon. The joy filled him for a moment, and that moment lasted forever.

ABOUT THE AUTHORS

JOANNA PARYPINSKI is a college English instructor by day and a writer of the dark and strange by night. Her work has appeared in magazines and anthologies including *Black Static, Nightmare Magazine, The Beauty of Death 2, Nightscript IV,* and *Vastarien.* She will also have a short tale in the upcoming *New Scary Stories to Tell in the Dark.* Her forthcoming novel, *Dark Carnival,* will be released by Independent Legions in 2019. Living in the shadow of an old church that sits atop a hilly cemetery north of Los Angeles, she writes, grades essays, and plays her cello surrounded by the sounds of screaming neighbor children. Visit her website at joannaparypinski.com.

JOHN CROWLEY teaches courses in Uptopian Fiction, fiction writing, and screenplay writing at Yale University. He received the prestigious American Academy of Arts and Letters Award for Literature. He is the recipient of many awards including the World Fantasy Award for Life Achievement. His novels include *Little Big* and the four books of the *AEgypt* cycle. His website is johncrowleyauthor.com.

KAREN JOY FOWLER is an American author of science fiction, fantasy, and literary fiction. Her work often centers on the nineteenth century, the lives of women, and alienation. She is best known as the author of the best-selling novel *The Jane Austen Book Club* that was made into a movie of the same name. She is the co-founder of the James Tiptree, Jr. Award and recipient of many awards including the Nebula Award, World Fantasy Award, Pen Faulkner Award, and the Shirley Jackson award. Her website is karenjoyfowler.com.

DAVID WELLINGTON is the author of more than twenty novels including his first zombie epic *Monster Island* and its sequels. His work has been published around the world and translated into more than a dozen language. His latest book, *The Last Astronaut*, is a hybrid horror and science fiction novel. David Wellington lives and works in New York City. Follow him on Twitter @ LastTrilobite, or on his website at davidwellington.net

LEANNA RENEE HIEBER is an actress, playwright, ghost tour guide and the award-winning, bestselling author of twelve Gothic, Gaslamp Fantasy and Supernatural Suspense novels for adults and teens for Tor, Sourcebooks and Kensington Books. Her *Strangely Beautiful* saga, beginning with *The Strangely Beautiful Tale of Miss Percy Parker*, hit Barnes & Noble and Borders Bestseller lists and garnered numerous regional genre awards. Her website is leannareneehieber.com

CASILDA FERRANTE is an Italian/Australian author of horror and weird fiction. Her stories have appeared in *SYNTH Issue 2*, *Nightscript V* and *Vastarien: A Literary Journal* (forthcoming).

As the son of an archeologist, RUDI DORNEMANN has seen his share of mummies and admits that, frankly, they creep him out. He doesn't mind writing about them, though, and appreciates that working on a story for Spirits Unwrapped gave him the excuse to disappear down a few particularly arcane research rabbit holes. His short fiction has appeared in *Strange Horizons*, *Conduit*, and *Realms of Fantasy*. He instigated and contributed to flash fiction website *The Daily Cabal*, occasionally writes for *The Rain Taxi Review of Books*. He lives in Portland, Maine, in house full of books and surrounded by gardens. He can be found online at rudidornemann.com

MARISSA LINGEN is among the top science fiction and fantasy writers in the world who were named after fruit. She has many opinions on Moomintrolls. She has been known to cross international borders in search of rare tisanes. Her personal relationships with bodies of water are intense though eccentric. She has recently branched out into essays, much to no one's alarm but her own.

Texas based author RHODI HAWK has been fascinated by storytelling since her earliest memory, when her grandmother read to her from *Peter Pan in*

Kensington Gardens. Rhodi has been reading or writing ever since. She is the author of the thriller novels *A Twisted Ladder* and *The Tangled Bridge* and part of the *Apocalypse: Year Zero* omnibus.

MICHAEL CISCO is an American writer, teacher, and translator currently living in New York City. He is best known for his first novel, *The Divinity Student,* winner of the International Horror Guild Award for Best First Novel. His novel, *The Great Lover,* was nominated for the Jackson Award for Best Novel of the Year, and declared the Best Weird Novel of 2011 by the *Weird Fiction Review*.

INNA EFFRESS is a former speechwriter who emigrated from Ukraine as a child. Her stories have appeared in *Santa Monica Review* and *The Wrong*. Her fiction has appeared in the *Nightscript* 3 anthology and been reprinted in the *Best Horror of the Year*. She writes in LA.

THANA NIVEAU was born to the wail of the Wendigo and the whisper of warp engines. So it's no surprise that her literary aspirations have combined both the mythic and the speculative. She is the author of the short story collections *Octoberland, Unquiet Waters*, and *From Hell to Eternity,* as well as the novel *House of Frozen Screams*. Her work has appeared in *Black Static*, *Interzone*, and numerous anthologies, and has frequently been reprinted in *The Mammoth Book of Best New Horror*. She has twice been nominated for the British Fantasy award—for her debut collection *From Hell to Eternity* and her story "Death Walks En Pointe." Originally from the States, she now lives in the UK, in a Victorian seaside town between Bristol and Wales. She shares her life with fellow writer John Llewellyn Probert, in a crumbling gothic tower filled with arcane books and curiosities. And toy dinosaurs.

JOHN LANGAN is the author of two novels, *The Fisherman* and *House of Windows*, and three collections of stories, *Sefira and Other Betrayals, The Wide, Carnivorous Sky and Other Monstrous Geographies* and *Mr. Gaunt and Other Uneasy Encounters*. With Paul Tremblay, he co-edited *Creatures: Thirty Years of Monsters*. One of the founders of the Shirley Jackson Award, he served as a juror for its first three years. He lives in upstate New York with his wife, younger son, and a collection of feral swords.

LEE THOMAS is the Bram Stoker Award- and two-time Lambda Literary Award-winning author of the books *Stained*, *The Dust of Wonderland*, *The German*, *Torn*, *Like Light for Flies*, *Down on Your Knees*, and *Distortion* among others. His work has been translated into multiple languages and has been optioned for film. Lee lives in Austin, Texas with his husband, John.

ABOUT THE EDITOR

DANIEL BRAUM is the author of the short story collections *The Night Marchers and Other Strange Tales* (Cemetery Dance 2016), *The Wish Mechanics Tales of the Strange and Fantastic* (Independent Legions 2017), and *Underworld Dreams* forthcoming from Lethe Press. Dim Shores published *Yeti Tiger Dragon*, a limited-edition chapbook of his stories in 2016. His work has appeared in publications ranging from *Lady Churchill's Rosebud Wristlet* to *Cemetery Dance*. His first novel is *The Serpent's Shadow* (Cemetery Dance, 2019). He can be found at bloodandstardust.wordpress.com.

www.ingramcontent.com/pod-product-compliance
Lightning Source LLC
Chambersburg PA
CBHW020446270626
47155CB00022B/1714